THE FISH THAT GOT AWAY

IN THE SAME SERIES

Fish Tales
Fish Nets
Fish or Cut Bait
Fish Out of Water
Fishy Business

THE FISH THAT GOT AWAY

THE SIXTH GUPPY ANTHOLOGY

20 TALES OF MURDER AND MAYHEM
BY THE RISING STARS OF MYSTERY!

Edited by
LINDA RODRIGUEZ

Introduction by
SUSAN VAN KIRK

WILDSIDE PRESS

Copyright © 2021 by the Guppy Chapter of Sisters in Crime
The copyright of each story is held by the author.

Published by Wildside Press LLC.
wildsidepress.com | bcmystery.com

CONTENTS

INTRODUCTION

The Fish That Got Away: The Sixth Guppy Anthology is a collection of twenty stories written by Guppies, more formally called members of the Guppy Chapter of Sisters in Crime. In this sixth anthology, you'll find stories that contain themes of criminal plans gone awry or the ones who slipped through the net. What might that mean? To me, it could be any number of possible scenarios. The criminal got away, but the case remains in the memory of the investigator. A felon gets out of prison vowing to discover the partner who got away with the money. A betrayed lover vows revenge on the person who is now off to their next conquest. Our Guppy writers imagined twenty different variations about the fish that got away.

Why Guppies? The Guppy Chapter of Sisters in Crime is a 1,000+ organization of mystery writers in all phases of writing careers. The chapter began as "the great unpublished" in 1995, a group of writers who were determined to share ideas and support each other. Today, the chapter has grown significantly, but the mission remains the same: "to create an environment in which members can share information, knowledge, opinions, motivation and inspiration without fear of ridicule or rejection." While SinC has many land-based chapters, the Guppy Chapter is wholly online with classes, manuscript swaps, critique groups, a listserv, and a sensational newsletter. The Guppy anthology, published every other year, is an opportunity for writers of all experiences to see their words in print. Various mystery genres are presented in this collection.

Linda Rodriguez is the editor of this edition, and the stories submitted were judged by three non-Guppies from the writing world who are experienced in short story and mystery writing.

Our entire chapter, 1,000-members strong, hopes you will enjoy *The Fish That Got Away*.

—Susan Van Kirk
Guppy Chapter President

TO EVERY SEASON

MARY ADLER

Summer

I'd begun to dread summer, a time I had once loved for its sunsets and temperate nights, for watermelon and heirloom tomatoes, and for the return of Monarch butterflies. Now, I thought of it as a killing season and feared for Jill Stoner, a hiker who had vanished six weeks ago. If we were honest, the most our search party could hope for was to find her body and something to tie her disappearance to Leonard Jackson, a recluse who had no family or friends and interacted only with the sick bastards who trained his fighting dogs.

Doug Cooper, the sheriff, called us together and gestured toward me. "I'm sure some of you already know Lucy Martin. She'll be here for anyone who needs medical help."

"No offense, ma'am, but aren't you a veterinarian?"

"None taken." I smiled at the man who had asked. "I'm also a volunteer EMT with the Sonoma fire department. I haven't mistaken an ankle for a hock yet."

Jokes about stubborn mules and old goats lightened the mood, but no one had forgotten why we were on Jackson's land. A woman had been murdered each summer since he had moved here from Idaho. After a walker found the first victim's body, someone reported having seen her with Jackson the day she disappeared. He denied meeting her and didn't seem to care whether Doug believed him. A background check revealed a few drunk and disorderly charges when Jackson was younger, but nothing serious.

When Robert Ames, a Boise detective, called to ask why the sheriff's department had run Jackson, Doug told him about our murder victim. Ames apologized. Said if he'd known where Jackson had moved, he'd have warned Doug that a suspected killer was heading his way. He wanted to know if our victim had blond hair, and when Doug said yes, asked if there was anything unusual about it. Any doubts Doug had about Jackson's guilt vanished when Ames told him chunks of hair had been cut from their victims, too. And that both their murders had happened in the summer.

The second summer, another woman disappeared. A few weeks later, boy scouts found the remains of her body. She had been murdered, and a section of her blond hair had been taken. Two summers, two murders, and now, in the third summer, another woman had gone missing.

When Jill Stoner disappeared, Doug hauled Jackson in again, but he denied ever meeting her. Then a week ago, someone sent the sheriff's office a photo of the hiker and Jackson by the creek on his property. After the lab authenticated it, the judge granted a limited warrant to search the woods on Jackson's land.

"You'll be searching in teams of two." Doug passed out walkie-talkies. "There's no cell service here, so use these to keep in touch. Be careful. Jackson has bragged that he's salted illegal leg-hold traps on his property. You all know what they can do." He lowered his voice. "If you find any, bring them in. Safely."

He nodded to the K-9 officer, who offered Jill's slipper to his Belgian Malinois. He kept the dog on lead, closer than he normally would, and headed to the creek.

As the searchers set off, Jackson shouted from his porch. "You're not gonna find nothin'. Shame all you people wasting a beautiful day like this." He laughed, then hate darkened his face, and he spat toward Doug and me.

We hadn't hoped for much but still felt let down when the search party straggled in empty-handed. As we loaded up in the waning light, Jackson yelled, "See you next summer."

A few weeks later, a worker inspecting utility lines found what was left of Jill. As with the other two women, a hank of her blond hair had been taken.

Autumn

One morning in September, the time of the autumnal equinox and of friends gathering to say goodbye to summer, Doug rushed into my clinic, carrying his dog.

"What happened?"

"Fox got him. I think it was rabid."

He laid him on the table and stroked his head, until the sedative I'd given him kicked in. I removed the shirt binding Max's wounds and examined every inch of his golden body. The fox had slashed his side, but the skin on his head and throat was intact. I cleaned the cut and put a drain in a nasty puncture wound on his shoulder. Then, I gave him a rabies booster and an injection of antibiotics.

"He's going to be fine."

Relief, then dread flickered in Doug's eyes. "The rabies."

"Did you…?"

"He's in a sack in the truck." He anticipated my next question, too. "Chest shot. I know you need the head."

"Max should be fine, even if the fox tests positive. You're the one I'm worried about."

"When the fox lunged, Max jumped in front of me." His eyes glistened, and he looked away. "He took the brunt of it."

"You touched the fox and bound Max's wounds with your shirt. Probably bare-chested." His red face confirmed what I said. "You could have come in contact with the fox's saliva, a carrier of the virus. I know of a case where a man was bitten by a rabid dog, got treatment right away, and recovered. Unfortunately, the friend who helped him didn't realize the dog's saliva had entered a wound on his own arm."

"What happened to him?"

"He died a horrible death. I'd rather that didn't happen to you." I folded my arms. "Take off your jacket."

I stared at him until he did.

"Didn't he see a doctor when he realized something was wrong?"

"It was too late. Once symptoms appear, it's fatal."

"How long? Till they appear?"

He was really asking when he'd know Max was okay. "Usually two to ten weeks. The nearer the infection site is to the brain, the faster it progresses."

I scrutinized his hands and arms and face for those scrapes and grazes that are a part of being sheriff in a rural county. His skin was unbroken.

While he washed up and slipped on a scrubs top, I bagged his shirt and put it in the hazardous waste.

"You always were a cautious one." He teased, but the worry hadn't left his eyes.

"That shirt is probably twenty years old and wasn't much to look at when it was new."

"Still has a good ten years in it."

"Not now, it doesn't."

I watched him take a deep breath and pull back his shoulders, changing from worried dog owner to keeper of the peace. He turned toward the door. "I'll get that fox for you."

"No." I grabbed his arm. "I'll get it. There's a protocol we follow. You go to Doc Pritchard and tell him I said you need a rabies inoculation. We don't want to take any chances."

"I'm fine. I don't want a big needle in my stomach." He made out that he was kidding about the needle.

"They don't do that anymore. Now, it's like getting a tetanus shot." Sort of. "When you're finished, Max will be ready to go home."

"Any chance the fox wasn't rabid?"

"We both know a healthy fox would have avoided you."

He nodded slowly and gave me a hint of a smile. "Guess I hoped it was a fluke."

"Stop worrying. You've kept Max's rabies vaccinations up to date, and the booster will protect him. You're the one at risk."

* * * *

I stroked the fox's dull flank, laid him on his back with his head hanging over the edge of the table, and sliced through the fur and skin of his neck. I was alone in the surgery, gowned, masked, goggled, and double-gloved, and I performed the decapitation with as little dispersal of fluids and brain matter as possible. I extracted a vial of virus-laden cerebrospinal fluid and locked it in the freezer with the brain tissue of a rabid raccoon.

After I showered, I looked for Daphne, my pit bull and self-appointed kitten nanny, who was where I expected her to be—in a pen with kittens who sparred and tumbled and leaped on her back, playing king-of-the-mountain—with Daphne as the mountain. She smiled that pitty smile and looked at me with the trust that had melted my heart when animal control laid her emaciated body on my table almost a year ago. She would have died if agents on a drug raid hadn't found her, when they stumbled upon a training camp for fighting dogs.

One of the men arrested said the dogs weren't theirs, that they belonged to Leonard Jackson. Daphne had been a champion fighter, but when Jackson realized she was worth more to him as breeding stock, he pulled all her teeth, so she couldn't defend herself or her puppies, and bred her relentlessly.

By the time Doug interviewed the men about the dog fighting, they all swore Jackson had nothing to do with it. Because he lived off the grid—no phone, no computer—Jackson conducted his business face-to-face at prearranged locations. There was no way to connect him to the dog fighting. He didn't go to jail, but he couldn't claim the dogs, either. They were safe with a group that rehabilitated fighting dogs and found them homes. Daphne had already found a home with me.

* * * *

When Doug brought Max to the clinic ten days later for his follow-up, I told him the fox brain had tested positive.

"About that rabies shot Doc Pritchard gave me…." He raised his eyebrows. "It wasn't in the stomach, but it also wasn't pleasant."

"Don't whine. It's not becoming." I glanced up at him. "Besides, more of you working with animals should be vaccinated—especially your deputies—, but you're all too darned stubborn. Probably don't have tetanus shots either." I removed the drain from the wound in Max's side. "We could be living in the nineteenth century."

I lifted Max off the table, took off my gloves, and gave him a treat. "He's going to be fine." We didn't talk about the outcome, if Max were to show signs of rabies. He was all the family Doug had.

Winter

Wind off the Pacific flung eucalyptus bark against the clinic siding, and rain pummeled the building so hard it sounded like a troupe of mad Irish dancers were practicing on the roof. When Daphne nose-bumped my leg—twice—I realized the pounding at the back door wasn't part of the storm.

I opened it to Smitty, a man who lived rough, doing odd jobs and pretty much keeping to himself. He couldn't abide roofs or walls, but he used the clinic's outdoor shower and sometimes spent rainy nights in a shed I had fixed up for him. He reminded me of the feral cat who had adopted me. We were good, as long as he could come and go as he pleased.

"My lord, Smitty, you're soaked."

"Don't matter." He pulled his rusty wagon into the clinic and uncovered a dog.

A golden retriever. One of the gentlest breeds.

"You okay, Doc?"

I forced a smile. "What happened to him?"

"Jackson's men dumped him in a field. For the coyotes. I waited for them to leave, then hid him in the wagon. Got here as quick as I could."

"You did good, Smitty." He looked at me with so much hope that I had to turn away. "Let's see what we can do for him."

He cradled him and carried him into the surgery. "You can't tell anyone he's here. We gotta hide him from Jackson."

"How about Doug? Will you tell him what you saw?"

He pursed his lips and nodded, then whispered. "You're gonna be just fine, Ranger. Doc'll fix you up real good."

I started an IV, phoned Doug before Smitty changed his mind, and called in my best tech. It was going to be a long night.

* * * *

Smitty slept in the clinic next to Ranger's pen for weeks. He sang to him and coaxed him to eat and helped him take his first steps outside. When I asked why he called the dog Ranger, he didn't answer. I knew from the pattern of Ranger's injuries that he had been a 'bait' dog, a dog who is chained and unable to defend itself from dogs whipped into a frenzy and set on it.

Ranger could have been taken from a car or a yard or a shelter anywhere in the country. I searched for his owner and was relieved when no one claimed him. I couldn't have borne separating him and Smitty, and they couldn't have borne it, either. Smitty worried that Jackson might see Ranger and want him back, but I assured him that, even if he recognized the dog, he wouldn't dare claim him.

Spring

The hills glowed with golden poppies. As the days grew longer, and I felt summer nearing, I threw myself into birthing lambs and calves and finding homes for the boxes of kittens left on the clinic porch. I wasn't the only one worried about summer and another woman going missing. Doug wanted to warn visitors about the three women who had been murdered, but county officials insisted the original newspaper articles were warning enough. Towns dependent on tourist dollars tended to downplay anything that might scare them off.

One afternoon, Max trotted onto the clinic porch with Doug close behind. "I have two dead foxes in the truck, Lucy. Hope this epidemic ends before a fox attacks a child."

"Fish and Game are strewing vaccine-treated chicken heads all over the county. If enough foxes eat them, we'll stop the epidemic." I sent a tech for the carcasses and asked Doug if he wanted to share my roasted-vegetable sandwich.

"You know, I've read that plants can feel things, too." He pressed his lips together, fighting a smile.

"I'll pretend I didn't hear you." If I started thinking about carrots having feelings, I'd starve to death. "How about coffee?"

"Can't stay. I need to make some calls." Anger roughened his voice. "Jackson is gearing up for another dog fight."

I set down my sandwich.

"Sorry. I spoiled your lunch."

I waved his concern for my lunch away. "What are you planning? Are you bringing in ATF and the DEA this time?"

"One person I trust at the DEA will ride along, but I'm keeping this quiet. So, it doesn't leak like the last time. A friend who heads a gang unit in Oakland wants in. He thinks the dogfights are connected to automatic weapons that are showing up on his streets."

"How did you find out about the fight?"

"Jackson's men stole a pack of beagles to bait his fighting dogs."

The betrayal of the dogs' trust was crime enough. They would be bewildered and frightened—and then—the brutality took my breath away.

"Their owner and his hunter friends vowed to put him out of business, so they told me what was coming up. They want to go on the raid." He looked toward the hills. "I think they're looking to beat the hell out of him."

A not-so-nice part of me needed to see Jackson bloodied. "Let them help."

* * * *

A few weeks later, I sat in my truck somewhere east of Geyserville, the smell of ashes from the Kincade fire filling the cab. My stomach churned. Luckily, I hadn't eaten. Instead, I'd used my dinner time to prepare my EMT kit.

The paramedics and I waited for our signal to join the raid on the dog fight. I chafed at the delay—a dog might need me—but Doug had to neutralize people with a lot to lose before bringing us in. Finally, he signaled it was safe, and I followed the ambulance into the site.

I took a moment to orient myself in the chaos. Deputies cuffed men and loaded them into a van, while K-9 teams searched for drugs and weapons. I ran toward the hay bales that formed the fight ring. A brindle pit bull with broken legs lay in the bloody arena. He looked dead, but when I knelt beside him, he growled, eyes still closed. I injected him with as much sedative and analgesic as he could handle and waited for him to relax.

I was fitting him with a basket muzzle, when an exchange of gunshots scared the hell out of me. When they stopped, I crept around the edge of the fight pit. A deputy in a Kevlar vest sat on a hay bale, clutching his chest, and a man lay bleeding from a stomach wound. When I saw Doug, I let go of the breath I hadn't known I was holding.

"This what you call safe, Lawman?"

"Damned fool tried to shoot his way out of here." He reset his hat. "My guess is he's wanted for something a lot more serious than watching a dogfight."

Paramedics started an IV on the wounded man and asked if I'd cover for them, so they could leave. I nodded and ran back to put splints on the brindle dog's legs. A few minutes later, siren bursts hung in the air, as the ambulance sped away with its patient. While I worked, animal control lured snarling dogs and trembling dogs and just plain shut-down dogs into crates. One of them carried a lifeless shepherd. I checked that they didn't need me and asked if someone would help me carry the brindle dog to my truck.

A tech wearing a sweatshirt that said "There's no such thing as Just a Dog" helped me slide a stretcher under him.

Doug hurried toward us. "I need your help."

"What is it?"

"Someone—probably the beagle guys—jumped Jackson. He was cut."

"Good." I motioned for the tech to lift the dog. We walked away. Doug caught up, as we slid the dog into a caged area of my truck.

"Lucy, I can't have Jackson bleeding all the way to jail. Will you…?" He nodded back toward the arena.

My helper spun around. "You've got to be kidding, sheriff. Look at this dog! Jackson deserves whatever happens to him. They all do."

"You know how I feel about him." I checked the dog's IV. "Let one of your men patch him up. They have first aid kits."

"He saw you. Knows you're an EMT."

I shrugged a *so what*?

"He asked for you."

I turned and met his eyes. "He must have a death wish. If he had any brains, he'd be afraid of me."

"He knows you despise him. He's taunting you, paying you back for taking Daphne. It kills me to ask you, but I don't want anything to screw up this arrest. You're the most qualified person here to treat him. I wouldn't care if he bled to death, but not tonight."

I'd wanted Jackson hurt. Seemed ungrateful to complain now.

I grabbed my kit and asked the tech to stay with the dog, then trailed behind Doug, telling myself I could do this.

Jackson held a bloody cloth to his face.

"Looks like dogfighting is becoming dangerous for you, Jackson. Why not give it up?" I felt obligated to ask.

"I've got the right to do what I want. A scratch like this won't stop me. Nothing will… Lucy." He said my name as if he were flirting, but the pause before it turned it into an ugly promise.

Doug stepped forward.

"Give me some room, Doug." I waved him away and opened my kit. "Ever think about the dogs, Jackson?"

"All the way to the bank." He lowered his voice so Doug couldn't hear. "And don't think I've forgotten you have something that belongs to me."

I clenched my teeth and double-gloved. I forced myself to clean the cut on Jackson's face as gently as I could and applied an analgesic I'd mixed that evening.

He flinched when the cold salve filled his open wound, then leered at me. "Be gentle. It's my first time."

I pretended I hadn't heard him. I closed the wound with butterfly strips, pressed on a leak-proof bandage, and told him not to take it off for a week, the time it would take to form a scab. I put the salve container and bloody gauze in a double plastic bag, pulled my gloves off inside-out, and stuffed everything in my pocket.

"Must gall you having to minister to me." His smile gave me chills.

I looked into his eyes. He must have seen something unsettling there, because the smile faltered, but then his lip curled in contempt.

I closed my kit. "It wouldn't hurt to have a doctor take a look at you."

"I can take care of myself. They're nothing but a waste of money." He spat. "Like vets."

I shrugged. "Suit yourself."

I made my way back to my truck and lied when the tech asked if I was okay. After he left, I pulled myself into the driver's seat and leaned against the steering wheel until I stopped feeling faint. I didn't have time to think about what had just happened. The brindle dog needed my help.

* * * *

I'd told Smitty about the raid and wasn't surprised to find him waiting on the porch. He and my tech put the brindle dog on a table, while I changed clothes and scrubbed my hands and arms.

We almost lost the mauled dog twice, and for a moment, I'd thought it might be kinder to let him go, but he'd made it this far and deserved a chance. I wondered how hard he would fight to stay in a world that had shown him nothing but cruelty. Smitty said he'd watch over him and unrolled a blanket next to his pen. Maybe the dog would choose to live.

Shortly after I cleaned up, Doug came by to check on the dog—and me. He apologized again for asking me to treat Jackson.

"Doug, we did what we had to do. It's over."

We drank coffee on the porch and watched pale yellow light rise behind the hills. We were both exhausted and unsettled by our night's work.

"The dog fighting world won't recover from this raid for months. Hope they blame Jackson." He looked into his mug. "You know he'll be out by this afternoon, and then his lawyer will get postponement after postponement, hoping the whole thing will go away, and Jackson will go back to his ranch and not come out until the next dogfight. Just like the other times."

I wanted to tell him not to worry—I had counted on Jackson returning to the isolation of his ranch without spending a day in jail. He would ignore the headaches and chills, thinking he had the flu, and by the time the convulsions started, and he realized he was dying, he would be too weak and disoriented to seek help.

I thought of Jill Stoner and the other women he had killed. Of the dogs who had suffered. Of Daphne. And I couldn't think of a more fitting way for him to die. Rabid and alone.

I breathed in the sweet scent of lemon blossoms and looked forward to a beautiful summer.

Mary Adler escaped her former life as an attorney and dean at CWRU School of Medicine for the gentler world of World War II and the adventures of homicide detective Oliver Wright and his German shepherd, Harley. She grounds the mysteries in the realities of wartime but tempers them with the warmth of friends, of food shared, and, of course, wonderful dogs. Join her in starting each day with the question poet Mary Oliver poses: "Tell me, what is it you plan to do with your one wild and precious life?"

BLACK ON BLACK IN BLACK

MB DABNEY

A guy in a late model station wagon flipped off Kendall Hunter after she changed lanes on Walnut Street on her way to her West Philly apartment. It was a minor annoyance, which she mostly ignored.

At only 7 o'clock, it was an early evening for Kendall, one of the FBI Philadelphia Field Office's best criminal profilers. Tall, slender and Black, she didn't look like your typical agent, which she used to her advantage.

Work was her main distraction in an otherwise dull life, and she threw herself into it. But for once, she was looking forward to a quiet night with her cat, a glass of wine, and mindless television.

Her cell phone rang. Situated in a holder next to the dashboard, she glanced at it quickly and immediately recognized the caller ID. It was an annoyance she could not ignore.

"Damn."

She touched a button on the steering wheel, which shut off the streaming audio of John Coltrane coming through her sound system, and connected the call.

"Hunter here."

"Kendall. It's Max."

FBI Special Agent Oscar Maxwell was her boss and the leader of a team on the trail of a serial killer.

"What's up?" Kendall said, swerving into another lane to avoid hitting a gray Honda whose driver wasn't paying attention.

"Our serial killer struck again."

"You sure?" she said.

"Yeah, I'm sure. I know you've quit for the day…."

"I'm on my way home, Max," she interrupted.

He didn't seem to notice. "But I'd like you to have a look."

A quick intake of breath preceded a brief silence. Then, "Describe it for me."

Max gave her the basic details and the address of the apartment. "It's up in Chestnut Hill, just off Allens Lane."

Kendall looked at her watch, then flipped on her turn signal for an abrupt right turn at 40th Street. "It'll take about 30 minutes to get there."

"We'll still be here."

Traffic was light on Lincoln Drive up into Chestnut Hill, an area of expensive homes and nice apartments, and at least Kendall could enjoy the ride. Her personal vehicle was a black BMW that she purchased three years ago after divorcing her philandering husband. She loved its power, and the gentle vibration of its engine was nearly a sexual experience.

She pulled up to the fashionable apartment building 27 minutes after hanging up from Max and parked across from the black and white medical examiner's van.

As a matter of habit, Kendall shoved her black Coach saddlebag under the passenger seat. This was Philadelphia, and despite all the police cars present, she never left anything of even the slightest value visible in the car. No sense in tempting a thief.

Marching up the stone stairs to the front door of the quadruplex apartment building, Kendall showed her government ID to two of Philadelphia's finest in blue, who stood as silent sentries at the entry doors. But once past them, it didn't take long to figure out where to go. The foyer and the first-floor apartment on the right were crawling with cops.

Fellow FBI agent Chris Columbus met her at the door and ushered her in.

Kendall surveyed the living room without speaking. The place was a mess but not because of any criminal activity.

There was barely enough space to sit down on the couch because of the litter of books, magazines, clothing, and a laptop. The coffee table was stacked so high with junk that it was difficult to imagine anyone seeing the television in the cabinet across the room. There was hardly any empty flat space in the first two rooms.

"Borderline hoarder," Columbus commented.

"Kendall, we're down here," came a voice from the far end of the interior hallway.

They headed down in the direction of a bedroom. Max and a heavyset, middle-aged man in an ill-fitting dark blue police captain's uniform met them at the bedroom door.

Max made the introductions.

"Captain Washington, this is Special Agent Kendall Hunter. I called her in because she is working on a profile of our serial killer."

"Nice to meet you," Washington said, sticking out his hand. She took it.

"And you, as well," she said warmly. "Tell me what we have."

"Why don't you have a look," Max said.

They entered the room and walked around an officer taking pictures.

The bedroom was in the same cluttered condition as the rooms in the front of the apartment. The bed was unmade and piled high with clothes, barely leaving enough room for someone to sleep. A laundry basket full of unfolded clothes was at the foot of the bed. It was hard to determine whether they were clean or dirty. An ironing board, converted to a shelf and stacked high with magazines, stood in the corner next to a broken floor lamp. The top of the dresser was full of personal items—hairbrush, makeup, earrings, and perfume—that didn't look like they had been touched in some time.

In all the disorder, there was one thing that clearly was more out of the ordinary than the rest.

In a chair next to the window was a woman, her head back, a blank stare in her eyes. Her arms were tied behind her back.

Blood congealed around the single bullet hole to the forehead.

She wore only a tight t-shirt that didn't cover her navel and a pair of neon yellow panties. She was pretty, even in death, and racially ambiguous in a way currently popular in media —a little too much color for a white woman but too little color to be considered black.

Max walked up to stand next to the body.

"She wasn't much for housekeeping," Columbus said behind him.

"Doesn't matter much now," Max said as he looked into the emptiness of the woman's brown eyes.

"Who is she?" Kendall said.

Washington ticked off the information from the top of his head. "Melissa Harris. Age 26. Single, lived alone. Worked as a financial analyst for an insurance company downtown."

"How long she been dead?"

"Last night some time. Last seen leaving her job yesterday. Didn't report to work this morning."

"Any evidence of sexual assault?" Max asked as he looked more closely at the body but didn't touch it.

"No," Washington answered. "No markings on her at all, except on the wrists where she was tied."

"Any evidence of how the assailant got in?" Kendall asked.

"It wasn't a break-in. No broken windows or door locks."

"Must have let them in," Columbus said, folding his arms across his chest, as if the gesture might help provide a better perspective.

"Seems that way," Kendall said. "Weapon?"

"Small caliber. Close range," Washington said. "I have officers checking the apartment and the surrounding area. Nothing yet."

"Look in here," said Columbus, who was standing in the bedroom doorway next to the bathroom. They walked over and looked at the mirror in the bathroom. "Same as in the case near Wilmington, Delaware, and the one in Delaware County."

“That’s why we called in you feds,” Washington said.

“I see,” Max said, absentmindedly scratching the stubble on his chin.

“But we didn’t find any evidence of the man,” Washington said. “We checked her laptop. She’s registered on a couple of adult websites as White Chocolate and looking for men to date, implying she was willing to do more. Could be one of these online guys found and killed her.”

“This is similar to the cases in Maryland and Delaware and the other two in Pennsylvania, all in the last 30 months,” Columbus volunteered. “This guy seems to be heading north.”

Kendall stood with her hands on her hips, looking at the victim. The ME would remove the body as soon as she finished. “You said it was a small-caliber handgun.”

“Excuse me, please,” Washington said. “I’ve got to go check on the others down the hall. And hopefully, someone’s found the murder weapon.”

Washington left, and Kendall continued to study the crime scene, asking only a few questions. When she finished, Columbus offered his opinion. Unsolicited.

“This is a perfect crime,” he said. Some guy finds women on the Internet, arranges to meet them, ties them up with their undergarments, shoots them in the head, writes two words on a mirror, and leaves no clues.”

“Besides all the known facts, I disagree with you on this being a perfect crime,” Kendall said, irritation creeping into her voice. “Killers make mistakes. There’s always a clue somewhere. A drop of blood. A stray hair. A small piece of fabric. The killer can’t cover everything. There’s got to be a clue. We just have to be clever enough to find it.”

“Well, that’s why you’re the best profiler,” Max said as he and Columbus headed back down the hallway to the crowded living room, leaving Kendall alone.

She went into the bathroom and looked intensely at the words scribbled in capital letters on the mirror.

SLUT WHORE

Kendall’s brows furrowed. She ran her finger close to the glass but avoided the lipstick-scrawled words. Then, in a reflection in the mirror, she saw something. She turned to look closer. It was small and on the floor near the wall just past the doorway.

She stooped down to pick up a small, silver stud and examined it closer. It was the type of thing a man might overlook, particularly given the disheveled condition of the apartment.

Kendall dropped the stud into her jacket pocket.

Max looked up as Kendall entered the living room moments later.

“We about done here?” she asked. “I’d like to get home in time to watch some TV before bed.”

"Yeah. We're good. I think we'll wrap it up for now. We can go over everything again in the morning," Max said. "File a report first thing, and then, we can talk. You have a nice evening."

"I will," she said with a dismissive wave of her hand as she reached the front door. Moments later, she was at the car, and she slid onto the black leather seat in the black BMW.

Black on black in black.

She reached into her pocket and pulled out the small, silver stud. Grabbing her purse from the floor under the passenger seat, she could see the stud was a perfect match for a missing stud on her black Coach saddlebag. She hadn't noticed before that it was missing.

Like I said. The killer always makes a mistake. Leaves a clue somewhere, she thought to herself. Just like tramps looking for married men online always get what's coming to them.

A smile of self-satisfaction spread across Kendall's face as she started the car, put it in gear and drove home.

Perhaps I'll have two glasses of wine.

MB Dabney is an award-winning journalist whose writing has appeared in local and national publications. A native of Indianapolis, Michael spent decades as a reporter working for *Business Week* magazine, UPI and AP, the *Indianapolis Star*, and *The Philadelphia Tribune*, the nation's oldest continuously published black newspaper, where he won awards for editorial writing. He has been a member of Sisters in Crime since 2008. His first novel, *An Untidy Affair*, is being published in early 2021. The father of two adult daughters, Michael lives in Indianapolis with his wife, Angela, and their dog, Pluto.

THE PEARL NECKLACE

E.B. DAVIS

Peggy Brant's heart raced as she peered into Galloway Department Store's display window on her way to work. She couldn't resist. The sign in the window proclaimed, "Congratulations Class of 1961." Graduation gifts for young men and women were showcased. Fancy pen sets, leather belts, luggage, watches, graduation charms, Smith Corona typewriters, and pearl necklaces. She pined for a pearl necklace, but the cheapest one was eighty dollars and the most expensive, two hundred and thirty dollars, more than a fifth of her yearly college tuition, room, and board. Her mother could never afford such luxuries. If not for the scholarships Peggy had won, looking for a full-time job would be on her agenda. Working part-time at the diner with her mother was all the menial work she ever wanted to do.

Having lost her husband in WWII, Peggy's mom worked long hours to scrape together the rent and grocery money. Her mother couldn't afford to buy her a graduation gift, but Peggy knew she deserved one. A pearl necklace would be such a nice reward for all her years of hard work and perseverance. A lump narrowed her throat. She swallowed. Tears wetted her eyes. Before she could clamp down her feelings, one tear ran down her face. Detachment. That's what she always resorted to when injustice and inequity won. With a slow exhale, she wiped the tear away and knew the only reward she'd get was four more years of hard work. But she had plans and dreams. She'd buy herself a pearl necklace and help her mother financially one day.

The window reflected a streak of apricot. The streak turned into a slowing car, which pulled into a diagonal parking spot behind her. Laughter shrieked out of the convertible. Three rich girls from her high school class sat in the brand-new 1961 Buick Flamingo. Betty Lou Harris drove with Margie Sharp in the front passenger seat that swiveled. Margie turned the seat to face Shirley Gibbs, who stretched out in the backseat. Peggy wondered if the car was a graduation gift. She watched the girls in the mirror-like store front.

Betty Lou cut the engine. "Let's hit the racks. I have to find a prom dress today."

"I can't believe your mother bought you a prom dress without even asking if you liked it. You didn't even try it on." Margie wrinkled her nose.

"Yeah, but Daddy said I could get another one if that one didn't suit me."

Shirley leaned in from the backseat. "It really is a nice dress. But your mom was thinking of herself more than you. Get a tight, low-cut dress like Jayne Mansfield wears." The girls shrieked with laughter.

"It's bad enough she's making me go to her alma mater." Betty huffed and patted her flipped hair. "I'll pick out my own dress." She opened the car door.

The girls were dressed in the new tapered-leg pants with stirrup straps, keeping their silhouettes sleek. Betty Lou patted the pearl necklace strung around her neck. Peggy wondered if it was another graduation gift.

The waitress uniform Peggy wore was a hand-me-down from her mother. Her fabric shoulder bag, also a castoff of her mother's, was boxy and middle-aged. So—1950s. But the bag contained her lucky shell. Thrusting her hand inside, she felt for the shell, a memento from the rare day she and her mother had spent at the beach a few years ago. She couldn't find it at first, but then felt it wedged in the hole of the torn lining. As she disentangled it, her fingers brushed against the hidden security pocket she'd sown into the bag's bottom. She rubbed her fingers over the shell's smooth interior, just like the nacre that formed pearls. As she rubbed the shell, her racing heart slowed.

"Peggy, what are you doing here?" Shirley asked. "Looking to buy a graduation gift for yourself?" Peggy had always thought Shirley seemed nicer than the other two. Then, she'd witnessed Shirley's quirky mean streak that occasionally struck some unsuspecting girl like Peggy's friend, who found herself in detention after Shirley accused her of cheating on a test. The accusation smarted all the more when the school administration decided to punish her friend without proof. Now, Peggy didn't trust any of these girls.

Turning toward the street to face Shirley, Peggy laughed. "No, Shirley. You know I couldn't afford anything in the window."

"If you could, which one would you get?" Shirley walked to Peggy with the others following.

Was Shirley serious? "Why? What's it to you?"

"Maybe I'll buy it for you. Which one?"

"Be serious, Shirley. I have to go to work," Peggy said, even though she was early. She made a quarter turn to walk down the sidewalk, but Shirley scooted in front of her, Betty Lou closed in on her side, and Margie stood behind her, surrounding her, pinning her against the window.

"Girls, this is ridiculous." Peggy crossed her arms.

"Which one?" Shirley asked again, crossing her arms, too.

Peggy sighed. She knew Shirley's question was frivolous, but then, she was rich. Would she buy her a necklace? Doubtful, but then why would she want to know? Peggy restrained herself from eyeing Betty Lou's necklace. "The pearl necklace," she said, trying to convey nonchalance in her tone.

Shirley stood aside. Peggy stepped forward to leave, coming level with Shirley, who took hold of Peggy's shoulders. "Come on, girls. Peggy needs to try on some pearl necklaces." The others brought up the rear, and before she knew it, the girls pushed her through the front door of the store. She thought about yanking herself free and fleeing, but she'd love to try on a pearl necklace.

They trooped past the cosmetics department to the back where the finer jewelry counters gleamed under the lights. Peggy wondered if they used brighter bulbs to make the jewels shine. She felt spotlighted and warm under their brightness.

Shirley led them to the counter, beckoning to the young salesclerk. "We'd like to see the pearl necklaces. Could you take out those four for us? Oh, and maybe that pearl ring, too." The clerk hesitated.

"I'm not really supposed to take out more than two at a time." She looked at the rich girls' smart outfits, dismissed Peggy. "But for you, I'll make an exception." The clerk lined the countertop with the four necklaces and ring on top of a display board. Covered with navy velvet, the background contrasted to the luminescence of the pearls. Peggy breathed through her nose so she wouldn't gasp. The pearls were stunning.

Shirley picked up one necklace and ran her fingers over the pearls, like she was an expert evaluating them. Squished between Betty Lou and Shirley, Peggy wondered why they pinned her in place against the counter, restricting her movements. She didn't like the close proximity. It made her feel powerless. Her forehead broke out in beads of sweat.

Margie looked at other jewelry while drifting away from them to the far end of the case. Didn't she want to see the pearl necklaces, too? "There's an adorable pearl barrette I'd like to see. Maybe it will match the pearls in one of the necklaces," Margie said to the clerk.

When the clerk walked to the end of the case to do Margie's bidding, Betty Lou put her arm around Peggy's shoulders and pointed to a pearl bracelet in the case. "Peggy, wouldn't it be divine to have the whole set?"

Peggy felt a tug on her bag. Her stomach dropped. Shirley had stuck something in her bag. One shoplifting charge, and her scholarships would be withdrawn and everything she'd worked for gone. Peggy wanted to jerk herself free, but then reined in her emotions. If she caused a commotion, security would be called, and whatever was in her bag would be found.

A cold, calm anger enveloped her. Peggy had never stolen anything in her life. They were framing and incriminating her as a team. Margie had walked away and gotten the clerk's attention. Betty Lou had tried to distract her with the bracelet, giving Shirley the opportunity to steal something and drop it into her bag. She'd worked too hard for these rich girls to wreck her life. She didn't understand people like them, destructive, nasty, mean.

Peggy slipped her right hand into her bag and felt a ring. "You are so right, Betty Lou. When the clerk returns, ask her if we could look at the bracelet, too," she said and slipped the ring on the tip of her finger, turned the pearls to the inside, and cupped her hand, concealing the it.

Margie walked over to them, carrying the barrette. She huddled next to Shirley. "Let's see which necklace the barrette's pearls most closely match."

Betty Lou asked the clerk about the bracelet while Shirley and Margie studied the barrette. "I wonder how the barrette's clasp works," Margie said, and slid the barrette into her hair. "Oh, it's easy. Press down to clasp, squeeze the little bars at the end to unclasp."

With the three girls' attention elsewhere, Peggy slid her hand out of her bag. She could place the ring back onto the counter, but then, maybe they needed to learn a lesson. She slid her hand into Shirley's bag. A light touch revealed an interior pocket where she dropped the ring. She slipped her hand back into her own bag, feeling around to make sure that was the only thing Shirley had placed there.

The clerk looked anxious. "Ladies, take a few more minutes, but if you could eliminate at least two of the necklaces, I need to get them back in the case. We aren't really allowed to have more than two items out at a time. With the barrette and ring, I've taken out six items. Please!"

Peggy felt in the bottom of her bag. She fingered smooth pearls. Shirley had made doubly sure with the ring and a necklace to snare her with shop-lifting charges. She coiled the necklace in her fist, ready to move her hand to the counter and release it, hoping the clerk would think the necklace had been there the entire time.

"Of course, honey. We don't want you in any trouble. Take the bracelet and ring back," Shirley said. She looked around the top of the case, let her mouth fall open, and feigned shock. "What happened to the ring?"

"I don't know where the ring went," Betty Lou said. "And look, I think one of the necklaces is gone, too."

With her hand still in her bag gripping the necklace, there was no time left to return it to the counter. Peggy's shoulders rose. What could she do?

Shirley stared at Peggy. "The last time I saw either, Peggy was holding them. What have you done, Peggy? I mean, I know you can't afford this stuff, but stealing is just wrong." Shirley turned to the clerk. "You'd better get the store management."

Peggy felt like she'd taken a stage role, the stooge. They'd set her up and now waited for her comeuppance. While the clerk dialed a phone number, Shirley smiled at Peggy. The other two girls backed away from Peggy as if she had cooties, and Shirley joined them. Peggy's hand was still gripping the necklace. She dropped it to the bottom of her bag and worked to conceal it with her fingers. Then, she stroked her lucky shell, hoping her plan worked.

A tall, lean man appeared at the counter. Peggy knew him from the diner. Mr. Tate. He was a serious man but tipped well. He spoke to the clerk and then addressed the four of them. When his eyes glanced at Peggy, he hesitated. She knew he recognized her. "Ladies, it appears a ring and a necklace have disappeared while you were looking at them. Let's take this off the sales floor." He pointed to a side door. "Follow me."

The cramped office contained a desk and three chairs. Mr. Tate moved behind the desk, and the girls took the chairs, leaving Peggy to stand. The name plate on the desk read "Mr. George Tate, Security Manager." Behind Peggy, the door started to open. She scooted to the side, allowing an older woman to enter the office. "This is Mrs. Campbell. She'll assist me today. She's going to pat you down. I'll check your bags."

Betty Lou stood. "This is outrageous. I want to call my father."

"May I see all of your drivers' licenses?" Mr. Tate asked.

All of them gave him their licenses. After looking at them, he smiled. "You've already had your eighteenth birthdays." Addressing Betty Lou, he said, "I have every right to search your bags and have Mrs. Campbell pat you down. We take shoplifting seriously at Galloway's, and we prosecute." Motioning to Mrs. Campbell, he said, "Proceed." To Betty Lou, he said, "Your bag first, Miss Harris."

Betty Lou gave her bag to Mr. Tate, "And to think I was going to buy my prom dress here today. You just lost your store a nice sale, mister."

After searching the bag, Mr. Tate handed it back to Betty Lou. "Thank you, Miss Harris." He pointed to Margie, took her bag, rummaged around in it, and returned it to her.

Meanwhile, Mrs. Campbell had already felt up and down Peggy's body and looked through her pockets. She was doing the same to Shirley when Mr. Tate asked to see Shirley's bag. With a growl, Shirley thrust her bag at him.

Mr. Tate removed Shirley's wallet, placed it on his desk, and let his hand roam inside. "Look what we have here, Miss Gibbs," he said, pulling out the pearl ring from the interior pocket.

Shirley screamed, and then stopped, crossing her arms and squeezing her biceps to get in control. "I didn't put it there. I have no idea how it got there." She turned to Peggy, her hand shaking as she pointed at her. "She put it in my bag to incriminate me. My parents belong to the country club. I have no need to steal. But Peggy does. She told us she wanted a pearl necklace."

Mr. Tate motioned for Peggy's bag. Her stomach muscles tightened as she handed it over. He looked through her bag, dumped everything out, held it upside down, and shook it. Bits of paper and pens from the bottom dropped out. He looked inside the bag and then at Peggy. "What do we have here?"

Shirley looked triumphant. Peggy swallowed hard. Tears started to form. There was no way she could explain away the pearl necklace. No chance of retaining her scholarships.

Mr. Tate pulled out her lucky shell and raised his eyebrows. Then, he gathered everything of Peggy's off his desk and dumped it back in her bag. "You're clean." He handed the bag back to her.

Shirley's hardened eyes glared at Peggy.

Mrs. Campbell had finished patting down Margie and started on Betty Lou. "Mr. Tate, this girl is wearing a pearl necklace."

"You don't say. You mean the indignant one?"

Mrs. Campbell stifled a laugh and then smiled. "Yes, that's the one."

Betty Lou fingered the pearl necklace. "But my father gave this to me. It's one of my graduation gifts. I didn't steal it. I was wearing it when I entered the store." Betty Lou looked over to her friends.

"Yes, she did wear it. I was at her house when she opened the gift," Margie said, elbowing Shirley.

"Yeah, it's hers. Her dad gave it to her." Shirley shrugged.

"If that's the case, then I'm sure your father will have the receipt. I'm calling the police." His hand neared the telephone on the desk, but before he could pick up the receiver, the phone rang. "Yes. Really? I wondered about that. Thanks." He hung up the phone. "That was the jewelry sales clerk. Seems a pearl barrette is also missing, just like the one Miss Sharp has in her hair."

Margie's hand rose to her hair. "I wasn't stealing this. I was checking the clasp to see how it worked." Her mouth remained open, but no sounds came out.

Mr. Tate quirked his mouth to the side and drummed his fingers on the desk. "Nice try." To Peggy he said, "You're free to go. But if you come back into the store, know that I'll be watching you."

* * * *

On the sidewalk, Peggy heaved a sigh of relief. She wanted to run, but that would have made her look guilty. The incident left her too weak to run, anyway. Entering the empty back room of the diner, she looked around to make sure no one was near. She sat down on a bench and felt inside her bag.

When the hole in the lining got big enough to be bothersome, she'd tried to sew it. Having sewn most of her clothing, she was a whiz with a needle. But the lining was so thin, it would have ripped again, even resewn. Her mother had warned her to find a way to keep some money hidden before going to college in the fall, in case her wallet was ever stolen. Every girl needed a few dollars for emergencies.

The solution came from the research project she'd done last year on new inventions from a 1958 Time magazine article. She couldn't sew the hole shut, but she could use it. She'd slipped a flap of heavy felt through the lining's hole and sown it into the bag's exterior material, inside near the bag's center seam. It wasn't easy sewing through the hole. Then, she fastened the flap with that new invention featured in the magazine article and seen in pictures from the 1959 New York fashion show. Velcro was a new-age marvel. Even NASA was looking into using it in space capsules to keep objects from flying around inside while in zero gravity.

Shirley had thrown the ring and the necklace in her bag at the same time. Peggy would have returned the necklace, had there been time. But the girls moved quickly to get her arrested. So, she had pushed it through the lining and into the felt flap, securing it with the Velcro closure. Then stuck her lucky shell into the lining's hole. When Mr. Tate dumped the bag upside down, she'd been nervous. But Velcro was truly the new miracle fastener.

Peggy would keep the necklace hidden. Everyone in town would be suspicious if she wore the necklace. But next fall, one hundred miles away at college, she'd wear and love it.

Betty Lou's father might have the necklace receipt, but Shirley and Margie would be stuck explaining the ring and the barrette. Peggy smiled. Maybe in a few years, she'd share the story with her friend, whom Shirley had accused of cheating.

E. B. Davis's short stories have appeared in many anthologies and online magazines, including *Kings River Life* and *Mysterical-E Magazines*. Look for "The Ice Cream Allure" a romantic mystery spoof contained in *Carolina Crimes: 19 Tales of Lust, Love, and Longing*. Her story, "Compromised Circumstances" appeared in the anthology, *Chesapeake Crimes: Homicidal Holidays*. A complete list and links to her other stories can be found at http://ebdavismysteries.com. She interviews authors at http://writerswhokill.blogspot.com, and is a member of SinC, the SinC Guppy Chapter, where she serves as Class Guppy on the Steering Committee, and The Short Mystery Fiction Society.

KNOW NOTHING

C. M. SURRISI

Makiline Price was a quiet woman who lived her life in and above her shop, the Olde World Bakery. My mother whispered to me that she was a "war bride from Poland," and, "It was a downright shame that Oren Price brought her all the way here, then up and died. She ought to go back to Warsaw. She'd be happier." I don't think my mother appreciated that, back in Warsaw, people were still struggling against post-war corruption.

Thirty years later, Makiline Price disappeared. It may have been to a better Warsaw.

As a boy, I was drawn to the Olde World Bakery by the smells and to Makiline by her crinkly-eyed smile. It may also have been because she gave me one free treat every time I went in. I always picked a slice of makowiec.

"Mak-ov-yetz," she made me repeat.

"Mak-ov-yetz," I said.

"The most Polish cakes. A thin layer sweet bread rolled around thick layer of poppy seed."

My selection was always followed by her swift admonition that one piece was all a person should eat in a day. For years, I thought her advice was about obesity. Eventually, I decided she was warning me off too much poppy seed.

She'd say, "Too much can kill you...." Then she would pause and shrug her shoulders. "Or bring you back from dead."

Despite the name Olde World conjuring up images of course-milled grains and raw sugars, it was far from that. Makiline was a master of refined Polish sweet breads, cakes, tortes, buns, and cookies. Their appearance and taste was so exquisite that they inspired me to become a baker, and by the time I was eighteen, I had signed up for the local trade school course. Even after I secured a second shift commercial baking job at a hospital, I remained among the steady throng of devotees who stopped by her shop the first thing in the morning for warm prune kolacky. I, of course, also had the quintessential slice of makowiec and each day received the requisite warning.

When I married and had children, I took them to Olde World on Saturday mornings for a paczki, the ancestor of the raspberry-filled Bismark but legions better for its delicate dough and orange zest. The kids watched me receive my slice along with the lecture. I explained what I had learned in baking school—that poppy seeds were chemically close relatives to opium, morphine, and heroin. They asked what those things were, and I explained that they were both prescription pain-killers and street drugs, which they should always stay away from. The explanation and warning sailed over their heads. They shrugged and took big bites into their paczki, dripping jam on their chins.

One Thursday morning, I was running a little later than usual. I arrived at Olde World at 9:30 a.m. and ordered my poppy seed delight. We bantered about my blue chef's coat and Croc shoes, and I cajoled Makiline for the thousandth time to give me her recipe for makowiec. She laughed and waved me away.

I sat at a small table by the window, polishing off my slice, when two men in leather jackets came into the shop. Their similar height, neck thickness, and pattern baldness made me wonder if they were brothers, possibly twins.

Makiline became all business when she saw them. The three conversed quietly, almost hungrily, in Polish. One of them jerked his thumb to the back room. The other handed her a brown paper grocery bag, crunch-rolled shut. She took it and retreated behind the beaded curtain, returning a few seconds later with two long loaves wrapped in white paper and trussed up with string. One of the men took the loaves. The other one smiled crookedly and saluted her with two fingers as he left.

She muttered what I took to be a prayer under her breath. It was probably my imagination, but the loaves were the size and shape of large makowiec. I guessed, if you were Polish he-men, you didn't get the warning about one slice per day. Of course, it could have been some special order of caraway rye.

Over the next months, out of concern for Makiline and due to my own curiosity, I kept my eye out for the two men. In fact, I altered my regular pattern and made a point of stopping by later on Thursday mornings. I was right. They came by regularly at 9:45 a.m., and the routine was the same. The three confabbed in hushed tones, the men handed over a sack, and she provided the loaves.

The repetition of the scene fueled my imagination and my concern. I worried for Makiline. What were they giving her? What was she giving them back? Where these men taking advantage of an aging war bride? She didn't seem to be coerced. If the loaves were indeed makowiec, were poppy seeds somehow implicated in this transaction?

It didn't help that I began to take note of Makiline's greying hair and deep facial lines. And that her clothes and apron hung loosely. Other patrons showed similar concern. "Makiline, how goes it?" "How are you feeling?" "Losing a little weight? Are you okay?" "Don't get sick on us now! We need you."

I drove my wife mad hypothesizing that the paper bag contained non-comestible poppy seed that Makiline was baking into something akin to Polish marijuana brownies for the local black market.

She laughed.

I protested that the simple poppy was a significant source for drugs, and these goofballs could be getting high on them—or getting kids high on them.

She just laughed harder. "Kids don't really like poppy seeds," she said.

"I did!" I argued. The whole thing made me want to save Makiline from her opium induced misdeeds.

Meantime, I fantasized about having my own bakery and serving fancy European pastries. But my efforts to duplicate Makiline's pastries convinced me that I couldn't do it without her recipes, if I wanted to do it well. There was something special in her touch.

Finally, one day, I waited until she was about to lock up and asked to talk to her. She secured the door and led me to the back, where I noted a commercial floor mixer, refrigerator, freezer, and tidy pantry. A clean stainless steel work counter occupied the center of the room. Across from them stood two perfectly-sized ovens. It was all just as I had imagined.

She offered me a coffee that could only be described as non-feeble. I took it and winced at the first sip.

I carefully approached the subject on my mind. "Makiline, I'd like to talk to you about something important."

Her shoulders stiffened.

"Oh, no. No. Nothing bad. I would like to buy the Olde World from you."

She laughed. "And I would like to go back Warsaw."

"I'm serious. You could go back to Warsaw. I can afford to pay you for your equipment and the value of your going concern. That would," I paused for a couple seconds, "include your recipes."

Makiline sank onto a stool as if in a sudden state of exhaustion. Her gaze roamed the room and settled on the small desk where a stuffed notebook held a wad of curled edge sheets. The recipes. I got a shiver up my spine at the sight of them.

"I have responsibilities," she said weakly, "...to customers."

"I can assume those," I said.

"You wouldn't want all."

I thought about the two men and their long loaves of makowiec. I'd already resolved this in my mind. I'd chalked it up to some form of stupidity. They were giving her a bag of non-food grade poppy seeds, and she was baking them into loaded loaves. My research told me there was no amount of poppy seed, comestible or otherwise, that could do serious harm to anyone. Since I didn't speak a word of Polish, I'd feign ignorance and refuse their paper bag. It would all be over quickly.

I could see her decades of fierce self-preservation dissolve before me. She asked, "What you think it worth?"

"Do you own the building?"

She laughed. "No. I rent the bakery and small apartment upstairs."

I'd done some calculations based on what I guessed was here, and I was pretty much on the nose…if I got the recipes. "With your recipe book, I think the equipment and good will is worth about $25,000."

"What about platters, curtains, pictures?" she asked.

She was referring to the antique china platters on which she displayed the baked goods in the glass cases, the handmade lace curtains, and the daguerreotype photographs of Poland in gilded frames. I'd imagined she would be reluctant to part with them. They looked so much like family treasures. Even though they delivered ambiance to the stark room with its rolling wood planked floors, ceiling lamps, and frosted glass windows, I was not going to press her for them. I hadn't placed a value on them, but if she was truly going back to Warsaw, what good were they to her?

"Whatever you say, Makiline. If you want to take them, take them. If you want to leave them, I can increase the price by..." I took a wild-ass guess within my budget, "five thousand dollars. I'm not asking you to leave things that are dear to you."

I fully expected her to say she would think about it, and take one week, two weeks, even let it drag on for months, before she made a decision.

She breathed quietly as her eyes roamed the kitchen. Complicated calculations appeared to be taking place in her mind.

"You sure? This can be rough business?" She moved her hand to show unevenness.

How rough could it be, I thought. I could bear some financial ups and downs.

"Yes, I'm sure."

Then she shocked me and said, "Okay. You keep all. You are big boy. I will go in the night. I'm ready to leave. But I don't want no one to know when I'm go, or where I'm go."

I sputtered. "Are…are you sure?"

She nodded with the fatigue of a woman who had baked too many babkas. She stared straight ahead. It was almost as if she was watching a movie of her life pass before her eyes: Poland, the war, a young soldier, a ship, a marriage, a dream, a death, a life of baking, then sunshine on her homeland—on a bright horizon. She walked to the desk, picked up the recipe book, and clasped it to her chest as if it were a child.

She took a few short steps and put the precious book in my hands.

"You study. You smart. You love them. I know you will bake very good."

I touched the edges of the pages with my fingertips, not wanting to fully open the book in her presence. It seemed too personal.

"Take home," she said. "Sunday when bakery closed, I will bake with you. One time. Then I will go."

My shock mushroomed into flushed cheeks. It was happening too fast. "Can I give you a deposit? To show good faith for borrowing the recipes?" I didn't want anyone to think I had taken advantage of her.

She pfffd. "I know from child. I trust you."

"Thank you so much, Makiline." I stood. "Please think about this overnight. You can change your mind, if you want to."

She pinched my cheek. "You are terrible negotiations man. I trust you."

I touched her wrinkled hand. "You are a great lady."

"I am running away lady. You are young risk taker."

Sunday came, and I arrived with my list. I also carried my own notebook, since I couldn't bring myself to make a mark on her pages. The script of her recipes, obviously written with a fountain pen, had an elegance to it that could be mistaken for sheet music at first glance. I was particularly intrigued with the title, "Makowiec Wielkiej Babci." It took me a while searching online to translate it to Great Grandmother's Makowiec. How lucky could I be?

We started with kotacki (foldovers), moved on to chrusciki (bowties), made paczki (doughnuts), szarlotka (apple tart), kolacky (filled buns), mazurek (fruit-filled pastry) and finally makowiec. The baking went on into the dark hours of the night and tantalized my senses with the aroma of cinnamon, apples, and cardamom, among other heavenly scents.

When it came time to make the poppy seed filling, Makiline pulled a gallon-sized plastic jug off the shelf. The label was from a commercial bakery supplier. I unscrewed the top and took a whiff. She laughed and pushed my face away.

We followed her great-grandmother's recipe, and she teased me with the reminder, "One piece per day." There was no hint about the two men or the brown bag. It was just another recipe. I laughed at my own imagination.

At the break of dawn, she went upstairs to clean up and gather her things. I watched the ovens and tended to the array of baking brilliance we'd produced.

As faint early morning light filtered into the bakery windows, Makiline carried one lone leather suitcase down the stairs. Her cloth coat hung on her shoulders. I imagined it was the one she'd clutched tightly around herself as she crossed the Atlantic thirty years earlier as a hopeful young bride. And just as in the black and white documentaries about Polish war refugees, she tied a checked woolen scarf under her chin. The pathos of her image shook me. I was convinced that the suitcase, the clothes on her back, and the money from the bakery were everything she had in the world.

So, despite having transferred $30,000 to her the day before, I dug into my pocket and pressed $40 in cash into her hand.

She laughed and pushed my hand away.

"You keep. You need." Then, she walked to a low cabinet near the stove and yanked at a drawer. She beckoned me to look in it.

I bent over and was shocked to see a pistol with a dark red mesh handle nosed into a leather case. My face flushed. I'd never been in the presence of a gun before. I stumbled backward.

She grabbed my arm and put her finger to her lips. "In case robbers. Yes?"

Suddenly, I was ready for her to leave. "Not to worry. I'm fine."

She patted my hand. "Okay. I go. No time, no place, know nothing."

Eager to see her on her way, I tried to drive her to the airport, but she refused.

She called a taxi and was gone.

As I unlocked the bakery door the next morning at seven a.m., the image of the obnoxious gun played on my mind. A quick internet search had revealed it to be a Rewolwer Nagant wz 30, a pistol used in Poland during the war. I reconciled that she had brought it with her years earlier, and she left it behind because it no longer worked. I resolved to properly dispose of it.

I walked up the steps to the small apartment, not knowing what to expect. She had to have left everything behind. I found a stark collection of furnishings: a bed, a three-drawer dresser, wooden table with two bent back chairs, a worn stuffed sofa. Framed black-and-white photographs still hung on the walls. They captured groups of three and four people: men, women, children. Wearing threadworn clothing and weathered faces. There was no other indication this intensely alive woman had occupied the space for her American lifetime.

I spent all day Monday, Tuesday, and Wednesday explaining to the regulars that I'd purchased the bakery and she had moved away. No, I didn't know where she moved to. Yes, she'd taught me how to make her recipes. Yes, I was very fortunate.

Thursday came, and I was a little nervous. I'd made two large loaves of makowiec, wrapped them in white paper and tied them with string. I'd steeled myself to decline whatever was in the brown bag.

At precisely 9:45, the two men sauntered into the bakery, holding the bag as usual. When they saw me behind the counter, they elbowed each and exchanged words in Polish.

"Where Makiline?"

"She's gone."

"She sick?"

"No. She's gone. This is my bakery now. But I understand this is your order." I pushed the two white logs across the counter.

They looked at each other, and one picked up a loaf and smelled it.

"How long she go?" One of them demanded.

I saw no harm in answering, "A few days."

Polish flew between them as they backed up. Their necks twisted left and right, as they looked both ways before bolting from the bakery and darting between parked cars across the street.

I found it odd, but great. I was finished with them. I picked up the loaves of makowiec and took them back into the kitchen, contemplating how well they would freeze. My thoughts were interrupted by a banging on the back door, followed by the uninvited entry of several men in dark suits. One flashed an FBI badge and handed me a search warrant. Another stuck a wanted poster in my face and asked. "Do you know this woman?"

It was, without question, Makiline. A much younger Makiline. A wartime Makiline. I stammered that I had bought the bakery from her a mere three days ago. They snorted, as if that was a likely story.

"Where is she?"

"I don't know."

Then, one of searchers reached the oven and opened the fateful drawer. I gulped.

He whistled low. "Look at this, Ed."

"Okay, mister—what's your name? We've been looking for her for years. Where is she?"

I couldn't take my eyes off the wanted poster: INTERPOL RED NOTICE: Lilliana Potzck. CHARGES: Illegal weapons dealing; Illegal transfer of weapons across international borders.

My hands trembled uncontrollably. I must have looked dumbfounded.

One of the agents snapped his fingers in my face. "She was an international resistance fighter, who supplied weapons to her buddies back in Poland."

It was too much to take in. I didn't know people were resisting in Poland all these years. I thought of the two thick-necked Polish men and their urgent retreat, the hushed tones, the paper bag, and the Thursday exchanges. I couldn't stop my mind from doing a quick calculation: two guns a week disguised as pastry for 52 weeks, for 70 years. That added up to over 7,000 guns. If, in fact, that was all she was doing.

"I'm sorry," I stammered. "I know nothing."

All I could think to do was make a conciliatory gesture. "Would you like some coffee and a slice of makowiec? I have two fresh loaves."

C. M Surrisi was nominated for a 2019 Agatha for her cozy middle grade mystery *A Side of Sabotage*, the third book in her series, The Quinnie Boyd Mysteries. She is the author of short stories "Actresses Are Like That," published in the *Malice Domestic Mystery Most Theatrical Anthology* (2020) and "The Bequest" published in the *Minnesota Sisters In Crime, Minnesota Not So Nice Anthology* (2020). She is the president of Minnesota TC Sisters In Crime.

GREETINGS FROM THE BOARD

MARY DUTTA

"Stabbing Santa was Ted's idea. We all remember that, right?" Guy looked at Ellen over his travel mug, his wedding ring beating a tattoo against its Porsche logo.

"We all said some crazy stuff," Ellen said. "I'm not sure—"

"It was Ted," said Guy, a statement now, not a question. "Just in case the police ask."

"There's no reason to think the police will get involved," Ellen said, her breath rising in the air. She was bundled up against the morning cold. Guy looked forward to the change of seasons when she would swap out her pantsuits. Even in a knee-length skirt and sensible pumps, there was no hiding the sensational legs. The one good thing about losing sleep over his financial situation was that he had been up early enough to catch a glimpse of her running every summer morning in her skimpy shorts.

"It was probably just kids," she said. "Who else would attack an inflatable yard decoration?"

"Someone who wants David Burke out of the neighborhood," said Guy.

"Well, that doesn't narrow things down." Ellen cast a glance down the platform. "Do you want to talk to Larry, too?"

Guy looked down to where the homeowner association board's treasurer stood waiting for the quiet car, working his crossword puzzle with a pen gripped in his gloved hands. "We'll see him at the meeting tonight," he said, raising his voice to be heard over the squealing brakes of the arriving commuter train. "Ted's idea," he said again, as the doors hissed open. "Just in case anyone asks."

The Cambridge Acres Homeowners Association board gathered that evening at the board secretary's house. Guy knew the woman's name, but thought of her only as "PTO mom." One of those women who spent all her time volunteering and, judging from pictures of her kids blanketing the family room, taking one too many trips to the portrait studio. The décor could not obscure the builder's grade finishes. Guy wondered again if he was ever going to recoup the cost of his own home renovations.

"Before we get started," he said, "I think we should discuss the Santa situation. I think we all know that Ted is the one who attacked David Burke's yard decoration."

"The hell I did," said Ted.

"You have history," said Guy. "You ran over his trash cans."

"That was an accident."

"Really? The day after you complained that he left them at the end of his driveway for days after trash collection? And that he hadn't raked his leaves all fall? And that he borrowed your ladder and never returned it? It's still sitting outside his garage. It's not surprising things escalated to violence."

"Violence is a strong word," Ellen said. "It's not like he stabbed a person."

"I didn't stab anything," Ted said, his voice rising.

"Would anyone like a treat?" PTO mom asked, grabbing up a plate of baked goods from the coffee table. Cookies spilled over the edge. "I'm sorry," she said. "I took cookies over to welcome David Burke to the neighborhood, and I never got my big plate back."

The interruption didn't placate Ted, perched now on the edge of his chair. "What about you?" he said, jabbing his finger toward Guy. "How many times have you called the cops on him for noise complaints?"

"If the HOA didn't have such toothless enforcement, I wouldn't have to call the cops."

"And I've always wondered how that gas leak happened with Burke's grill last summer," Ted said. "So, maybe you're the Kris Kringle killer."

"Look," said Ellen. "We all agreed that something had to be done about our problem neighbor. And the board has limited options in dealing with these situations."

"The only official thing the board can do is charge interest on unpaid dues," said Larry, "and David Burke is paid up. We even talked about him taking over as board treasurer one day." He reached for a cookie. "You know, he's not such a bad guy. He's interested in military history. He's been over a few times to look through my collection." A maniacal gleam flickered in his eyes.

"Well, if Burke's such a nice guy," Guy said, hoping to stave off yet another description of Larry's incredibly costly, yet spectacularly boring, colonial crap, "why was Ellen leaving dog poop on his front porch?"

Ellen bridled. "It was his dog's poop!" she said. "He lets the thing run loose, and it keeps doing its business in my yard. The homeowner covenants clearly say dogs can't be off leash."

"I could send him another notice," said PTO mom.

Another Greetings-from-the-Board missive riddled with exclamation points and emojis, no doubt. Guy knew how effective that would be.

"Reminding him of the rules never helps," he said. "We've all tried to make our feelings clear, but with this stabbing, I'm worried that things are escalating to a point where we might have bigger problems."

"Bigger problems like you being unable to sell your house with all that crap in the yard across the street? And the sagging fence? And the dying trees?" said Ted.

Larry made a production of pushing back his sweater sleeve to check his watch. "I think we should move on to official business," he said. Guy checked his own watch, a diver model that cost as much as a lifetime supply of the style of cardigans favored by both Larry and Mr. Rogers. Although Mr. Rogers' probably weren't cashmere like Larry's. There would be time to deal with David Burke later.

The conversation turned to cost estimates for power washing the sidewalks. Guy and Ted let the others carry on, casting cold glances at each other, until the meeting broke up an hour later. On the porch, Larry waved vaguely and made a beeline for his car. Probably wanted to get home in time for Antiques Roadshow. Ellen walked off with a plate of leftover cookies. Four houses down, she lifted the lid of a trash can and tipped them in. Guy was glad to see her commitment to keeping in shape. He didn't want her spoiling his view.

Ted and Guy were left standing in the driveway. "I know it was you," Ted said. "The Santa stabbing. And really, I don't care. Whatever it takes, right? The guy's dragging down everyone's property values." He took a step closer. "But I do care about you trying to pin it on me."

Guy held up his hands. "Fair enough," he said. Ted held his gaze a moment longer, then turned and got into his car, unnecessarily gunning his engine. He had a lot of attitude for a guy who drove the lowest tier Mercedes. Even Larry drove something better, even if it was a station wagon.

* * * *

Guy paced his way through his insomnia late that night. He looked out the front window at the silent neighborhood, where a streetlamp shone down on David Burke's front yard. Guy felt as gutted as the deflated Santa. But it was going to take more than duct tape to hold him together.

As he gazed, a dark figure emerged from behind the Burke house and passed through the side yard. Guy leaned forward until his forehead touched the cold glass, but even when the figure skirted the edge of the street lamp's glow, he couldn't see more than dark pants, jacket, and hat. Whoever it was hustled down the sidewalk and was soon out of sight.

Guy might have mentioned what he'd seen to Ted the next morning, but the other man barely acknowledged his greeting at the train station. He brushed past and was soon deep in conversation with Ellen, who kept casting glances back at Guy. They broke off their conversation as an ambulance screamed past. Larry looked up from his crossword puzzle. Ted walked to the end of the platform and craned his neck. He jogged back. "They just turned into Cambridge Acres," he said.

The four of them hurried to their cars. When they arrived back in the neighborhood, the ambulance had pulled up in front of David Burke's house. Neighbors had gathered, leaning into the sagging fence until it threatened to finally collapse. David Burke lay sprawled in his front yard, as motionless as his mutilated Santa, a string of Christmas lights clutched in one hand. A metal extension ladder lay next to him.

A police car arrived, and two officers jumped out and ran to where the body lay. A short time later, the EMTs ceased their efforts. The police officers asked the neighbors to move back from the scene, and the younger one started taking names and contact information. The board members retreated across the street to stand in front of Guy's house.

"Is that your ladder, Ted?" Guy asked.

"I don't know. They all look alike."

"But you lent him yours."

"So?"

"The police look awfully interested in it." Guy gestured toward the police officers, one of whom was squatting over the ladder. He called his partner over from where she was collecting information and pointed something out to her.

They watched the scene a little longer, staring at the officers' backs. "If we leave now," Ellen said, "we can make the 8:47 train." They each slipped away and made their way back to the station. They spread out along the platform, avoiding eye contact. Guy tapped his ring arrhythmically against his travel mug. Larry clicked his crossword puzzle pen repeatedly, but didn't fill in any words. Ted stood with his hands in his pockets, looking intently at the platform. Ellen stared down the track for the incoming train.

The next day, the police had taken away the body and the ladder, along with the mutilated Santa. But crime scene tape still stretched across David Burke's front yard. Guy felt as though his neighbor were reaching out from the grave to thwart his home sale. He flipped again through the mail he had retrieved from his mailbox. The others better show up soon. There was only so long he could pretend to be this interested in credit-card offers and overdue bills.

He looked up and saw Ted approaching. He wore running clothes but made no effort to move quickly. Ellen appeared from the other direction, holding an empty glass plate in one hand. She didn't look pleased.

"What was that text all about?" she asked when all three met at the mailbox. "And why the big charade about just bumping into each other? I had plans today, and returning this cookie plate wasn't really one of them."

"The police are all over me about that ladder," Ted said. "It looks like someone sawed through one of the steps so that it broke free, and Burke fell."

Ellen gasped.

Guy looked thoughtful. "Who do they think did it?" he asked.

"I don't know," said Ted, "but it wasn't me. Why would I tamper with my own ladder? I would be the one killed."

"This sounds like a personal problem, Ted," said Guy.

"The hell it is. Anyone of us could look guilty, if the police start asking questions about what's been going on."

"What's been going on has nothing to do with murder," Ellen said. "We all just wanted him out of the neighborhood. We didn't want him dead."

"I don't know what you all wanted," said Ted. He turned to Guy. "You're the one who had the most to lose, if he didn't go. It's pretty clear you need the money from selling your house."

Guy flushed and crumpled the mail in his fist. "That better not be what you're telling the police."

"And you better not be telling them that I'm responsible for attacking his decorations or my own ladder. Anyone could have done it. He left it outside. Hell, Ellen's out running every morning at 5:30. She could have sawed through the thing before anyone else was even awake."

Larry's station wagon came around the corner, and they stood silent as he slowed and waved. Guy stared at the Louis Vuitton golf bag in the back. Something about the accountant just didn't add up.

Once the car had passed from view, Ellen spoke. "I'm going to return this plate before someone else gets killed," she said, and headed off. Guy turned and walked back up his driveway, leaving Ted to jog halfheartedly away.

The board members kept their distance after that. PTO mom sent out a Greetings-from-the-Board memo, asking everyone to share any relevant information with the police. Guy kept one eye on the investigation and one on the Burke house, watching for any sign that someone was swooping in to fix it up and sell it. No heirs had yet appeared to clear away the ragged police tape. Some shingles had blown off the roof and lay in the yard, the only markers for either the late David Burke or Santa Claus.

The first day back to work after the new year brought them all together again on the train platform. The police were sending someone the next evening to update the HOA board on the case. A courtesy they said, but Guy was worried. Had Ted or Ellen been talking? He looked for them along the length of the platform, relieved to see them standing apart.

Larry stood in his usual spot doing his usual puzzle, but next to him stood two large suitcases. Guy recognized the brand, which was far sexier than Larry. Larry was a bit of a puzzle himself. The high-end luggage, the expensive sweaters, the luxury car. In putting together the pieces, Guy realized, he just might have found a solution for his own problems.

Larry had said that David Burke had been to his house and talked to him about his treasurer position. Maybe Larry's pricey lifestyle had been bankrolled by money siphoned from the HOA coffers, and the dead man had somehow stumbled across that information while poking around the muskets and powder horns in Larry's study. Larry had found a way to get himself all the money he wanted. And for a reasonable share, Guy was willing to keep that possibility to himself.

He approached the treasurer. "Fleeing the jurisdiction?"

"I'm off on a tour of revolutionary battlefields," Larry said, but his eyes lacked their usual maniacal gleam on the subject. He fixed Guy with a steely glare more befitting a murderer than a mild-mannered accountant. Guy took a step back from the platform's edge. He lowered his voice and told Larry his suspicions about the HOA money. "As a board member, I could request an accounting," Guy said, then named the price for keeping his silence. A figure just large enough to get him out of the financial hole he was in.

Larry nodded. "I'll be in touch," he said, then wrestled his bags into the quiet car of the train that had pulled in.

The car couldn't have been any quieter than the board meeting the next night as they waited for the police to arrive. Guy tapped his ring on the arm of his chair. PTO mom worked a crochet hook at a frenetic pace. When the doorbell rang, she cried, "Oh, dear," and leapt up to answer it, returning in a moment with a middle-aged woman wearing a wrinkled blue suit and carrying a large tote bag.

The detective wasted no time in bringing them up to date on the investigation. "I also have some questions for all of you," she said.

Ted and Ellen exchanged glances, and Ted held up a hand. "I think you should know," he began, "we—"

"I saw something," Guy shouted over him. "The day before David Burke died." Everyone looked at him. He licked his lips. "I saw someone walking around his yard in the middle of the night."

The detective stared at him. "Why haven't you told us this before?"

"Yeah, Guy," Ted asked, "where is this coming from all of a sudden? What have you been hiding?"

This time the detective held up her hand. "Go ahead," she said to Guy.

Guy told her what he had seen. "I didn't see who it was," he added, "but I think it was a man, about Ted's height." Or Larry's, actually, but there was no payoff for him in sharing that information.

PTO mom stood suddenly, yarn cascading from her lap. "It was me," she whispered. Then louder, "It was me." Guy didn't care if it was her, Ted, or Santa, as long as the police's attention was turned away from himself and Larry.

She looked around the room. "I just wanted my plate back," she said. "I thought maybe the back door would be open, and I could just slip into the kitchen and take it." She collapsed onto an ottoman and burst into tears.

"You're both going to have to come in and make statements," the detective said. She turned to Ted. "Was there something you wanted to say?"

He looked at Ellen, who gave him a quick shake of the head.

"No, never mind," he said.

"Right," the woman said. She reached into her tote and pulled out two plastic bags, one containing a hacksaw and the other a newspaper, and placed them on the coffee table. She picked up the saw bag. "We found this hacksaw in the woods behind your subdivision. We have reason to believe it's the one used to tamper with the ladder Mr. Burke was using. Do any of you recognize it?"

Everyone shook their heads. "Those things all look the same," said Ted.

"It was wrapped in that newspaper," she added.

"Everyone subscribes to that paper," Ellen said. "You'd find it in anyone's house in Cambridge Acres."

Guy stared at the newspaper where it lay on the table. Through the plastic, he could see a completed crossword puzzle. In ink. But then, Larry's gloved hands wouldn't have left any prints.

The detective left with no more information than she had brought when she arrived, reminding Guy and PTO mom to come in and make statements the next morning. Guy would have nothing to say. The money that had arrived in his bank account had ensured his silence.

A month later, an email landed in his inbox, the subject line a sad emoji. He opened it. "Greetings From the Board!" it said. "We are sorry to inform you that the new treasurer has discovered..." Guy didn't need to read any further.

Mary Dutta traded New England and a career as an English professor for a job in college admissions in the South. She is the winner of the New England Crime Bake Al Blanchard Award for her short story "The Wonderworker," which appears in *Masthead: Best New England Crime Stories*. Her work can be also be found in *The Best Laid Plans: 21 Stories of Mystery & Suspense*. She is a member of Sisters in Crime and the Short Mystery Fiction Society. Follow her on Twitter @Mary_Dutta.

QUARRY

SUSAN ALICE BICKFORD

The moment Katy Harding arrived at the deserted quarry with Brian and his friends, she knew she had made a mistake. She should never have squandered Senior Ditch Day—her last day of high school—to hang out with a bunch of misfits she barely knew. Now, she counted the minutes until she could escape.

Cushioned only by a thin towel, every bone from her head to her heels objected to being forced to lie on the granite slab overlooking the quarry. Katy tried to wiggle her shoulders into a more comfortable position, her sense of irritation growing with each twitch.

This was not the soft beach experience Brian had promised. The air was still and stifling. The water in the old quarry was cloudy with a sheen of algae on the surface and smelled of rotting vegetation. Worst of all, she had nothing in common with Brian's friends, Lisa, Matt, and Gretchen.

A persistent zing sounded around her left ear. She slapped and sat up to study the results on her palm: a flattened mosquito and a tiny black fly, both full of blood. Probably hers. Mosquitos were annoying. Black flies were evil. They loved to tuck themselves behind her ears and suck to bursting.

She ran her fingers under her bikini top, readjusting it to her upright position. Sweat coated her hands. She rubbed them against her damp cutoffs.

How could a place that was so cold and nasty for nine months of the year turn so hot and sweaty and full of bugs in the course of a few weeks? She couldn't wait to leave Central New York.

"I thought you said we were going up to Oneida Lake. Sylvan Beach," she said to Brian, her voice a low grumble.

Brian raised up on his elbow, inhaled deeply from his e-cigarette, and blew out a cloud of vapor. "I said we were going swimming. Here, we can smoke and drink. And get naked." He waggled his eyebrows and pointed to Lisa and Gretchen. Both were topless.

Katy ignored the hint. Next, he would want to make out. A couple of hours ago that had seemed like an enticing option.

Now, stripped down to his cheap bathing trunks, Brian wasn't nearly as cute as he appeared in French class. Where did all that chest hair come from? He even showed the beginnings of a paunch. At least, he didn't have man boobs. Yet.

She pointed to the water below. "No swimming for me. That stuff looks vile. And I don't like sitting on this ledge with black flies for company."

Brian leaned in closer. Katy could smell the mix of stale sweat and musty stink from his swim in the quarry.

"I'm all the company you need. Live a little. Take off that top and get an even tan." He reached over and snapped her bikini strap.

Katy scooted sideways and pushed to her feet. She inched closer to the edge of the quarry and leaned forward to peer at the copper-colored water.

She heard a scraping noise on the stone and wheeled to find Brian bent over, creeping up behind her.

"Stay back, Brian. If you push me in there, I will chop you into little pieces." She braced her feet and scowled, hoping he would forget he was taller and heftier.

Brian stood up straight and raised his hands. "Stop being such a coward. It's just water."

"It's a deathtrap, unless you lower the rope, so I can climb out."

"Yeah, guys. Toss down the rope. I'm tired of paddling around down here." Matt's voice wafted up from the water, followed by echoes that bounced off the sheer granite walls.

"Are you in danger of drowning?" Lisa asked with a giggle and kicked a loose stone into the water.

Matt splashed in a circle. "Hell no, but I'm thirsty. No way I'm drinking this stinky stuff. I want a proper drink. Either toss me the rope or toss me a beer."

Matt was laughing, but Katy thought she heard a higher note in his voice. Pulling up the rope after he had jumped in wasn't funny, in her opinion. She didn't want to be the next victim of that so-called joke. She sidled over to the left corner of the quarry wall where the rope lay tethered to a nearby tree and tossed the slimy coils over the edge.

"Hey! You're spoiling our fun." Gretchen's voice was a petulant slur. "Brian, I told you not to bring her."

Katy grinned at Gretchen. That probably looked as fake as it felt. *I couldn't care less about your opinion.* She moved to the cooler and rummaged inside. "Don't we have anything else to drink, besides vodka and beer? I'm parched." She grabbed a chunk of ice and popped it into her mouth.

"Oh, please," Matt said. Now safely out of the quarry, he reinhabited his usual slacker mode. He reached for Lisa, who squealed and pushed him away.

"You stink. That water is truly gross."

"It's magical. Full of ancient mysteries." Matt grimaced and clutched his stomach. "Jump in, and they fill your soul, take over your being. Aggh. Help!" He rolled into a ball.

"It's probably filled with nasty stuff. That's because it's completely stagnant. Plus, anything that falls in never gets out," Katy said. "I wonder how deep it is."

She scanned the perimeter of the jagged edge. Roughly thirty feet across by fifty feet long, it definitely didn't qualify as impressive, but there was no sign of the bottom. The surrounding woods, fringed with dense poison ivy, had grown up to the edges along three sides, leaving their semi-flat picnic slab as the only open area.

"Thank you, Professor Katherine. No wonder you're getting those honors tomorrow." Brian's voice was a bit fuzzy, and he listed to one side.

Katy pulled her cell phone from her bag and checked again for coverage. *Nada.* She wanted to leave, but they'd all come in Matt's car. The thought of a very long walk home in the hot sun with no water was not appealing.

"It's almost four. I have to be home by five," she said and slapped at another mosquito.

"Or what? You're an adult now." Brian lay down and rolled onto his stomach with a groan.

"You don't know my father. If he smells anything like booze or even this water, he'll give me what for. I really don't want to have a black eye for graduation. Besides, I'm not eighteen yet. Which means that, in his opinion, I'm still his property."

Katy clamped her lips shut. She wanted to pull the words back inside. She never talked about her family life, particularly her father. She moved away from the others and stood closer to the woods.

Gretchen stood up and came to join her, just out of earshot of the others.

"You do know you're standing in poison ivy, right?"

"For some reason, I'm not sensitive. It's my superpower." Katy stepped back further, daring Gretchen to join her.

"If you say so. That's a good one to have around here. I catch it just looking at it." Gretchen gave her head a quick tilt to one side. Katy inched closer, into neutral territory.

"I heard about your dad," Gretchen said, her voice low. "My stepfather is not a nice guy, and he told my mom he'd never mess with your father."

She shifted her gaze to the far side of the quarry and tossed a small pebble into the water. "I turned eighteen in April. My bags are packed. I'm skipping graduation tomorrow and hitching up to Syracuse. My sister says that, if I catch the bus to Rochester, I can stay with her for a while."

"You'd really skip graduation?" The very idea was a foreign concept to Katy. School was her safe place. "Won't your mom be upset?"

"Mom hasn't figured out I'm finished with high school, or that there's an event. She dropped out in her junior year to have me, so she's not big into ceremonies."

Gretchen swatted at a pesky black fly. "I got through high school without getting pregnant or using anything stronger than vodka. I'm picking up my diploma, and I'm getting out."

"Hey, girls," Matt called out in a teasing voice. "Come on back here, and be sociable."

Katy started walking, but Gretchen grabbed her arm. "Why's your dad so mean?"

Katy looked down and studied her bare feet. She wanted to give her nails a new coat of red before graduation.

"The army," she said. "He didn't have a regular job or anything, and my arrival was kind of unplanned. My parents needed money. So, he enlisted and left for a while."

"PTSD?"

"I guess it's something like that. My mom says he was so different before he went to Afghanistan, but I don't remember him any other way. She's always telling me how funny and sweet he was. And he hardly drank at all. He's a golem now."

"A goblin?"

Katy chuckled. "Kind of. A golem is like a zombie in Jewish folktales. A thing made from mud and body parts that comes back to life."

Gretchen put a cigarette to her lips and lit it. "I get it. Golem, *ghola*. Like Duncan Idaho in the *Dune* books. Lots of religious stuff in there." She handed Katy the cigarette. "See? I read books, too. You don't have to smoke that. Just wave it around to keep the bugs away."

Gretchen reads. Who knew?

Katy joined the others but settled back in the shade of a maple tree. No point in getting sunburned, even if the bugs were worse in the shade. She needed to be patient. Her so-called friends would have to leave, once the sun dipped below the tree line and the mosquitos came out with a vengeance.

And maybe these guys weren't so bad—as long as she didn't have to go into the water. She closed her eyes and thought of the impressive gray fieldstone buildings at Middlebury College. That was the place she planned to call home for four years, starting in the late summer—just a few short months away.

She was so close. Her planned escape from this remote hole in Nowheresburg, New York, dangled like a bright gem. She pushed away the thought before she could jinx it.

Her reverie was interrupted by a growl, growing closer to their hidden parking place. *Motorcycle?*

The engine cut off abruptly. Brian and Matt leaped to their feet. If the cops or the sheriff's department came calling, drugs and alcohol needed to be moved out of sight.

"This is a raid. This is a raid." A man's voice from the woods was followed by a deep laugh. A young man stumbled into their clearing. Despite the hot weather, he sported black jeans tucked into leather boots, a black leather motorcycle jacket open to the waist, and no shirt.

"Shit," Brian said, his voice a low hiss. "Reggie. Who told him?"

Matt offered a lopsided smile. "Hey. There are five of us. An odd number."

Once she heard his name, Katy recognized Reggie Brochu. He'd either graduated or timed out of high school a few years ago. As the school's football quarterback, he'd been popular and had his pick of girlfriends. She remembered he had enticed a girl named Elaine into having sex and then bragged about it before dropping her very publicly at a school dance.

Fortunately, he was out of her league, and their paths had never crossed. Until now.

Despite being a chronic screwup, Reggie was considered untouchable. His father was Charles Brochu, Sheriff of Oriska County. Many people loved the sheriff, but almost as many hated him, including her father. And the feeling was mutual.

Reggie was taller than Brian and Matt, with six-pack abs visible under his leather jacket. Dark-brown, wavy curls fell across his brow and around the base of his skull with just the right number of natural streaky bits.

But his eyes were bloodshot and narrowed, and a lit cigarette dangled at a precarious angle from his lips. The stubble on his chin was uneven. He walked with more stagger than swagger.

Not good. Katy had seen that look on her father's face. Reggie was on the hunt and looking for easy prey.

Reggie shuffled with his knees slightly bent to the edge of the ledge. From his jacket pocket, he pulled out something and touched his cigarette to it. Sparks leaped from the thing in his hand. *Cherry bomb.* Katy hated firecrackers, especially the big ones. She plugged her ears.

She hoped he would blow his own hand off, but he let it fly at what must have been the last possible second, and it detonated just above the water level. The noise would have been deafening, even in an open field. Trapped by the walls of the quarry in the dense woods, the noise echoed and reverberated. She could feel the thump in her chest and stomach.

Reggie wasn't done with his surprises. He pulled out a pistol from the back of his jeans and aimed it at a beer can next to Brian.

Brian's eyes widened, and he scrambled away. Not surprisingly, Reggie's shot went wild. They all ducked. Where the bullet landed after its ricochet off the rocks, Katy wasn't certain, but she thought it smacked into a tree to her right. *Too close.*

"Fuck, Reggie." Brian's voice squeaked in the soprano range.

Reggie sloughed off the jacket and tucked the gun into his waistband. He helped himself to a beer. "Who's the new one?" He pointed at Katy. "Why's she wearing that?" He waved his hands over his upper chest to indicate her bathing suit top. "It's not like she has much to cover up."

After a long pause, everyone chuckled, including Katy.

"Have we met?" Reggie asked. He walked over, his eyes fixed on hers. The smell of body odor, mixed with alcohol, tobacco, and other less savory sources, preceded him. He pursed his lips for a juicy kiss, but Katy stepped back, and he kissed open air.

"Hey, Reggie? Sorry to cut out on you." Matt's voice stuttered. "I have to get home now, and I'm the one with the car, so..."

Matt must have changed his mind about inviting Reggie. The others took his hint and started gathering their belongings.

"Oh, come *on*!" Reggie twirled around. "I just got here."

"Yeah, well. Sorry." Matt was already headed down the path to the car, Gretchen and Lisa close behind.

Katy scrambled for her shirt. She could put it on in the car. Where were her sneakers? By the time she found them and her bag, she and Reggie were alone on the ledge. Brian stood at the top of the path.

Katy looked from Brian to Reggie and back to Brian. He wouldn't meet her eyes.

"You can stay here." A crooked smile lurked under Reggie's fixed stare. His hand traveled around to the back of his pants.

"I'm going with Brian." Katy stepped toward the path.

"No, no, no." Reggie spread his long arms, cutting off her route, the gun in his right hand. "We'll spend some time here, and then I'll take you home on my motorcycle. You'll like it. Trust me."

Katy felt her body temperature drop. "That's not what I want." Katy made her voice low and firm. "Brian! I want to go with you!"

"Brian, just go home," Reggie said, keeping his eyes on Katy.

The hair raised on the back of her neck at Reggie's soothing tones.

"Brian, no! Call the cops." Katy made her final appeal, as Brian faded into the dark woods, down the path.

"You do that, Brian, and you're dead." Reggie's voice had a singsong lilt at the end. He turned his head over his shoulder to watch Brian disappear.

For a few brief seconds, the woods fell silent aside from the buzz of mosquitos and the pounding of Katy's pulse in her temples. She heard the noise of a car start and gradually fade away.

She refused to meet Reggie's stare. She kept him in her peripheral vision and edged her way toward the path, only to be cut off again. The prospect of his sinewy embrace frightened her more than the gun. They worked their way back and forth in a half circle along the rim of the quarry.

She considered dashing into the woods. Of course, she would be at a disadvantage, shoeless in the growing gloom and dense brush. Easy prey.

Reggie released the buckle at his waist and pulled his leather belt free. He swung it around and snapped it into the air, then dropped it onto the rocky surface.

The crack of the leather released a moan in Katy's chest. Her pulse picked up. Would he settle for a kiss or some fondling? She didn't think so. She was about to become a victim. She would end up raped. *Or dead.*

Reggie picked up Katy's bag and held it over the edge of the quarry, watching for her response. "What have we here?"

"Stop." That bag held her driver's license, her student ID, her bank card, and her phone.

"Stop." Reggie raised his voice to a high falsetto, ending in a chuckle.

Katy felt a new pounding in her temples. The knot of fear in her belly uncoiled, and rage took over. Her chest swelled, and every nerve in her body tingled. She would not be a victim.

When Reggie looked down at the bag, Katy lunged. She crashed into his chest and brought her head up under his chin.

The bag hit the slab. Reggie wrapped his long arms around her upper body. Katy's feet stuttered along the rough stone, as he dragged her toward the edge.

"Give up, or I'll toss you in." His voice was deep and hoarse.

"No way."

She stopped flailing and leaned back, becoming dead weight. He grunted. She knew he was ready to swing her over the side and drop her in the water.

She wrapped her pinned arms around Reggie's waist and grabbed onto the belt loops of his jeans. She coiled her legs around his.

Reggie yelped and let go of her. He tried to pry her hands free from his pants. "Let go, you stupid bitch."

Katy leaned forward, pressing her body against his. Unbalanced by the weight shift, Reggie lost his footing and tumbled into the quarry, taking Katy with him.

The slimy filth swallowed them up, and stagnant water filled her mouth and nose. For a few moments, cold and shock knocked the breath from her lungs. She kicked free and splashed her way toward the far side.

Reggie surfaced with a gasp and flailing arms. His cries echoed from the walls.

Katy spat out oily water. *I'm dead. I've killed myself.*

From a safe distance, Katy rotated to tread water. She could see Reggie wasn't much of a swimmer. He wasn't coming after her. In fact, he was thrashing like a drowning man.

A rational thought was trying to break through. *Think. Think.*

Katy was a good swimmer. She knew she could swim and float for a long time, as long as she kept calm. But she couldn't climb out without the rope. She could see it in her mind's eye, coiled on the ledge above where they'd left it after pulling up Matt.

Her thoughts circled round and round, timed to the slow motion of her backstroke around the edge of her prison.

Where was Reggie? The sun still shone brightly on the ledge above, but it was twilight inside the quarry.

A faint whimpering led her to him, wedged onto a narrow ledge just below the waterline. He was still in a panic, clawing at the granite wall, the whites of his eyes visible from across the water.

"Reggie," she called out, floating on her back. "Reggie, you need to shed those heavy clothes."

Reggie didn't answer, but he stopped squealing.

"Start with your boots."

"What?"

"Fine. Go ahead and drown."

She listened to his splashing. After a minute, she called out again. "Now your jeans. They're too heavy."

"Got no underwear."

"As if I care."

While she waited for Reggie to lighten his load, Katy tried to come up with a plan. Her brain was not engaging. Just as she thought she had an idea, it slipped away from her.

Maybe the others would come back if she didn't show up for graduation the next day.

That did not seem like a good bet. Even if she and Reggie could rest on little ledges below the water line, sooner or later, they would succumb to exhaustion and hypothermia and drown. Morning was a long time away.

The idea of being close to Reggie was repulsive. Still, a small plan was gaining traction. She had to find a way to enlist Reggie in order to escape.

Katy swam to the opposite side from Reggie and studied the granite walls in more detail. All the upper edges of the quarry were well above the waterline. Six feet? Eight? Maybe one of them could reach one of the lower edges—if they worked together.

She floated on her back to study the sky. High above, the summer equinox guaranteed daylight for hours, but they would have to act soon.

"Reggie?" The walls of the quarry bounced her voice back and forth.

"Hunh? Hunh?" Sniffling grunts from Reggie's side of the quarry.

"Reggie, listen to me. You're about six foot, right?"

"Six two."

"If I stood on your shoulders, and you pushed up my legs and feet, I could get onto that ledge over your head."

Reggie stopped whimpering. The buzz of hovering mosquitos sounded like the wheels turning in his tiny brain.

"And then what?"

"Then, I'll toss down the rope."

"How can I trust you to do that?"

Katy paddled in a small circle.

"I don't want your death on my conscience. You're an asshole. But that's not the same as wanting to kill me," she said after her third turn. "And I'm not going to complain or anything. My dad would kill you *and* me if he found out."

Was that too complicated?

"Okay," Reggie said, after a long pause.

"Find a good ledge along your side that you can stand on. Not too deep," Katy said, gliding through the slimy water in a silent sidestroke.

"Got one." Reggie stood with the water waist high.

Katy slid closer. "Face the wall and crouch down. Put your hands on your thighs. I'm going to climb onto your left thigh, then the right. And work up to your shoulders. At that point, you stand up."

She moved closer to Reggie, floating just out of reach.

"Pay attention. Turn around and bend over," she said.

Reggie looked as though he was having second thoughts. *Idiot.*

"Reggie. No fooling around. If you screw with me, I'll drown you myself. Now, bend over."

Reggie coughed and spat, but he turned and bent over. *Good boy.*

Katy reached her left foot around Reggie's hip to his left thigh. Pressing her hands on his back, she hoisted herself up and leaned forward. She gagged and clenched her teeth. Grabbing at crevices in the granite wall, she placed her right foot on his upper right arm.

As she moved her left foot to his left shoulder, Reggie grabbed her left ankle, holding her steady. They paused, panting.

With a grunt, Katy pulled her right foot up onto his other shoulder. "Now stand. Slowly."

Reggie obeyed. At last, her hands scrabbled along the rim of the ledge.

She could feel the poison ivy vines with the tips of her fingers.

She swore. She couldn't pull herself up.

"I need more height. Grab my ankles and push." Her voice came out in a breathless groan.

Reggie grabbed her calves and worked his hands down to her ankles. He bent down, straightened quickly, and tossed her upward.

* * * *

Katy lay with her upper body resting in the sun on the granite ledge covered with poison ivy, while her legs still hung down into the murky pit.

"Wow. I can't believe it. It worked," Reggie said. "You okay? Did you make it? Whatever you do, don't slide back."

"Shut up, Reggie."

Katy tried to grasp the rock with her hands and wriggled her arms and upper body back and forth, pulling at the vines. She measured her progress in tiny increments, until she could lift her right knee, followed by the left, onto the ledge.

The mosquitos and black flies were waiting for her, and the ledge was hot. Katy pushed to her feet. She hoped immunity to poison ivy really was her superpower.

"Hey! What about me?" Reggie's voice was high and squeaky.

"Hold on. You're not getting out of there, until I'm ready to leave."

She found her shoes and shirt. Her bag and the pistol rested where Reggie had dropped them at the rim of the quarry. Reggie's keys to the motorcycle lay nearby, along with his belt.

Katy dressed and assembled her thoughts. She leaned over the edge, fondling the keys in her sap-covered hands.

"Let me tell you how this will work. If you say anything to anyone—if I hear even a snicker or someone trolls me—I'll tell my dad, and you'll pay. He won't care who your father is. He's that kind of guy."

She stepped back from the edge. The burning anger in her chest had settled into a soft glow, filling her body with energy. Even her vision seemed sharper. She tossed the keys into the woods.

She picked up the pistol and hefted its weight, centered on the temptation of its menace. Reggie wasn't watching her, as he panicked in the water alone. With the flick of her wrist, she tossed it into the quarry, where it would undoubtedly join many other dark secrets.

Out of the corner of her eye, she caught a flash of a white shirt. Gretchen, half ghosted by the dark woods, stood at the top of the path.

"I came back. I couldn't..." Gretchen's voice trailed off. "You stink."

"I wasn't being very cooperative. He tossed me in."

"How'd *he* fall in?"

"I panicked. I grabbed him, and we both went over."

Gretchen took a step back. "That wasn't very smart. You both could have drowned. He probably would have pulled you out."

"Probably wasn't good enough."

Gretchen peered over the edge. "Do you plan to let him up?"

"Catch and release. It's the right thing to do for the puny ones." Katy walked over to the rope and tossed the tasseled end over the rim.

"Be good, Reggie," she said. "Remember our deal."

Grunts and groans echoed from the quarry. As Reggie hauled himself onto the flat rocks, Katy and Gretchen picked their way down the path toward the dirt road.

"Where are the others?" Katy asked.

"Matt dropped us off, and everyone scattered."

"Brian. What a chivalrous asshole. He and I will need to talk. He thinks he got away, but he's mistaken." Katy stopped, tears rising at last. "I was all alone."

Gretchen reached out and pushed Katy's hair off her face.

"How'd you get here?" Katy asked.

"I took my mother's car. She and my stepdad are out drinking someplace. Now come home with me."

Another groan from the woods. Katy pictured a naked Reggie looking for his keys.

"Won't your mother mind?"

"Not likely she'll even notice. You call your folks and say you're having dinner at my house. To celebrate. You can take a shower and clean off all that smell. We'll wash your clothes. I'll drop you home later."

* * * *

Parked next to a thick patch of poison ivy, Reggie's bike appeared to glow in the dark woods. Katy dropped her bag and kicked the bike over. She waded in to give it an extra kick and toss sticky leaves and vines on it for good measure.

Gretchen's eyes were round, and she backed away. "More poison ivy. Are you nuts?"

"I'm already covered with it."

"Well, then, you aren't getting into my car like that. I'll put something down on the seat, but don't touch anything, until you climb into the shower. Not even the seatbelt."

At the car, Gretchen spread newspapers and an old towel across the passenger seat. She stepped back to let Katy settle into the car with her bag in the footwell and gently closed the door. "Remember. Keep your hands to yourself," she said through the open window. She climbed in behind the wheel and turned the ignition.

"Let's get going," Katy said. She swiveled to look over her shoulder. "Reggie might insist on a ride."

Gretchen put the car in gear. The sound of the tires crunched on the dirt lane, and Katy put her head between her knees, gulping deep breaths.

When they reached the paved road, Gretchen came to a full stop and looked at her passenger. "I came back for you. Would you have come back for me?"

Katy sat up. "I wouldn't have left."

"I suppose not. You scare me a bit, Katy."

Katy's laugh came out as a cackle. "I'm the least of your worries. Are you waiting for the light to change? Let's go. And come to graduation tomorrow. There's a party at my house after. Stay over. I'll give you a ride to Syracuse."

Gretchen shifted her foot from the brake to the accelerator. "I don't know. I might stick around a while to see what happens with Reggie. He's a total snake. I can watch your back. You might wish you'd kept his gun."

Katy leaned over to look out the passenger-side mirror. No Reggie.

"Not as long as he *thinks* I did."

Susan Alice Bickford was born in Boston, Massachusetts, and grew up in Central New York, the setting for many of her stories. Her passion for technology pulled her to Silicon Valley, where she became an executive at a leading technology company. She splits her time between Silicon Valley and her family's home base in Vermont. *A Short Time to Die*, was a Left Coast Crime Debut Novel nominee. Her second book, *Dread of Winter*, was an Edgar nominee. Contact Susan at: www.susanalicebickford.com.

CATCH AND RELEASE

MARK THIELMAN

I let a murderer go today.

I knew Edmonds was guilty, but the jury saw the case differently. Maybe the problem lay with the proof that they couldn't see. They didn't see the smirk, that small, irritating, self-satisfied smile he flashed during the pre-trial hearings, the confidently upturned corners of his mouth that he wore like a designer suit whenever he walked into court. Thomas Edmonds' smug look seared itself into my brain, as I watched him sit through testimony, implacably calm, his face unshadowed by doubt while the witnesses testified.

On breaks, he'd turn to his defense lawyer and chat, shoot the bull about the weather, like a guy locked up should have any right to an opinion about the outside temperature. Other times, I'd hear him chuckle as the two discussed the betting line on the game. He'd be doling out advice like a sports handicapper. Maybe that's how he paid his lawyer's fees and the price tag for the assortment of bespoke suits he wore.

On a break in the middle of the trial, he and his lawyer huddled close, like they were discussing some strategic move or maybe preparing a surprise motion. Suddenly, Edmonds pulled his head out of the cluster and started talking to me.

"Hey, Stevie," he said.

No one ever calls me Stevie.

"Stevie," he repeated, "take Minnesota to win the game tomorrow. I guarantee it, you'll make some good money. Buy your wife a fancy present. You'll get some."

All the while, he's sporting that smile of the virtuous. He acted like Saint Raymond Nonnatus, patron saint of the wrongfully accused, who had returned to earth in a pinstripe suit to bestow a blessing on his captor.

During his entire lesson to me on the betting line, I never got the sense that Edmonds saw my face. His presentation seemed more theatrical, a stage performance to flash his level of non-concern across the DMZ separating the defense table from the prosecutor's side. I began to wonder if Thomas Edmonds ever saw whole faces, maybe he only looked for fear in the eyes, heard a tremble in the voice, or noticed the bullet hole in the teenager he killed, the case for which I prosecuted him. Perhaps, seeing parts separated from the whole enabled him to be a soulless killer.

Pretending not to hear the comment, I turned and filed some papers. I don't talk with defendants; I talk with their lawyers. The snub did nothing to push the smile off his face.

I didn't bet the game. I should have. Minnesota won without the points; I could have made a bundle.

Later, my mind returned to the brief encounter. I wondered how Edmonds knew I was married. I finally decided that my wedding ring must have given me away. Gunmen, I suppose, get used to looking at hands, too.

I admit he got inside my head. Edmonds sat in comfortable repose at the defense table, always existing at the edge of my peripheral vision. He resided there, seemingly carefree amusement across his mug, the pads of his fingertips quietly tapping time on the tabletop, as he patiently waited for the end of the court case. Defendants take notes during trial. They scribble denials and pass their lawyers questions demanding answers. I've seen it with every trial I've done over the years. Defendants become totally invested in the most insignificant of misdemeanor trials. They churn through legal pads, often distracting their attorneys.

Edmonds sat, the relaxed palm of his left hand resting against his cheek, supporting his head, while the right hand silently drubbed on the table. His sly smile remained ever-present, teeth occasionally showing, like the shirt cuff beneath his suit jacket.

I once read an article about the ancient Aztecs. A condemned prisoner, staked for execution, would be shown his still-beating heart after it had been cut from his body. He would be the last to grasp what the world around him already knew.

I fantasized about wiping that grin off Thomas Edmonds' face, visualizing the details with cinematic perfection.

"The defendant will rise," the judge would command.

In my mind's eye, the judge would read out the jury's verdict. The defendant's smile would remain for just a fraction of a second, a delayed reaction as his brain processed the news of the conviction. Then, the smirk would flicker and fall, eyes widening as the news spread throughout his brain, registering the late firing neurons of understanding.

Thomas Edmonds' knees would wobble, his body still uncomprehending. This, I would think, is how the girl felt as she saw the gun raised to her face, a mixture of fear and confusion. The judge would begin his sentencing recitation. Edmonds' lids would blink with rapid eye movement as his face searched for a familiar sign in a landscape suddenly unrecognizable. His lips would purse as he drew shallow, panicked breaths. His fingers would clench and release as his brain struggled to process the news and decide whether to fight or flee. Drips of realization would fall as his mind began to absorb all of the things he would never again get to do: order off a menu, drink a beer, choose his own shoes or brush those now vanished teeth in the privacy of his own bathroom.

He would watch the last beat of his disembodied heart.

In my dream, I do not focus on a single feature. Instead, I watch Thomas Edmonds' entire face. I savor the moment, filing the expression away in the album of my memory. This is what justice looks like.

Maybe I let my desire to wipe away that grin affect the way I tried his case. Perhaps my fantasy became my obsession. I am left to second guess my every question and argument.

I let a murderer go today.

I know that his self-satisfied look wormed its way into the minds of others. Antonio Silva, the lead detective, told the jury about driving Ridge Way, the road hugging the edge of the hills overlooking Horseshoe Lake just outside of town. He described combing the area looking for the gun used in this homicide. Silva testified to searching the steep crags which run alongside the shoulder. His delivered his testimony crisply and precisely. He gave me everything I wanted. I glanced over at Edmonds. He sat unperturbed.

Before cross-examination, Edmonds leaned over and whispered something to his attorney. Defense lawyers ordinarily hate it when clients talk to them during trial; they're trying to concentrate. This time, I saw the lawyer smile and ask to approach the bench. He and I huddled near the judge. Although the jury could not hear the conversation, from the corner of my eye I saw Silva lean closer. "Your Honor," Edmonds' attorney whispered just loudly enough for his words to reach the witness stand, "during questioning, I may need to review some…personal peccadilloes…of this detective."

"Objection, relevance," I fired back, clueless as to what he meant.

"Sustained," the judge said.

Edmonds' lawyer did not appear disappointed as he returned to his chair. He had never really been addressing the judge. He had been speaking to Silva the entire time.

Back at counsel table, the lawyer asked Silva to show the jury the locations on a map. As he approached the easel, Thomas Edmonds brushed a lock of his perfectly coifed hair. His hand momentarily shielding his face from the jury, he winked at Silva. The detective stopped mid-sentence. He seemed flustered and disoriented on the map. Silva pointed to one spot and then corrected himself. Edmonds smiled. Silva's face reddened. He became tentative, his voice shaky and halting. An experienced detective shouldn't fall apart on a wink. Somehow, Edmonds' sorcery affected him. Silva gave me an apologetic look as he walked off the witness stand. Edmonds smiled again.

Weakness spread through my case like a virus. The patrol officer who canvassed the area came to court with a head cold. He held a tissue throughout his testimony. Perhaps the cold medicine dulled him. He promptly fell for one of the oldest weapons in the defense attorney arsenal.

"Isn't it possible that there might have been witnesses swimming at the lake?"

"Isn't it possible that there might be video recordings?"

"Isn't it possible that you overlooked something?"

"I suppose it's possible," he said.

The hand gesture he made was, I'm sure, meant to look dismissive of the questions. From my chair, however, he appeared to be signaling surrender. The white tissue waved back and forth. My case's foundation seemed rooted in sand. Edmonds, meanwhile, sat, the twinkle in his eyes flickering more brilliantly with each struggling witness.

I watched the cross-examination of Christi Stone, my star eyewitness, the one who identified the defendant.

"And how long did you have to look at the gunman?" Edmonds' lawyer asked.

She quickly glanced my way. Then she slowly turned toward his attorney, stopping just before her eyes reached the table. "Maybe a minute."

He slid back his French cuffed shirt exposing his Rolex. "Tell me when a minute is up?"

Her eyes again flicked toward me and then to the clock on the back wall.

"Ms. Stone, don't cheat. Just tell me when a minute has lapsed."

Time stopped Silence filled the court. Every eye watched her.

"Stop," she said.

Edmonds smile broadened. His lawyer looked at her, saying nothing.

"How long was it?" she asked.

"You said a minute, didn't you?" the attorney answered.

"Yes."

"And you were as sure about that as everything else you testified to?"

"Yes."

"As sure as your identification of my client as the murderer."

She shifted in her chair before making a thin nod, "Yes."

"You stopped me after twenty-seven seconds," the attorney said.

Christi Stone looked as if she had been punched in the stomach.

"You were wrong about the time, weren't you?"

"I guess."

"Guess is a good word to describe what happened, isn't it, Ms. Stone?"

Her shoulders slumped forward. "Yes."

"And you testified that you were as sure about the time as all of the other things you testified."

"Yes."

I pulled every advocate's trick I knew to rehabilitate Christi's testimony. Despite my efforts she never regained her energy. She spent the redirect examination afraid of saying anything that might offend Edmonds or his lawyer.

He didn't bother to cross-examine her again.

Christi Stone slouched down off the witness stand, head hung, utterly defeated. The theater of the courtroom compelled me to sit iron-stiff in my chair and watch her go. My own posture wanted to mimic hers as each witness added another ingredient to what was quickly becoming a giant soup bowl of reasonable doubt.

Edmonds still wore the smile. He flashed it during his jail book-in photo, and he carried it as my case collapsed.

I let a murderer go today.

The jury quickly acquitted Thomas Edmonds.

I knew that I should find solace in taking on the battle. Somewhere in my head, a motivational speech by Michael Jordan or Babe Ruth rolled, detailing the shots missed or the strikeouts accrued. Inevitably, failure accompanies everyone to the biggest stage. Much can be learned and achieved through losing, the speech concludes, more from losses than from victories. Failure force us to scrutinize our decisions, our assumptions, and our conduct. Losing puts our complacency under a microscope. Hard and valuable lessons flow from defeat. Think of To Kill a Mockingbird or Thermopylae.

Do I remember the Alamo?

All acquittals hurt, but this one cut deep. After the judge read the verdict, the defendant turned and faced me. His face showed no relief; he took the news of his verdict the way he might take the news of warm weather in July. The jury had just confirmed what he already knew. He was walking out of my courtroom. I had watched him, hoping to see his face fall. Instead, his eyebrows merely bobbed one time, representing the full measure of his surprise, if he had any at all. Instead, it was he who had the square-on view of my crestfallen expression.

"Shame you didn't get a conviction," he said as he brushed past me, the deputies escorting him to the holdover cell to begin the release paperwork. Soon, he'd leave the courtroom, using the same doors I used. "Some people just aren't made for guilty."

I have sometimes found solace after courtroom defeats. Some defendants learn, I tell myself. They've had an epiphany. St. Raymond pulled them from the penitentiary, and they recognize the gift they've been handed. Not all of them succeed; some defendants slide back into crime, giving the prosecutors another opportunity to balance the scales. In that moment, however, each culprit sincerely intends to use the opportunity to turn away from his past life mistakes and begin anew. Not Edmonds, I could see. The lesson he learned, another layer of non-stick paint had been applied to his armor.

I took a long drive in the country to unwind after the trial. I needed some time alone with my thoughts, some space to get to the place where my mind could listen to that inspiring speech full of sports metaphors. Motoring through the hills north of town, I came upon a car wreck on Ridge Way. A sports car hadn't held the curve and skidded on the loose gravel near the shoulder. The vehicle had spun before coming to a rest, torn through the guardrails, and lodged between the boulders lining the cliff's face, the last line of defense before the steep drop to the lake below. The driver's side of the car hung out over the edge. A nearly empty bottle of Talisker single malt lay in the gravel, thrown free through the open passenger door.

Pulling to the shoulder, I jumped out and ran to the car wedged precariously between the rocks. The driver's door had been torn off and lay, armrest side up, below on the lakeshore. I stood on the high side of the car, and looked across the bucket seats to the driver, still seat-belted in place. He moaned as I approached, the sounds of confusion rather than pain.

"Are you all right?" I yelled.

The driver pawed at the remains of the deflated airbag, limply hanging from the steering wheel, the right side of his face marred by a bloody nose and the rash of the exploding airbag.

"Take my hand," I shouted, thrusting my arm into the vehicle.

Moving slowly, his reactions dulled by alcohol and the high-speed punch of the air bag, he reached for my hand, the arm swinging back and forth in the air, before, finally, catching hold of my outstretched hand.

"Undo your seatbelt, and I'll pull you out," I shouted.

The driver cocked his head, as if not understanding my words, his eyes red and unfocused.

"Undo the belt," I yelled again. "I can't get you out when you're strapped in."

Nodding slowly, he reached down and unclicked the buckle. The belt hung freely alongside him. The driver looked back at me. I felt his weight, freed from the restraint, pulling against my arm, and I gave him a reassuring tug. Thomas Edmonds smiled, his teeth glossy and slick, smeared with blood from his cut lips.

I let a murderer go today.

As Thomas Edmonds fell, he may have realized who had let him go. His eyes widened in surprise, and his mouth gaped, as if to shout in protest.

But I didn't hear a word nor catch a single sound until impact.

I also didn't see that smirk.

I let a murderer go today. Perhaps I should feel guilty, but I guess some people just aren't made for guilty.

I'll let St. Raymond sort it all out.

Mark Thielman is a criminal magistrate working in Fort Worth, Texas. Formerly, he spent 27 years as a prosecutor for the Tarrant and Dallas County District Attorney's Offices. He has a law degree from the University of Texas as well as a Bachelor of Arts and Master of Liberal Arts degrees from Texas Christian University. A two-time Black Orchid Award-winning novella author, Mark's short fiction has been published in Alfred Hitchcock Mystery Magazine and anthologies including the Mystery Writers of America collection, Odd Partners. He lives in Fort Worth with his wife, two sons and an over-sized dog. MarkThielman.com

DEAD ARMADILLOS DON'T DANCE

KARI WAINWRIGHT

Rain slashed my windshield. My headlights barely pierced the dark night.

Lightning zigzagged through the sky. In that moment, I could clearly see the country road and the small armored animal crossing in front of my car. An armadillo. He jumped three feet into the air, as I frantically swerved around him. My car fishtailed, spun around, and slamdunked sideways into the deep ditch by the side of the road.

My head thudded against the window. My body slumped against the driver-side door, held in place by a now-taut seatbelt.

I was surprised the air bag didn't go off, but maybe, going in sideways, rather than head-on, had saved me from getting whomped in the face and torso.

Indulging in a brief moment of self-pity, I wished I'd stayed home in Colorado, but when my best friend from college had asked me to be her bridesmaid, I couldn't say no. All things considered, I doubted I could make it to her home in Austin tonight, as planned. With the wedding still three days away, I hoped I would find a way to get there in time. Right now, I just felt lucky to be alive, even though I was miles away from my destination.

I tried to ascertain how bad my situation was. My Kia Optima was wedged deep in the gully. My totally useless headlights focused along the muddy bottom of the ditch. Then, I saw the armadillo tap dance on the tippy-tip of his claws right in front of my car again. It looked like the little bastard was giving me a mocking nanny-nanny-nuu-nuu salute.

I gave him a one-finger salute in response but doubted that he saw it.

I had to face the facts. My car was stuck, half swallowed up by a deep Texas ditch. I turned off the engine.

I was stuck, too. With my weight against the seat belt, I couldn't unfasten it. Then, I remembered a tool Dad had bought for me thirteen years ago when I got my driver's license. I'd never had an occasion to use it. I couldn't think of its name but knew where it resided. I turned on the car's interior light and fished the thing out of the console. Its bright orange color made it easy to find. One end had matching heavy metal points on each side of its head to break windows, while the other end contained a recessed blade for cutting. Worried about hurting myself, I worked my fingers along the seat belt, until I found a place at my side. There, I sliced the seatbelt. Voila, I was free. And, voila, my arm hit the steering wheel and honked the horn. Loudly.

Take that, you overgrown armored rat!

With some serious maneuvers, I finally managed to finesse my way around the steering wheel and up onto the passenger side of my cattywampus car. Now, what?

I dug my cell phone out of my raincoat pocket and punched in 911. Nothing. Nada. Zippo. There was only one little, useless bar. I tossed the phone across the car in disgust. Smartphone, indeed.

Looked like I'd have to go for help the old-fashioned way—by foot. I found my purse and flashlight after a quick search. Realizing it might come in handy later, I tried to reach my rejected phone, but it would have taken a contortionist to get it, and I'd already used up all my circus-acrobat movements for the night. I couldn't find my umbrella, either, but since I was wearing a raincoat with a hood, I told myself I'd be fine.

I shoved against the passenger side door above me. Nothing doing. It wouldn't open. So, once more, I got my handy little nameless tool, pulled my hood over my head, closed my eyes, and struck the window above me. Pieces of pebbled safety glass bombarded me, followed by heavy, wet raindrops. I shook off the glass pieces, striving to leave them in the Kia.

Carefully, I pulled myself out of the vehicle through the window, wound up slipping in the mud, and landed on my keister. As I thudded to the earth, I saw the armadillo one more time. He skittered sideways, then waltzed away. I remembered my father's advice when he taught me to drive. Do not swerve for wildlife. All you are doing is endangering yourself.

Sorry, Dad. I didn't recall your advice in time. If I had, my lovely sedan wouldn't be consumed by a ditch. And there would have been one dead armadillo, one who couldn't have danced away into the night.

For a moment, I felt like a child again, but Daddy wasn't coming to his little girl's rescue. Abigail, I told myself, let's get going.

I tucked my long, reddish-brown hair further back into my raincoat's hood. It took a couple of tries to scramble my way out of the ditch and back onto the road.

I had no idea how far it was to the next house, or business, or town up ahead. But there'd been lights on at a farmhouse about a mile back. There'd also been a sign announcing, "Fresh Farm Eggs for Sale." Maybe I could get an omelet, along with some help.

Flashlight on, I started my trek, propelled by the wind at my back and the rain smacking my calves and shoes. Nothing like squelching along the road in squeaky sneakers.

After a long and very damp eternity tramping up and down hills, I found myself at the farmhouse driveway. The rain had tapered off from its pounding tempest, and the angry wind had dissipated. I shook my fist at the cloudy sky and cursed the weather god for not stopping the storm sooner.

I trudged up the drive, dodging puddles whenever possible. After weaving my way amongst the various vehicles and farm equipment, I saw light creeping out the glass panels of a side door. I stepped up on a small porch, raising a hand to knock and announce my presence.

Then I stopped, my fist poised in mid-air.

Inside was a dark hallway, leading to a pool of light in a nearby room. And in the center of that light sat a man and woman, both tied to straight-back chairs.

A brutish menace of a man hovered over them. He slapped the woman's face. Hard. I drew back. I wasn't the only one needing help tonight.

I reached for my phone to call 911, then remembered—I'd stupidly thrown it across the car.

Maybe I could go for help, but how far away was the next house? I couldn't remember. I heard the woman cry out in pain. They needed help now.

I put my hand on the doorknob and eased the door open a fraction of an inch. I wasn't about to enter right now but needed to know I could when ready.

I circled behind the white clapboard farmhouse and discovered a window to the room where the couple and their tormentor were located. I risked only a quick peek to ascertain their whereabouts, before moving to the front of the house. I carefully opened the front door and peered around it into a foyer. A worn Persian runner lined the floor for several feet. I saw a staircase on the right and two rooms on the left. The first room was cloaked in darkness, the second well-lit, showing a stone fireplace and a maroon wingback chair to the side. I'd glimpsed those when I looked in the last window. Now, I knew how to get into the house.

I needed a diversion. Too bad I hadn't brought the armadillo with me. Tossing him into the house would definitely get someone's attention, just as he'd gotten mine earlier. I looked around the yard for something to use against the bad guy but found nothing. Where was a damn armadillo when you needed one?

Chickens! The place advertised fresh eggs, which meant they must have chickens.

I crossed the dirt parking area, no longer caring about puddles, and found a rustic wooden shed next to the barn. It was surrounded by a yard fenced with woven wire.

I unlatched the gate and moved across the small yard, hoping I wasn't stepping in too much chicken doo-doo. Upon opening the building's door, the smell of ammonia assaulted my nostrils. I gagged as the acidic stench trailed through my nose and seeped into my mouth.

I flicked my flashlight beam through the interior. Chickens galore. Some asleep, some stirring on their roosts. Boldly, I reached for one and captured her under my arm. I was immediately sorry. The creature turned demonic and started pecking at my hand, my wrist, and any other part she could reach.

I still wanted one more, but now they no longer acted domesticated. They squawked, flapped their wings, and chased their shadows around the henhouse. They flew past my head and into my face. I wound up spitting out feathers. I reached for one, only to get pecked on my other side. It took five tries and countless wounds to catch another by her legs. Now, I had one under one arm and the other upside down. At some point, I'd lost my purse. Who knew what mess it had landed in?

Armed with my feathered diversions, I headed back to the house, adrenaline racing through my veins like ice water. I couldn't close the gate to the chicken yard, but after all I'd gone through dealing with them, I didn't care if a fox got in there or not.

The one blasted bird kept pecking me. My hand was now raw and stung like the dickens. The other blasted bird kept flapping her wings, trying to get out of my grasp. She screeched. "Shut the cluck up!" I ordered. She didn't.

Back at the side door, I threw the angry birds inside without looking. Much squawking and flapping of wings ensued.

I ran to the front door as fast as my squelchy sneakers would take me. Once inside, I sidled up to the living room and peeked around the corner. Both the man and the woman were restrained with duct tape, but now her chair was overturned. She was on her side on the floor. The bad man wasn't there. I guessed he was in the hallway, investigating the distraction I'd provided.

I headed over to the couple and whispered, "I'm here to help you. mister, I'll try to free you first." I pulled out the trusty nameless tool from my raincoat pocket and sliced through the tape binding his chest and his hands with ease. But before he could stand, and I could free the woman, the bad man returned, kicking the two chickens in front of him.

At least, he wasn't armed. I noticed a gun on the fireplace mantle, but it did me no good. The bad man stood between me and it.

"What the hell is going on?" the menace said. The chickens left the room, clucking and flapping some more. Then, he noticed me kneeling behind the farmer's chair and stepped toward me. "Come out from there."

I flinched and knelt lower. I dropped my tool back into my pocket. The farmer kept his hands behind his back, as if he were still constrained.

"I said get out here. Now!"

I rose slowly and stepped out from behind the farmer with my hands raised.

The bad guy grabbed my right arm and pulled me closer. "Who are you?"

My mind spun on its axis. What should I tell him? Then, I remembered seeing a placard asking folks to reelect Sheriff Dalton. I raised my chin, glared at him, and put on my best Texas drawl. "My name is Billie Sue Dalton, and Sheriff Dalton is my daddy. Y'all harm one hair on my head, and he will hunt you down. And what do I call you?"

He grasped both my upper arms, then scowled. "You're all wet." He flung me onto the nearby couch. "I'm not telling you my name. You must think I'm an idiot."

"Well, I have to call you something. How about Gus?"

"I don't like that name."

If this had been under different circumstances, I would have laughed. Here was a man not only refusing to tell me his real name, but he dickered over my choice of a moniker for him. "How about Pete?"

He shrugged. "Whatever."

"Pete" was tall, or maybe his threatening manner just made him seem so, as he loomed over us. A scar dissected his right eyebrow, hardening his appearance even more. "Well, Billie Sue, do you know these people?" He pointed to the farm couple.

I studied the poor woman on the floor, her housedress bunched up around her thighs, her grey hair askew, her face streaked with tears and blood from a cut lip. She choked back a sob. Her husband's stoic demeanor hid behind full, bushy eyebrows and a brown thicket of a beard. He remained still, not giving away his new-found freedom.

"No, sir, I do not know these folks."

"Then what in the world are you doing here?" he asked.

"I had an accident down the road apiece. My car wound up in a ditch at a real uncomfortable angle, so I called my daddy and told him I was coming to this farmhouse, because it was the closest," I lied. Surely it wouldn't hurt if Pete thought a sheriff would be arriving soon. "What are you doing here? What do you want from these people?"

"None of your damn business."

The farmer raised his thick eyebrows. "He thinks we have a pot full of money hidden on our property. But we don't."

Pete raised his fist, as if he would clobber the man. With a stern gaze, he slowly lowered his arm.

One of the chickens came back on the scene, clucking like a crazed creature. Pete picked up his gun from the fireplace mantle and pointed it at the bird. "Anyone up for a fried chicken dinner?"

Looking down at the blood oozing from my left hand and wrist, I should have found that to be poetic justice. But I didn't like the idea of the man getting comfortable firing a weapon in the house. "You know if you shoot that gun in here, the bullet might ricochet, and no telling where it would wind up."

"Is that something Sheriff Daddy taught you?" the bad guy asked.

I nodded. "Sure. My daddy taught me lots of stuff," I said, hoping my fake Texas accent was holding up.

"Did he teach you how to dodge a bullet?"

"N-n-no," I stuttered. He pointed his revolver at my torso, his finger caressing the trigger. I sure hoped it wasn't a hairtrigger.

"Listen, Farmer Prewitt, if you don't tell me where the money is, Miss Billie Sue is going to get her chest aerated."

The woman on the floor struggled against her bonds. "I have some money in my dresser drawer. You can have that." She choked out the words.

"Upstairs bedroom?"

"Yes."

He waved the gun in the direction of the stairs on the other side of the foyer. "Get up, Miss Billie Sue. Beings the money's in a lady's dresser, I think you should be the one to do the rifling through the undies and such."

He made me precede him up the stairs. I peered into the first room. A bathroom. I fumbled for the light switch in the next room. There, I saw a bed, two Early American dressers, and a rocking chair. All was neat and tidy. A colorful, Lone-Star quilt covered the bed, but I didn't have time to appreciate its beauty.

He motioned to the closest dresser. "Check that out."

I opened the top drawer with my non-bloody hand and found men's socks, neatly folded and stacked. Tried the next. Men's briefs.

"Check the other one." He kept using the gun as a pointer. I kept hoping it wouldn't go off.

Once again, I opened the top drawer. Lady's granny panties. I wondered if the woman downstairs might find this invasion humiliating. I felt through the underwear but found no money. Next drawer was bras. Not quite so neat as the other drawers. Stacking bras wasn't easy. Third drawer held scarves. And cash. I removed it and held it out to Pete.

"Count it," he said.

Being held at gunpoint was getting to me. My hands trembled as they separated the bills—all twenties. "There's two hundred and twenty dollars." I held it out to him again, bloodstains and all.

He grabbed it with his left and stuffed it into his jeans' pocket. Some of the bills' edges stuck out, and he pushed them down harder.

Now he waved the gun, motioning me back to the stairs. The walk felt like a death march. I swallowed my saliva, trying to swallow my fear along with it.

I noticed the front door at the bottom of the stairs. Wide open. I gasped.

Pete's gun poked me in the back, urging me to descend faster. Outside the door, I couldn't see anything, except the circle of light that escaped from inside.

As we crossed the foyer, we could tell the living room was empty, the farm couple gone. Apparently, Farmer Prewitt had managed to free himself completely, then help his wife. Good for them. I was glad they'd escaped. Though I sensed it could be bad for me. Really bad.

"What the hell?" Pete raged, as we moved through the chaos of wadded-up strips of duct tape and turned-over dining room chairs.

He shoved me. I stumbled, and then, turned to face him, my nerves vibrating like a terrified tuning fork. Was he going to shoot me in retaliation for their escape?

"You have some money now," I pushed the words past my quaking vocal cords. "You should just go. They've probably called the police."

He shook his head, giving me a questioning look. "Don't y'all mean the sheriff? Your daddy, Miss Billie Sue?"

With a shudder, I realized I'd lost my Texas accent, as well as my standing as sheriff's daughter. I shrugged, trying to look cool. "You can't blame a girl for trying."

"Beings I got the gun, I can place blame wherever I want."

A furtive movement on the foyer's Persian rug behind Pete drew my attention. I screamed.

Startled by the noise I made, Pete shook his head and laughed. "You think I'll fall for that old trick? Hey, mister, there's something behind you."

The armadillo that had entered the house left the long rug and clacked his way over the hardwood floors. Tappy, tap, tap—an out-of-sync Terpsichore.

Pete finally realized I wasn't trying to fool him and turned toward the new sound. His back was to me, and the way he took control of the gun in both hands told me he meant business.

I didn't think I could overpower him, but I remembered my trusty nameless tool, residing in my pocket. I smashed the metal hammer end into his skull. Immediately, blood rivulets ran through his brown hair and down his neck.

He dropped the gun. It skittered and spun across the hardwood, alarming the armadillo. The little guy jumped three feet off the floor and squealed before racing for the door as fast as its little hairy legs would carry it.

Both Pete and I went for the gun. He got to it first, but with hands bloodied from trying to staunch his wound, he had problems getting it under control in his slippery grasp. The revolver fell to the floor again.

This time, I got the gun. I aimed it at his torso, even though I hated touching its sticky surface.

"Bet you won't use it," Pete challenged.

A rough drawl came from the front door. "If she won't, you can bet I will. I've shot many a varmint in my time." Farmer Prewitt raised a shotgun to his shoulder.

Mrs. Prewitt appeared behind him. "You better believe him."

"You didn't leave?" I felt incredulous, grateful, and a lot less alone.

"Of course not, child. We couldn't leave you alone with Pete."

They entered the house, and then, the woman saw the blood still streaming from Pete's head. "Keep the gun on him, old man, while I tie him up and stop the bleeding. He's making a mess."

After he was secured to a chair and had a big bandage positioned on the back of his head, Pete cursed and called us vile names. "I shoulda shot all of you when I had the chance."

Mrs. Prewitt approached him one more time. "Stick a sock in it," she said, and then, did it for him.

I hoped it was from the dirty clothes hamper, but it looked clean. Dang it all. I wondered if I was suddenly thinking in "Texan."

Now that Pete was taken care of, the farmer sat in the maroon wingback chair with his gun across his lap. "I'm curious. What exactly did you use on him?"

I pulled my trusty nameless tool from my pocket one more time. "I don't know what it's called." I got up and reached over to show him.

"Why, that's one of those car-safety hammers," he said. "Cuts through seatbelts with one side and breaks windows with the other."

"Not to mention cracking heads open," the woman said. "Serves him right."

Now that Pete was muffled, she introduced herself as Jean. "We called the sheriff. He's on his way."

"By the way," Farmer Prewitt said, "he was surprised to learn he had a daughter named Billie Sue." He chuckled. "First time tonight I could smile."

I smiled back. "My name is really Abigail Parsons, but I thought being a sheriff's daughter might be more effective."

Jean motioned me to the comfortable-looking couch. "Sit, child. We need to take care of that injured hand. I'm afraid you have some nasty scratches there."

She gently cleaned the wounds, applied petroleum jelly, and wrapped my wrist and hand in sterile bandages. She also suggested I see a doctor to ascertain if I needed a tetanus shot or not.

I was about to mention the armadillo invasion, when we heard the sound of sirens piercing the night. Colored lights strobed the farmhouse and night sky. Sheriff Dalton and a deputy had arrived in separate vehicles.

It didn't take long for the two of them to get a fuming, handcuffed Pete out of the house.

The sheriff reentered, just as Jean called us to the kitchen. "I'm making tea," she said.

After we all sat, she held a cold pack to her cut lip. Dalton asked for details of the night's events. Once Farmer Prewitt had related their ordeal, the sheriff turned to me. "So, you're the daughter I never knew I had."

"I hope you don't mind."

"Young lady, you probably saved the lives of my friends. I'd be proud to be the daddy of a heroine like you."

"I'm not the only one. An armadillo not only caused my accident, thus leading me here, but a bit ago, one entered the house and distracted Pete. Do you think it could have possibly been the same animal?"

The Prewitts laughed, deep big-throated chortles, until Jean moaned and put the cold pack back on her lip.

"Most likely you met Jedidiah," the farmer said. "I don't think he would have traveled that far, especially with all the rain tonight. He'd probably stay in our front yard, where he knows the best worms come out after a storm."

"Jedidiah? You name armadillos around here?"

The farmer continued, "He's sort of her pet. Jed has a burrow on the far side of the yard where he spends his days. But every night about nine, my Jeanie here, puts a treat outside the door for him. Tonight, he probably came in looking for his bowl of cat food, since it never made it outside."

Sheriff Dalton harrumphed. "Most people discourage the beasts or kill them."

"I know," said Jean, "but I've known him since he was orphaned as a youngun. 'Course, I never encouraged him to come inside." A worried wrinkle stretched across her forehead as she looked at me. "You didn't touch him, or the other armadillo, for that matter, did you, Billy—I mean Abigail?"

I thought of those hairy tanks the animals wore, not exactly pettable "No. Of course, I was a little busy both times I had run-ins with them. But why do you ask?"

"About twenty percent of them have leprosy and can transfer it to humans."

I leaned back in shock, almost bringing my chair and myself crashing to the floor.

Sheriff Dalton pulled me forward, so that didn't occur. "Can't have anything bad happen to my daughter."

I gulped. "Leprosy, who knew? Actually, there's a whole lot I don't know about them. I thought they rolled up into a ball when they felt threatened."

"That's the smaller three-banded version. The kind we have here is nine-banded and too big to curl into a ball. But they often jump when scared."

"Well, I guess Pete scared him, which gave me the chance to get the gun." I raised my teacup in a salute. "As far as I'm concerned, he's a hero armadillo." We clinked cups and sipped in honor of him, the armored tank version of the Texas cavalry.

Kari Wainwright belongs to Desert Sleuth Sisters in Crime as well as Mesa Writers. She's been published in Desert Sleuth anthologies as well as That Mysterious Woman, Busted! Arresting Stories from the Beat, Landfall, and A Murder of Crows. The story, Dead Armadillos Don't Dance, was a finalist in the Bill Crider Short Story Contest in Texas. Kari shares her Arizona home with husband Tom, son Travis and ShihTzu Oscar Wilde.

THE CASE OF THE ABUSED ARTICHOKE

CYNTHIA SABELHAUS

I'm generally a laid-back woman, immune to road-ragers, line-cutters, and the angst of my teenage daughter. But on that hot, muggy Indiana evening at the checkout counter of Meadow Spring's newest grocery store, I'd met my match. The young cashier bounced to the beat of some tune only she could hear. A wad of gum bulged in her jaw. I was mesmerized by her nametag, attached to the top of her skimpy red dress: MONICA. The tag seemed to vibrate even more rapidly than its wearer.

It had been a long day. I was beginning to have doubts about the promotion at United Indemnity that allowed me to move back to my hometown. I hadn't counted on the twelve-hour workdays or the resistance from my daughter, Allison. She wasn't happy about leaving her friends back in Chicago and moving to a small town where nothing ever happens.

My feet hurt, and my head throbbed. I watched Monica grab the first of my items, scan it, and toss it toward the bagging area. A dozen donuts slapped the counter. A gallon of milk quickly followed, tipping precariously toward the donuts. The artichokes hit the milk carton with a thud and began spilling from their plastic produce sack. I grabbed one as it rolled toward the edge and impaled my finger on a spike-tipped leaf. That did it!

"Monica," I said, louder than I intended. The girl raised her heavily made-up eyes toward me but continued to scan and toss items. I reached out and grabbed a carton of eggs just before it, too, was flung onto the pile. "Please stop throwing my food."

Monica stopped mid-scan and glared at me. "S-s-sorr-y." She rolled her eyes.

I felt Alli shrink away from me. She was at that age. Fourteen trying for twenty-one. I smiled weakly, noting the similarity between Alli's clothes, make-up, and attitude, and those of our sulky cashier. Even their too-short red dresses were similar. I had longer shirts in my closet.

Several nearby customers looked my way. Great, I thought. My first week back in town, and here I am, behaving like a raving maniac. I forced a smile toward Monica, which she mistook for permission to continue the grocery abuse.

A bottle of chardonnay rolled toward the end of the counter. Oblivious to the danger of broken glass and spilled wine, Monica picked up the phone above the cash register and asked for a price check on a bag of dinner rolls. I considered pointing out the bag contained hamburger buns, and the price was clearly marked. Instead, I glanced out the store's large windows.

With the exception of the frames for its large doors, the front of the store was made up entirely of glass. A coating blocked much of the incoming light and obscured the parking lot while reflecting the checkout counters. It was darker outside than it should have been, and rain began pelting the glass. I sighed. If my groceries survived Monica's rough treatment, they were sure to get soaked on the way to our car.

Then, the lights went out. Somewhere, a woman screamed, but it was quickly drowned out by an explosion of thunder. I heard my groceries roll around on the counter. Was Monica trying to bag them in the dark?

Another round of thunder erupted. In the quiet that followed, customers murmured. Someone laughed. Feet shuffled. "What next?" I said to no one in particular, then turned in the direction where I had last seen my daughter. "Alli, are you all right?"

"Mom," Alli stretched the word into at least four syllables.

I couldn't think of anything else to say. A male voice emerged from the din. "Ladies and gentlemen, please stay where you are. We are checking our emergency lighting. It should be on in a moment. Please—"

But the voice was lost under the nerve-shattering blare of a fire alarm. This time, I reached back and pulled Alli toward me.

Over the din, she yelled, "Terrific! A fire drill. Well, I'm not going out in that storm until I smell smoke." With that, she pulled away from me.

I had to agree with my daughter. As obnoxious as the alarm was, it beat going out into the driving rain. Just thinking about it gave me a chill.

My mind drifted. I was mid-way through planning the next day's agenda, when the alarm suddenly stopped, and the lights came on. I blinked, then looked around. The area just inside the doors was wet. People were milling about, but Alli was gone, and so was Monica. Some of the customers began to talk. I stood on tiptoes and scanned the store, but I wasn't particularly concerned. It wasn't like Alli was still three years old and likely to take candy from strangers.

Employees were scurrying in and out the store's small office in the front corner of the building. I recognized the portly, balding man standing in the doorway, holding a towel to the side of his face where blood had seeped down to his shirt collar. Bobby Williams. We'd gone to high school together. His father owned the only grocery store in town back then, and it looked like Bobby had stuck with the family business. He must have hurt himself during the blackout, but it didn't look serious.

Soon, the police arrived, followed closely by an ambulance and two fire trucks, although there was no sign of a fire. Uniformed men and women of every description entered the store, and the pandemonium increased to a roar. I heard something about a robbery from the cashier on the next aisle. Someone else said something about a fire.

The store's PA system hummed for a moment. "This is Charlie Burk. Most of you probably know that I'm the acting police chief while Ted's on medical leave. Looks like we've had a robbery here, folks. I'm going to have to ask all of you to stay where you are, until one of the officers can speak with you. We'll try to make it quick. I know you all want to get home." The PA system hummed again and then clicked off.

Charlie Burk. Another familiar name. If it was the same guy I remembered from high school, I supposed we were all in good hands, at least if testosterone would solve the current crisis. The Charlie Burk I remembered was full of it--and of himself. He was the top jock.

Dismissing Charlie and all that ancient high school history, I began to worry about Alli. She still had not returned. I moved to the other side of the counter, where Monica had been working, to get a better view of the store. Something scraped my foot and snagged my stocking. Absently, I bent down and retrieved an artichoke. Despite my best efforts, one had escaped the conveyor. Placing the prickly vegetable on the counter, I noticed a sticky red smear on my palm. I might have guessed ketchup, but I hadn't bought any for Monica to drop. There was a matching stain on the floor where the artichoke had fallen. It was dark and red. My stomach turned.

Charlie Burk approached.

"Maggie Sanders?" he said. "I had no idea you were back in town."

Now that was a shock. He knew who I was. "It's Maggie Evans now. My daughter and I just moved back." I looked beyond him, searching for Alli.

Charlie cleared his throat. "I…uh, I'm sorry. I mean, I heard about your husband."

"Thanks," I said quickly, continuing to scan the store. After two years, the pain of my husband's death had dulled, but I still couldn't talk about it, especially not to someone like Charlie.

"I've only been back here for a year myself," he said. "I did twenty in the Marine Corps and then took a job with the city police. My folks used to keep me informed about everything that went on in this burg, at least, until they moved to Florida last year."

Charlie was looking at me, instead of the floor, and walking straight toward the red smear. I hopped out of the cashier's spot and stopped him. "I don't know what's going on here," I began, ignoring his broad smile, "but I think you should see this." I pointed toward the congealing spot.

Charlie bent over and studied it. "Looks like blood," he said, as he straightened.

"I was afraid of that." My stomach twisted. I needed to find Alli. I took a deep breath. "Look, my daughter seems to be missing. She was right behind me when the lights went out. I haven't seen her since. And the cashier who was working at this register also disappeared during the blackout."

"How old is your daughter?"

"Fourteen. Alli's an independent kid," I said, "but I don't like not knowing where she is, especially given the circumstances." I pointed toward the possible blood.

Charlie grabbed my hand and twisted it to examine the red smear. "What's this?"

I pulled my hand back. "I don't know. It came from the artichoke, I think."

Charlie frowned, took me by the elbow, and began ushering me toward the front of the store.

"Wait. What about my daughter? I need to find her."

"You need to come with me," he said.

I pulled away from him and widened my stance. "I need to find Alli. Now."

Charlie sighed. "Look, we'll find her. Come with me for just a minute to let one of the officers take a sample of the blood, or whatever it is, on your hand. I'll have someone page your daughter. We'll ask her to come to the office."

When we reached the office door, Charlie pulled a note pad from the pocket of his sports jacket and jotted down Allison's name. He spoke to two officers. One headed toward the checkout lanes while the other, a woman, joined me outside the office. She swabbed my hand, gave me a disinfecting wipe and stayed by my side. We were both leaning against the wall next to the office door when I heard Alli's name announced on the store's PA system.

Glancing into the office, I could see Bobby hunched over a desk, supporting his battered head with his hands. A paramedic treated his injuries, while a policewoman applied gray powder to the open door of the safe.

The room was crowded. Charlie pulled a chair up to the desk and placed his pad and pen in front of him. I heard him say, "Bobby, I need to get some information from you. Can you tell me what you remember?"

Bobby nodded. "I always make the night drop at the bank on my way home around eight. All the cashiers had turned in their checks and big bills, and I was opening the safe to get the rest of the day's receipts. Next thing I know, the lights go out, and I'm seeing stars and hearing bells. It took me a few seconds to realize the fire alarm had gone off. When the lights came back on, the safe was empty." He looked sheepishly at Charlie. "I wish I could tell you more."

"Where is the breaker box for the lights?"

"In the back. Why?"

Not answering, Charlie turned his attention to the paramedic who had finished bandaging Bobby's head and was replacing his equipment in a plastic box. "Can you tell me what caused the wound?"

The paramedic shook his head. "Not really, but it's odd. There are two lacerations, one on each side of his head. It looks like he was hit on the right side, causing his skull to strike the safe door. I doubt the first blow would have even knocked him down, but that's where all the blood came from. I don't know what caused it. There are two punctures, and I found some fibrous material lodged in one of them."

"We'll get it to the lab," Charlie said.

I stepped into the doorway. "Artichoke," I volunteered. Everyone looked at me, as though I had lost my mind. "Well, it would explain the bloody artichoke at the checkout counter. I think the thief used it to hit Bobby."

Bobby groaned and slumped deeper into his chair. "I was robbed at artichoke-point. I'll be the laughingstock of the next grocers' convention."

An officer stepped around me and motioned to Charlie. "You'd better come out here, sir. They just found one of the checkout girls wandering around in the parking lot. She says she was abducted."

Charlie, the officer who had swabbed my hand, and two paramedics dashed out, leaving me alone. I followed them. Monica was standing just inside the store's double doors, her hair streamed with water, and most of her make-up was gone. A ragged rip in her black tights exposed a scraped knee, and blood was trickling from several scratches on her right hand. As we approached, her eyes widened. Then, the lids slammed shut, and her body went limp.

"She's fainted," someone announced.

One paramedic supported her head, while another snapped a vial, holding it under her nose with only limited effect. Monica opened her eyes slightly and mumbled nonsense. "Shock," one medic nodded to the other. "Let's get her to the hospital."

As the ambulance faded from view, my fear for Alli intensified. Since the police seemed to have lost interest in me, I thought I'd try to find my daughter. As much as her choice of dress sometimes bothered me, she was levelheaded and mature for her age. We'd helped each other through the grieving process after her father's fatal car accident. We were close.

I fumbled in my purse for my cell phone and stepped outside to place a call to her cell. The rain had stopped, at least for the moment.

I dialed her number, counted the rings, and got her voice mail. After six tries, I hung up and looked across the parking lot. A few customers were trickling out of the store. I looked back through the store window to the office. There was still no sign of Alli.

"Where are you, Alli?" I whispered.

I couldn't go back inside to sit and wait. Every muscle in my body was coiled. I had to do something. I walked to the end of the sidewalk and looked down the pavement along the side of the building. It was deserted. Following the windowless block wall, I went to the back of the store, just as a police cruiser pulled away. Two young men stood smoking on the loading dock.

"Hi," I called up to them. "Did either of you happen to see a young girl out here? She's about my height. Long, blond hair. Wearing a short red dress and black tights?"

"Yeah, maybe," one of them said. "About half an hour ago, I saw somebody down by that car." He pointed toward a rusting Datsun sitting under a tree, several yards past where the pavement ended. "I couldn't see too good with the rain and all," he added.

"Do you know whose car it is?"

The other boy tossed his cigarette butt off the end of the dock and stepped toward me. "It's been out there a few days. We figured someone dumped it. Looks like a piece of junk."

I thanked them and ran to the car. The driver's door was slightly ajar. I yanked it open and leaned inside, noting stained and frayed upholstery. Fast-food wrappers and beer cans littered the floor. It looked pretty much like an abandoned car was supposed to look, with one exception. There was a key in the ignition. I sat down in the driver's seat and twisted the key. Nothing.

I removed the key and went to the back of the car. I knew I was being irrational, but the image of Alli stuck in the trunk flashed through my brain. I turned the key in the trunk lid, and it popped open without a squeak. There was no one inside. At first, I thought it was empty, but then I noticed three zippered bags bearing the imprint of Chase Bank. I had found the loot.

I closed the trunk, locked the car, and put the key in my pocket. The loading dock was now deserted. I climbed the cement steps and went inside where cartons filled the large storage area. The lighting was poor. Cautiously, I worked my way toward a door that I hoped would lead into the brightly lit sales area. I passed an electrical panel. Someone would have had to come back here to turn off the lights. Could the same person have gotten to the front of the store in time to hit Bobby? A foot beyond the panel was a fire alarm, its glass cover was shattered.

A flight of metal stairs enclosed by rough, chain-link fencing took up the rest of the wall. I could see a piece of fabric caught in the wire about halfway up. It was red.

One of the boys from the dock came through the swinging door from the main part of the store. "Where do these stairs go?" I asked, keeping my voice low.

"There's some storage space up there. It's empty. The store's only been open a couple months, so we haven't had a lot of junk to store."

"Look, I'm going up there." I dug in my pocket for the car key and handed it to him. "Take this to Charlie Burk and tell him Maggie Sanders said he should have someone check the trunk of the car out back." I started up the stairs. "And tell Charlie where I've gone, would you?"

"Sure. The cop told us to come to the office as soon as we finished our smokes, anyway." He shrugged and disappeared through the door, leaving me alone on the stairs.

I reached the fabric twenty steps up. It felt cold between my fingers. It could have come from Alli's dress, I thought. Or Monica's. Or perhaps from some other source that had nothing to do with the robbery.

There was a door at the top of the stairs. I opened it slowly and stepped into a large, open room. High windows across one wall let in a little light from the parking lot. Allison was sitting on a plastic milk crate a few feet away. I heard her say, "It's okay. Nobody will blame you for the robbery."

Across from her, a tall, skinny boy cleared his throat. Shadows covered his face. "Monica loves me. She said so. We were going away together."

"Yeah? And where is your darling Monica now?" Alli asked.

"I don't know—" The boy hesitated. It sounded like he was trying to stifle a sob. "Something went wrong."

Alli shook her head. "That's about the dumbest thing I ever heard. Monica's old, like maybe thirty. And you've got your whole life ahead of you. College. A great career. Can't you see, Monica is using you?"

"Stop it," the boy screamed as he rushed toward Alli.

I stepped behind her. "So, this is where you disappeared to, dear." I put a hand on her shoulder and tried to channel a bright, ditzy 1970s sit-com mom. "Aren't you going to introduce me to your friend, sweetie?"

Alli caught on quickly. "Mom, hi. I was just going to come looking for you. This is Howie Benson. He's sixteen and a science tutor. Sometimes, he helps me with chemistry or algebra."

"Hello, Howie," I said. "I'm glad to meet you, but I wish the circumstances were better."

He wiped his nose on his sleeve. "What do you mean? What circumstances?"

"Well, the robbery and all. I'm sorry. I didn't mean to eavesdrop, but it does look like you're the one who cut the electricity and set off the fire alarm. I'm afraid you're going to be in a bit of trouble. Monica's in the hospital. You'd better talk to Officer Burk before she has a chance to blame you for everything. By the way, I do think Monica was trying to dump you. She went straight from the robbery out to her car, but the battery was dead."

"Oh, yeah?" His tone was belligerent.

"Yes." I nodded. "If she'd made a better choice in weapons, maybe she'd have had time to get away."

Howie shrugged. "That shows how much you know. She was supposed to use something soft—"

Charlie Burk shouted from the stairway, "Maggie, you up here?"

"Here," I yelled back.

Charlie arrived with two officers in tow. He looked at the three of us, but then walked to Howie. "I think you and I need to have a little talk over at the police station," he said. "Your parents are going to meet us there."

Howie looked at his feet but followed the officers down the stairs.

"Hey, you don't have to do that," Alli yelled after the officers. "Howie didn't do anything. I know. I was with him."

Charlie patted Alli on the shoulder and assured her that the boy would be fine. When he told her one of the officers would need to take her statement, she brightened, no doubt ready to continue her campaign to free Howie.

The female officer who'd taken the blood sample from my hand what seemed like days ago came up and spoke quietly to Charlie. She nodded as he gave directions, and then she turned to Alli. "We need to get your statement while everything is still fresh in your mind," she said. "Let's go to the employee lounge for a few minutes. I'll buy you a soda, and your mom can pick you up there." She looked at me. "In about fifteen minutes?"

I nodded and watched them walk away. Then, I was alone with Charlie.

"You know," I said, "there are a couple pieces that still don't fit."

Charlie shook his head. "What did you say you do for a living?"

I smiled. "I'm the new Vice President of UI's Fraud Division."

Charlie shook his head. "I should have known. Let's go talk to Bobby."

We found the store manager where we'd left him, still sitting at his desk in the office. He grinned when we entered. "Hey. I heard you caught the guy. Good work!"

"As it turns out," Charlie said, "there were two of them. We lost the girl, but we got your money back."

Surprised, I turned to Charlie. "Monica escaped?"

Charlie continued, as though I wasn't there, directing his attention to Bobby. "Monica, one of your clerks, disappeared from the hospital. We're still searching, but it doesn't look good."

And then, it clicked. I knew what had happened. "How's your head?"

I asked.

Bobby reached up and gingerly rubbed his bruised and bandaged face. "I'll live."

"When you told Monica to choose something soft, you probably didn't expect a vegetable with prickly spines."

"What?"

Both Bobby and Charlie stared at me. Once I'd plunged in, I had to continue. "I doubt the police will be able to prove it, Bobby. And with Monica gone, you might be able to keep quiet and watch as that poor kid gets sent to jail. But my guess is, you were in on it, too. It's the only way the artichoke and the timing make any sense. You weren't planning to hit your head on the safe, were you? The kid let slip that Monica was supposed to use something soft to hit you. The only way that makes sense is if you were going to fake an injury and then call the police after Monica got away with the money."

Bobby's jaw dropped open, but he didn't make a sound.

"You hadn't planned to hit your head on the safe. You got knocked out, but only for a second. When you came to, you blew it. You called too soon."

Charlie nodded. "What did she have on you, Bobby?"

The chubby store manager jumped up and pulled the office door closed. "Okay. Look, you guys. I didn't know what else to do." He rubbed his cheek, wincing when he made contact with the injured area. "She came on to me, you know. And me and Louise, we were having some problems. Hell, I was flattered."

"And she used your affair to blackmail you into helping with the robbery?" I asked.

"She said she had pictures," Bobby shrieked. "She wanted money, and I didn't have any, what with opening the new store and all. Then she came up with this plan. I'd let her rob the store, and she'd disappear for good."

"Well, it looks like she kept her part of the bargain," Charlie said. "You're going to have to explain why the store isn't filing charges against the boy. And you're going to have to convince me that you weren't planning a bit of insurance fraud as part of this scheme."

"You know I wouldn't do that," Bobby said. "And you guys found the cash, so no harm done. I'm happy to see the boy get off. He can keep his job, and I'll even pay for some counseling if he needs it."

* * * *

I picked up Alli from the employee lounge and drove us to the closest pizza parlor. We'd have to grocery shop all over again tomorrow. For tonight, I wanted something hot and quick.

While we waited for our pizza, Alli surprised me by throwing her arm around my shoulders and saying, "I'm glad you're okay, too." Then she turned back to her Coke, as though the brief show of affection never happened.

I smiled. "I don't suppose you want to tell me how you ended up with Howie?"

"Well, I was just going to grab one of those bags of chips at the end of the aisle near our checkout lane. You know, kinda throw it in the with groceries so you wouldn't notice. But I guess I got turned around in the dark. I saw Howie hit the fire alarm. He had a flashlight. I figured I should find out why he did that."

I thought about lecturing her but decided to save my breath. We were well into the super jumbo deluxe pizza when Charlie came in. I insisted he join us.

"I'm glad to see all the excitement hasn't ruined your appetite," he said to Allison.

Alli looked up at him in surprise. "Naw. Is Howie okay? He had a crush on that awful Monica. I think it's all her fault. Will he be in a lot of trouble now?"

"His folks came down to the station. I talked to them a bit. They're planning to get him a therapist. I don't think the store will press charges."

Alli nodded, finished off her fourth slice of pizza and motioned toward the video games in the corner.

"Of course, you may be excused, dear," I said to her back.

Charlie sat quietly, eating pizza and sipping coffee, courtesy of our waiter. The silence was growing uncomfortable when he said, "I'm sorry I didn't take your worries seriously tonight. I hope you won't hold it against the Meadow Springs PD."

"Not a chance," I said.

We chatted about people we both knew from school, until the evening caught up with me, and I had to stifle a yawn. Charlie was getting ready to leave when Alli rejoined us.

"It was nice meeting you, Allison," Charlie said. "I hope you're okay after such a hectic evening."

"Nice meeting you, too," she replied. "Actually, tonight was pretty exciting. I guess life in a small town isn't always dull."

Charlie looked at me. "Nice seeing you, too, Maggie. I think I owe you dinner. Can I call you tomorrow?"

Alli grinned, but I gave her a poke before she said anything. "I guess you'll need a statement from me, too. How about I drop in at the police station after work? Around 5:30?"

"See you then," he said before he walked away, his grin matching Alli's.

Alli started giggling. "Mom's got a boyfriend," she said in a sing-song voice.

I smiled and pushed her out the door. I had to agree with her, though. Life in this small town had suddenly gotten a lot more interesting.

Cynthia Sabelhaus is the editor of Calliope: A Writer's Workshop by Mail (CalliopeOnTheWeb.org). Her publication credits include chapters in the Mechanical Engineer's Handbook (Wiley) and the original Lowe's Garden Center Manual. She received the William F. Deeck-Malice Domestic grant for unpublished writers for her novel, and her story, "Soup," was published in Seascape: Best New England Crime Stories in 2019. Cynthia lives with her husband and fellow writer, Ralph, in Green Valley, Arizona.

WILD ABOUT SAFFRON

MARCIA ADAIR

A rib bone and what looked like human toes lay in the tall grass at the edge of the cabin. Guarding the find was a sleek Dachshund with dirt on her muzzle and bared teeth. Her eyes flashed with feral excitement, and a soft growl rose in her throat.

"Come on, Ruby. Be a good girl, and let me see what you've got there. How about I trade you for a yummy pastrami on rye?" Sheriff Amy Finley waved her sandwich toward the dog, letting the aroma work its magic. As Ruby wagged her tail approvingly and approached, the sheriff tossed the bribe twenty feet into the weeds and watched with satisfaction as the dog dashed after it. She moved quickly to secure the area with crime scene tape.

"No, no, no. What are you feeding her? Ruby is on a very special diet." Trudy Pennerton stormed around the corner of the cabin, clearly upset at what she had witnessed through the window. She ran after Ruby and scooped her up protectively, as the dog was about to enjoy her reward. "No, baby. Mama says no."

"Ma'am. I told you to keep your dog away from this site. You reported suspected human remains under your cabin; it's a potential crime scene. That means no one—not even Ruby—comes beyond this tape."

"Well, she's the one who found the bones," Trudy defended. She pointed her chin toward the hole Ruby had dug under the crawl space. It was where she'd slipped through and made her discovery.

"No one. Crosses. The tape."

Sheriff Finley watched, as Trudy welled up at the mild reprimand. Oh, jeez, she thought. A weeper. She changed tactics to keep the waterworks at bay. "Let's step over by my car," she invited softly.

Trudy sighed and nodded. Still carrying Ruby, she surveyed her new land purchase. Its several acres in rural Minnesota sat on a small lake with four run-down cabins that once might have been an inviting dusky blue. Now, they were in dire need of paint and repairs, or—in the sheriff's opinion—a bulldozer.

"I just bought this place," Trudy sniffled. "It has such a romantic history. Did you know that back in the '40s, some sweet couple built this as a family resort? They gave it to their daughter — I think she was named for some spice. Curry, maybe? Cumin? Anyway, she had a little art commune or something here in the '60s. Isn't that delicious? There's love here. Soul. Deep history. I was going to fix it all up and start a retreat center for writers. Make it vibrant again, you know? And now…this." She flapped her hand toward the bones. "Who would come here now?"

The sheriff gave a sympathetic shrug. Hoping to keep things calm, she excused herself and stepped away to call the Minnesota Bureau of Criminal Apprehension agent who served Dogwood County. She described the scene and her suspicions. The agent promised to send a BCA crime scene team right away. "We'll see what they say, Chuck, but I'd bet a pastrami sandwich we're gonna need the forensic anthropologist, too. These bones have a story to tell—and I think it's murder."

She concluded the call and returned to Trudy.

"Ms. Pennerton," she began, "perhaps you can shed some light on this situation for me."

"I really don't know anything. Like I said, I only recently bought the place."

"Let's start there. Who did you buy it from?"

"Some lawyer in St. Paul. He was representing the owner. I have his name inside, if you want it."

* * * *

A sharp rap on his office door startled Roger Hoffman.

"Come," he called, miffed that his secretary would interrupt him when he told her not to. He was wrapping up estate issues for a client and didn't want to be disturbed.

The door opened, and Hoffman did a double take. He stood and extended his hand to the visitor, giving her a quizzical look. "I'm Roger Hoffman. And you are?"

"I'm Sheriff Finley from Dogwood County. I'm working on a cold case, and I hope you can be of some help."

"My goodness. Well, of course, if I can." He spread his arms out magnanimously. "Sit, please." He indicated a low seat in front of his sleek desk. After straightening his tie and smoothing his blue suit over his lean frame, he settled in his chair.

"Nice office," the sheriff said, scanning the mid-century modern décor of the law office. "Is that a Vasarely?" She was studying the disorienting geometrics of an op-art painting on the far wall.

"You know art," Hoffman said, impressed.

"My parents collected back in the '60s. I'm afraid some of their knowledge of the times rubbed off on me." She flashed a peace sign, to Hoffman's amusement. He relaxed.

"It was a great art movement," he said. "So groundbreaking. These pieces sure make you think about what's reality and what's illusion, don't they?"

Sheriff Finley leaned forward slightly and leveled her gaze at Hoffman. "I generally can tell the difference, Mr. Hoffman. It goes with the job."

"Well, yes, of course. I didn't mean you…." he sputtered.

"You recently represented Osgood Peterson in the sale of a property up in Dogwood County," the sheriff continued.

"That's right. I'm his attorney."

"It was a bequest to him from Saffron Ardmont, I gather from courthouse records."

"Also correct. I've been Mrs. Ardmont's lawyer for years. I'm the executor of her estate."

"So I understand. What can you tell me about Mrs. Ardmont and that particular property?"

"Nothing, I'm afraid. All communication with a client is confidential. Even after death. Of course, you already know that."

Sheriff Finley raised a cynical brow. "Human remains were found under one of the cabins, Mr. Hoffman."

He paused for half a beat, then drew in a sharp breath. "How gruesome," he exhaled.

"According to the crime scene team, they were buried in a shallow grave, which certainly suggests foul play. Our forensic anthropologist pegs the death to the late 1960s. About the time Mrs. Ardmont abandoned the place, we understand."

"I need to stop you right there, sheriff. The place was never abandoned. Mrs. Ardmont retained me years ago to handle those legalities. If you check the records, you'll find the mortgage was paid off. All taxes were filed on time. Critical maintenance was performed. Et cetera."

The sheriff took out a notebook and jotted something down.

"Do you have any leads?" Hoffman tapped a silver pen on the desk.

"Did you know her husband?"

"Again, that would be confidential, wouldn't it?"

"DNA testing will confirm it, but we have reason to believe the bones are those of Frank Ardmont. According to some old-timers with long memories, he disappeared back when the place was a hippie hangout. Locals called it Stoner Henge. Funny, right? Lots of transients and druggies passed through in those days. Everybody with hippie names—Sunshine, Moonglow, Boho, whatever. Free love and furtive affairs at every turn.

"Rumor has it that Frank abused his wife, cheated his friends, and dodged his debts. Apparently, it wasn't a disappointment to anyone when he hitched to California to 'find himself.' Curiously, though, no one ever heard from him after that. He has no line of credit, hasn't paid taxes in all those years. He simply disappeared."

"Well, there you go. Sounds like he was a creep, who abandoned his wife and then went off the grid. When his poor wife couldn't run the collective anymore, she must have left, too. A lot of people probably had it in for this Frank fellow. I suppose over the years when my client wasn't actively enjoying the cabin life, any number of trespassers could have used the place for criminal activity. Even Frank himself, when he returned from California. If the bones are his, I'd guess he was done in by a drug dealer who didn't get paid. No end of suspects, eh?"

"You called the place a collective. Do you have personal knowledge of Stoner Henge?"

He watched the sheriff study him, his silver hair, and the '60s décor of his office. She was, he was certain, trying to visualize him 50 years younger, maybe place him at the scene. "Saffron told me about it, of course," he replied. "I was her lawyer."

Sheriff Finley gave him a steady look, put her notebook away, and rose to her feet. "Thank you for your time, Mr. Hoffman. I'll let you know if I have any more questions."

He showed her to the reception area. Returning to his office, he gave his secretary a scowl for having allowed the law to barge in on him, and then, locked himself behind the thick oak door.

Retrieving a key from the wall safe, he unlocked the bottom drawer of his desk. He pulled out a bottle of Glenfiddich, a glass, and a thin envelope worn with age. Slowly, with ceremony, he gave himself a four-finger pour of the amber liquid and lifted it heavenward. "Oh, Saffron, my darling. The cops were just here." His voice dropped to an urgent whisper. "They found Frank."

He quaffed the scotch and wiped a little sweat from his brow. Had Sheriff Finley noticed the engraved gold nameplate on his desk: Roger Bodie Hoffman, Esquire? Had she already put it together? Bodie Hoffman, Boho? She'd even said that name as one of the monikers locals remembered from Stoner Henge.

After another deep draw on his drink, he carefully opened the envelope. Out fluttered an old photo of a willowy, long-haired woman with her head tipped back in sun-kissed laughter. Standing in front of a dusky blue cabin, she wore a white peasant blouse and long colorful skirt. Hoffman traced the outline of her lips with his finger and kissed her face.

Then, his gaze traveled to what was in her hands: A plush throw pillow, bright with a psychedelic paisley design. He stared at the curving, feathery teardrops that swirled across the cushion. He looked at the riot of purple and red and yellow spirals. An explosion of color, then an extinguished breath. Frank's breath.

"Saffron," he whispered. "I'm scared. I think they're finally on to us, after all these years." His voice grew tense, hot with fear, as he realized their one slipup. "They have DNA testing now. We cleaned up everything, didn't we? I ditched the shovel. But what did you do with that pillow?"

Two thoughts fueled his fear: If the cops found that pillow, DNA could tie them both to Frank's murder. If the pillow still existed, it would be at Saffron's house. He laid a plan to find out.

* * * *

The next afternoon, Hoffman drove from his Crocus Hill condo in St. Paul to the Minneapolis bungalow Saffron had shared with Ozzie Peterson for decades. Ozzie answered the knock on the door and beamed when he saw who it was.

"Are you here as my lawyer or my friend?" he teased. "I can only afford one of you."

"Then, I'm here as your friend. I can't afford to work for nothing," he joked back. "Just stopped by to say hello and see how you're doing."

Ozzie made coffee, and the two sat amiably in matching armchairs in the living room. The 1920s Craftsman was always lovely, with original woodwork, gleaming hardwood floors, and homey touches throughout—souvenirs from world travels, photos carefully arranged on the mantel, handmade quilts in a big basket by the hearth. Those touches were Saffron's doing, ever the hippie, ever the artist. He felt a jealous pang, wishing that this was his house, his memorabilia of life with the woman he had always loved.

Hoffman scanned the area, zeroing in on an uncharacteristic mess in the dining room. "So, what's with all that stuff?" He pointed to a pile of women's clothes on the floor and a table rife with attic detritus. Next to that was a box with linens and pillows spilling out the top.

"I'm working on an estate sale," Ozzie explained. "I've decided to move. Too many memories here, too many reminders that my Saffron is gone. It's time to let the past go."

More like bury it, he thought, eyeing the box of pillows. Hoffman sipped his coffee and considered his strategy. It took all his willpower not to leap up and rifle through the box, to tear through the whole house, if necessary. Slow and steady, he counseled himself. There would be time to search, time to do it casually, methodically, without suspicion, if he stayed cool.

"You've sure got a lifetime of memories here, right down to the lava lamp. What was it—fifty years you two were together?"

"Forty-nine. Too bad you didn't know Saffron back in the day. She was something else. We met the last day of Woodstock. She always said it was an easy anniversary to remember, so I better not forget." His eyes crinkled at the corners as he remembered. "It was love at first sight. For me, anyway," he said. "She was still hung up on some guy. 'Course, I quickly won her over with my charms." He winked.

Another pang tore at Hoffman's heart. Ozzie never knew about him and Saffron as anything other than lawyer and client. It was better that way, of course. No way to link them romantically, to tie them both to Stoner Henge, to Frank. It was part of how they kept their word to each other to never reveal what happened. Still, it hurt to be erased.

"Then, she caught that awful flu and pneumonia this past Christmas," Ozzie said, choking back tears. "I didn't think I'd get through losing her. My world fell apart," he said. "Well, thank heaven for you, Roger. I couldn't have handled all the estate details. The whole thing was so complicated, since we never actually got married. She always quoted that Joni Mitchell song about not needing any paper from city hall. You know that song?"

"Hmm? Oh, yeah. Sure. I know it."

More to the point, Hoffman knew the real reason why Saffron wouldn't marry Ozzie. She couldn't. According to public records, Frank was still alive and married. Saffron would be bound to him until her death did them part. Ozzie never knew about that relationship, either. It was how Saffron wanted it.

In the melancholy silence that grew between them, Hoffman's mind wandered back to 1967. It was the Summer of Love. He'd drifted into Stoner Henge, and there she was, the loveliest, most winsome thing he'd ever seen. Even her name was beautiful: Saffron, earthy, exotic, costly.

It fit with his name: Boho, unconventional and artistic.

She was the one who pointed out the harmony of their names. Soon, they discovered the harmony of their bodies, and then their souls.

Then came the night she showed Boho the deep bruises on her arms and back. "My husband did it," was all she said, tears spilling down her cheeks.

He had drawn her close, promised to protect her, though he didn't know how, not at first. The plan emerged slowly, as night after night, they talked and made love. His resolve deepened as Frank's abuse grew. One clear August night, when the Milky Way made them dizzy with its impossible beauty, they knew what had to be done.

Hoffman thought again of the photo he had in his office—his love standing by the dusky blue cabin, holding a pillow. The musty smell of the cabin rushed back to him, the gritty feel of dirt in the crawl space, the shrill buzzing of cicadas pulsing on a hot summer night. Then, the scraping of a shovel, the feel of Frank's head under a psychedelic paisley pillow, four hands pressing him hard against the ground. Frank was so strung out that night that he only clawed at the pillow a few times. Enough to get fibers under his nails, Hoffman thought. He could still feel the man's weight in his arms, as he dragged the body under the cabin and rolled him into the grave.

The lovers started the rumor that Frank and some chick had split for California to find themselves. It wouldn't have been the first time he'd run off. No one doubted it. Frank had no family, no friends, and no employer to report him missing. No one particularly liked him or cared he was gone. People drifted in and out of the community all the time.

Boho and Saffron made a pact: She'd close the art collaborative and keep the remote property unused. They'd post No Trespassing signs. Their secret would go to the grave with them. They sealed it with a kiss.

They were free. Hoffman smiled as he remembered the two years they spent hitching, busking, making their way, barefoot and in love. San Francisco, Woodstock.

His face darkened, as he remembered the first night of Woodstock, when he told her he wanted a more secure future for them and was going to law school in September. He could still see the sense of betrayal in her eyes, hear the disgust in her voice, as she accused him of being square and working for the man. She left him on the spot, standing in the mud at Yasgur's Farm, as drizzle turned to torrents and Joan Baez sang "Joe Hill."

"Did I tell you the cops came around here yesterday?" Ozzie said. "Some lady sheriff from up north."

Hoffman tried to tamp the panic rising in his chest. Breathe, man. Easy does it. "Really? What'd you do, forget to pay a parking ticket or something?" He hoped it sounded casual, unconcerned.

"No," Ozzie said, seriously. He leaned forward, elbows on knees. "It was about that land Saffron left to me, the place you convinced me to sell."

Hoffman's brain was racing. Selling the property, if Saffron died first, was part of the plan to distance themselves from the murder. They'd launder it through unsuspecting Ozzie; she'd will it to him, and Hoffman would get him to sell it. Since Saffron had never taken Ozzie to the cabin, he could honestly say he had no connection with the place or people who passed through it. There'd be no link between Saffron and Hoffman, except as her lawyer, years after the murder. They'd be in the clear. That's how it was supposed to work, anyway.

"They found bones buried under the cabin, Roger. Human bones. Kinda freaked me out."

Hoffman felt dizzy and flushed. He let out a low whistle. "No kidding. That's awful. What'd the sheriff say?"

"Well, she asked if I knew anyone named Frank back in the day, and if

Saffron was ever married before. No and no, I said. She seemed surprised Saffron and I weren't married. Asked how long we'd been together and why she left the place to me. She seemed particularly interested in how often I'd been to the property and why I decided to sell it. I told her Saffron never took me there, not even once. When I told her that my attorney advised me to sell the place, she already knew your name."

Hoffman's chest tightened.

"It kinda shook me, you know?" Ozzie continued. "Like she thought I was involved in this death or something. I was glad when she stopped asking questions and started shopping." He nodded toward the estate sale piles. "She seemed especially interested in those crappy throw pillows."

The walls were closing in. "Seems odd, doesn't it?" Hoffman said. He got up from his armchair and walked over to the box of cushions. "Who would want used pillows?"

Ozzie shrugged. "The sheriff, I guess. She bought one."

Hoffman started rummaging through the stack, slowly at first, then faster and faster, searching for the one pillow that held his future. Canvas stripes, corduroy polka dots, avocado green shag, polyester yellow smiley faces. No cotton psychedelic paisley. Nothing. He ran his fingers through his hair, hands trembling.

"You okay, man?" Ozzie had a note of concern in his voice. "You seem really uptight. Why don't you come over here and sit by the fireplace?" He put a friendly hand on Hoffman's shoulder and led him to a cozy sofa. "You're shaking, buddy. Are you cold? Here, wrap up in this." He grabbed a quilt from the basket and draped it over Hoffman's shoulders. "I'll get you more coffee—unless you'd like something stronger."

"Whiskey, if you've got it," Hoffman said, his voice tense. He pulled the quilt closer around himself and tried to calm his racing mind.

Ozzie returned with a glass of whiskey and sat on the couch. "Ugly old thing," he said, patting the quilt. He handed the glass to Hoffman. "Saffron made it ages ago, not long after I met her. I never cared for it, but she always said it was her favorite one. What'd she call it? Her bohemian hippie quilt, I think. No, her boho hippie quilt."

Her boho hippie quilt. The words struck Hoffman like thunder. He pulled the blanket off his shoulders and unfurled it over his lap to better see the design. A slow smile turned up the corners of his mouth and spread across his face. He touched the patchwork, piece by piece. First, squares of the long colorful skirt he remembered from so long ago, the one she wore in the photo. Then, strips of the shirt he wore that fateful night. At the center, an explosion of color, a burst of psychedelic paisley cut into the shape of a heart. He stared at the swirl of curving, feathery teardrops and at the riot of purple and red and yellow spirals and flowers.

He hugged the quilt hard and sighed in relief. Then, he leaned back and let out a long, deep, rolling laugh. She'd gotten rid of the pillow, all right. Her own way. Sheriff Finley had nothing.

"Man, you like this old cover-up that much? You'd better have it, if it makes you that happy. Consider it a bequest from Saffron. She'd like that."

"That'd be cool, Ozzie. Beyond cool. It means more than you know. Thanks."

"No problem, man. You've helped us out so much over the years. And you were right, by the way, about selling off that lake cabin—bones or no," Ozzie added. "I'm glad to be rid of that albatross. And thanks to you, I made a mint on the sale."

Hoffman grinned. "Yeah. I always knew it was the kind of property you could make a killing on."

Marcia Adair spent her childhood reading mysteries by flashlight under the covers. By the time adulthood rolled around, she had earned a master's degree in journalism and launched her career as a professional writer and editor. Her short stories appear in anthologies, including *Dark Side of the Loon* (2018) and *Minnesota Not So Nice: Eighteen Tales of Bad Behavior* (2020), from the Twin Cities Chapter of Sisters in Crime; *Restaurant in Peace* (Cooked to Death, Vol. 5, 2020); and *Malice Domestic 14: Mystery Most Edible* (2019). She received the 2018 Dorothy Cannell Scholarship. She is a member of Sisters in Crime. https://www.facebook.com/MarciaAdairAuthor/

GOOD NEIGHBORS

VICTORIA KAZARIAN

Em fastened Ethan's carrier into the big-as-a-tank stroller and tucked a blanket around his feet. His blue marble eyes locked onto her with utter trust.

She wedged her 48-ounce water bottle into the slot on the broad plastic inset on the handle that resembled a big dashboard, with a place for everything. Toys, keys, phone. She was piloting the equivalent of a stroller SUV.

As they rumbled down the walkway to the street, she glanced wistfully at her sleek gray Lexus coupe in the driveway, with its bumper sticker for her recent product marketing launch. *LegiPro Platinum. There's no substitute.*

Of course, it wasn't her job anymore. The new product was now Melissa's baby, so to speak. After planning the launch, Em had handed everything off to the assistant who had taken over her job. But it had been three weeks since the developers conference, and Em had heard nothing from Melissa.

Em carefully weighed the pros and cons of quitting LegiPro to stay home. She and Matt had decided they could afford it, even with their purchase of a bigger house. The plan was to stay at home with Ethan until kindergarten. Em and Matt had looked at each other and said, nearly in unison: *By the age of five a child's sense of self is set.*

It was an overcast day that threatened rain that evening. The street looked deserted. Across the street, a lawnmower droned lazily, as landscapers pulled trimming equipment out of a trailer.

Walks through the neighborhood were the highlight of Em's day. She'd given up trying to plan her time. Day blurred into night, night into day. While Ethan napped, she compiled to-do lists. By evening, all she'd done was feed and change. And quell her ravenous appetite with whatever Matt had brought home.

After Matt left for work in the morning, she'd bundle Ethan up in his car seat carrier and snap it into the stroller for a loop through the neighborhood. If she was feeling energetic, she'd push the stroller up the hill, so she could see a view of Silicon Valley, and the crowded swath of highway 17, the route she'd driven every day to work in Santa Clara.

On their walks, she sometimes got to talk to actual adults. The few who weren't working long Silicon Valley hours.

Em sometimes had to hold herself back, wanting to latch on to anyone she saw who would talk. A couple doors down, Mrs. Derosio, a wiry woman in her 70s, always came out for a good convo about everything from babies to politics to her thoughts on the neighbors.

Right away, she'd learned. Mrs. D had *opinions.* The Saldanas across the street shouldn't have given their middle schooler a cell phone. The newly single man down the street with the roses was sad and needed to talk to someone. The Lews on the corner were putting in cheap new carpet and would sell their house soon, *mark my words.*

Today, as they neared Mrs. Derosio's gray split level, Em felt herself perk up, happy at the chance for conversation. Maybe a little gossip.

But as they approached the house, an unfamiliar car was angled in the driveway. A dented, rust-colored sedan. The kind of car Matt called a beater.

A stocky, older man came down the driveway, smoking a cigarette and dragging a wheeled suitcase behind him. He opened the car door, collapsed the handle, and pushed it into the back seat. Then, he dropped the cigarette on the pavement and ground it out with his shoe.

"Hey, I'm Em from down the street. Is Margie home today?"

"Who?" The man looked at her from under heavy eyelids. "My ma slipped and broke her hip last night. She's over in Good Samaritan."

Em felt a drop in the pit of her stomach. Breaking a hip could be the beginning of the end for an elderly person.

"Is she—will she be there long?"

"She's supposed to be in the hospital a few days," he said, his eyes unfocused and bleary. "Then she'll go to a convalescent home for rehab."

Feisty Mrs. Derosio in a care facility. She couldn't imagine it. Tears flooded her eyes. *Damn hormones.*

"Can you tell your mom that Em and Ethan said hi?"

The man slammed the car door. He looked her up and down with the brazen purity of someone with a limited set of social skills.

"Sure thing, hon."

The man stood there, his big hand resting on the top of the car, looking at her longer than she was comfortable with. Em nodded her thanks, then pushed the stroller a little faster, as they continued down the street.

A hole was opening in the milky clouds near the hills. Sunlight filtered through in a fan of lines, the way kids draw it in kindergarten. She wondered if she and Ethan could go visit Mrs. D in the hospital.

They followed the street as it curved toward the hills. Just ahead, a man was trimming a hedge of roses, snipping the blooms off, letting them drop to a canvas below. Deadheading. That's what it was called. She assumed he was a hired landscaper. Then, she realized this was Dan, the one Mrs. Derosio had called *sad.*

"Good morning." She smiled cheerfully. "It's so worth it when they come back stronger, right?"

"It's a risk you have to take." Dan stepped back from the roses, a pair of clippers dangling from one hand like oversized scissors. His skin stretched tight across his cheekbones, and he had shadows under his eyes. "My wife always did this. I didn't want to lose the roses, too, so I'm trying to take care of them."

So that was it. She'd left him. Probably not that long ago. He had the look. Beaten, emptied out.

The man laid the shears on the canvas and wiped his hands. He stooped down to look at Ethan, and his face brightened. "How old is the little guy?"

"Almost six weeks." With all the changes Ethan had brought, it had felt a lot longer. "We moved into the neighborhood a week before he was born. He wants to eat all the time, but other than that he's a good baby. Do you have any children?"

Dan looked down at the rose heads on the canvas, and his smile faded. "A five-year-old. Connor. I stayed home with him."

"A stay-at-home dad? Great." Em decided not to pursue further questioning about Connor. She wasn't sure what custody arrangement had been made, but it didn't sound good. "I quit work to stay home with Ethan. I managed a department and reported to the CEO. Now I'm just—home. I feed. I change. I do lots of laundry."

Sharer's remorse swept over her. Why was she telling a stranger this? But as she talked, recognition sparked in his eyes.

"I worked in IT for ten years. Kept the company network up and running. Fought fires all day. When my wife went back to work, I decided I'd stay home." He wiped his sweaty forehead with a tissue from his pocket. "It was—a gift."

"My name's Em. We live just past Mrs. Derosio's house. Where the McKendrys used to live."

"I know exactly where that is. I'm Dan, by the way. Guess I'll be seeing you around." He shook her hand, and then bent down again, peering under the stroller shade at Ethan. "Ethan, you be good to your mom, you hear?"

Ethan looked up at him, one eye open and one closed, suspicious.

Em turned the corner, and in a few blocks, they passed the elementary school, where students always seemed to be at recess. Screaming with sheer joy, as they ran across the grassy field, scrambled up green plastic play structures, and kicked balls at each other.

"Someday, that'll be you, Ethan," she said out loud.

Then I'll be free again. She didn't say that out loud.

Refreshed by her conversation with Dan, she decided to take on the cardio challenge of pushing the stroller farther up the hill. Then, her phone rang. Melissa's ringtone.

Em paused on the sidewalk, hit the brake on the stroller wheel, and held the phone to her ear. Melissa kept her voice low, almost whispering.

"Em, things are bat shit crazy here."

"How was the developers conference?"

"That? The launch went smoothly. *PC Computing's* doing a feature on Platinum. We followed your plan, and it was spot on."

"So what's up?" Em lifted the stroller shade to see Ethan staring up at her plaintively. His eyes crinkled up like camera apertures. He was into his windup, 30 seconds from the hungry cry.

"It's Rick. He's totally checked out. Rumor has it, he's dealing with some legal thing. Probably a sexual harassment charge or DUI. He's the CEO, and I'm reporting to him, but I get zero time with him. I need signoff on the ad concept by Friday."

"Talk to a VP. Rod Demming will put in a word with Rick. I told you—make friends with Rick's assistant, Karla. Bring her a caramel macchiato from the cafeteria. She'll get you on his schedule."

Ethan's whine built up to a shaky, vibrato wail.

With a rushed goodbye to Melissa, Em took the brake off and looked around at her options. No convenient place to nurse. Ethan would have to hold out for a few more minutes.

At home, she parked and unstrapped Ethan. His crying lapsed into shudders as he felt the comfort of her arms. She unlocked the door and headed for the couch.

As soon she picked him up to nurse, he turned his head toward her, his mouth opening and closing like a goldfish, until he connected with his mid-morning meal. Em leaned back and waited for a satisfying dose of hormonal motherhood to kick in. Sometimes it came—a deep, settled rightness. Other times, she felt like a cow hooked to a milking machine.

She'd just begun to relax, when the doorbell alarm went off. Before Ethan was born, Matt installed a doorbell with a video camera. She could check the app on her phone to see a recording of who'd been at the door. As time went by, she discovered that the alarm went off for any number of reasons. A man handing out flyers. The mail lady. A kid's bike whizzing past on the sidewalk.

For the next few hours, as she fed Ethan and folded laundry, the alarm went off three times. Later in the afternoon, it beeped twice. She checked her phone and saw no footage recorded.

Once she laid Ethan in his crib in the back bedroom, she stepped outside in front to look around. She circled the porch, then followed the walkway to the street. She took in the sharp smell of smoke. She walked a few steps toward the street and saw a cigarette butt ground into the curb.

Matt came in at 6:30 with a bag of Indian takeout. She could smell the spices from the door, and her stomach rumbled.

"Em, there's something out here. You want me to bring it in?"

She looked up from her copy of *Marketing Week*. Ethan was still asleep, and she'd finally gotten a nap herself, snuggled among the unfolded clothes on the couch. The Em of a few months ago would have been disgusted, but she was past that now.

Matt set a clay vase filled with red roses down on the coffee table. Homey and lovely.

"You want me to open the note?" Matt pulled out an envelope and frowned. Em racked her brain. Could be a delayed thank you from Melissa for the work on the launch.

Matt ripped open the envelope. "Welcome to the neighborhood, Ethan and Em. - Dan." He looked up. "Who the hell is Dan?"

"From down the street. I met him on our walk today. He's just gone through a tough divorce."

"Weird that he didn't mention *my* name."

"I don't think I talked about you. It was a short conversation."

"We just moved here, Em." Matt pulled out cartons of curry and rice and laid out paper plates. "You need to be careful. We don't know these people. I know you're an extrovert, but you can't make friends with everybody you meet."

After Matt had been home for an hour, Em noticed it. The doorbell alarm wasn't going off, at all.

The next morning, Ethan woke up at 5 a.m. After nursing him, she laid him in his carrier and slept on the couch, until Matt woke her, dressed in work clothes. His briefcase strap was slung across his chest like he was the CFO Bandito. He smelled like toothpaste and aftershave.

"Be careful today, Em. And take it easy. You don't have to do everything on your list, okay?"

Em yawned at him and got up to get dressed. She felt lazy, grubby and claustrophobic. She wanted to breathe fresh air.

After she finished her weak-sauce decaf tea, Ethan began to stir. She nursed him again, then dressed him in a warm sleeper. As she buckled him into the stroller, she inhaled his soft, faintly sour smell and was surprised how good it made her feel.

When she bent down and kissed him, his fat, moist hand hit her on the nose.

"Don't take my whining personally, Ethie." She stroked the silky hair on his almost-bald head.

Today, the street was damp from last night's rain. Dry patches remained where cars had parked all night and left in the morning. Apparently, everyone had somewhere to go but her. They rolled past Mrs. Derosio's. Mail peeked out from the flap of the mailbox.

They neared Dan's house. The lawn looked tidy, the porch clean and swept, with ferns and white impatiens thriving in a clay planter. She should thank him for the flowers. There was something about him she identified with. The tired circles under his eyes. The staying-home transition he'd struggled with.

She was turning the stroller into his driveway, when she was startled by footsteps behind her. She turned her head quickly.

How long had he been behind them?

"Hey there, Em," Dan called out, as he caught up with her.

He wore a clean white t-shirt and jeans. His eyes looked brighter today, as if someone had flipped them on with a switch. He moved with ease and energy.

"That was nice of you to leave the roses for us last night. They're gorgeous."

"I thought you'd enjoy them. As you can see, I've got more than I need here."

"You weren't, by any chance, passing by our house yesterday, were you?" She watched his face. She wanted badly for him to say no. "Our doorbell alarm kept going off."

He smiled sheepishly. "I could be responsible for that. I go for a run in the afternoons. Keeps me grounded."

He squatted down next to the stroller, bouncing on his heels. He reached out his hand, and Ethan reflexively grabbed his finger. Something deep and fierce stirred in her. It felt wrong for someone else to touch her child's hand. She corrected herself: *Don't overreact, girl. It's the hormones.*

"I was heading your way, because I found some boxes of Connor's baby clothes. I thought you could use them." He pointed to boxes just inside his open door. "Otherwise, I'll take them to the Goodwill truck, later."

Babies outgrew clothes quickly, every mom at work had warned her. She'd been planning a trip to the local kids' consignment shop to get 6-to-9 month sizes for Ethan.

"He'll need them, at the rate he's eating." Ethan flung a plump arm against the side of the stroller. "The books say six weeks is when the first big growth spurt happens."

"Need a bouncy seat?"

Em shifted on her feet. She wasn't used to accepting this kind of charity.

"Sure. Thanks."

Ethan was squirming, so she parked the stroller and unstrapped him. She held his warm body close, as she followed Dan through the door into his house.

Once inside, Em looked around in admiration. The house was decorated in muted brown, orange and green, with pops of red from throw pillows tastefully scattered over the sofa and easy chairs. The furniture was midcentury, warm, burnished wood and green upholstery. Photos in rustic wooden frames sat on a Scandinavian-looking end table.

"Your house looks like something out of *House Beautiful*, Dan."

"Gina's good taste, not mine. Can I get you anything to drink, Em?"

Em realized she'd forgotten her enormous water bottle.

"Yes, water. Please." Her mouth felt dry. She lay Ethan across her lap.

Dan brought out the bouncy seat. Then, he poured her a tall glass of cold water from a pitcher in the fridge.

She hadn't kept up with her water intake this morning, and her body was screaming for it. She took a gulp.

"He's a big guy for six weeks." Dan bent in close to Ethan and made a big-eye face at him. "Aren't you, Connor?"

Electricity rippled through her. It traveled up her spine and landed with a small explosion in her brain.

"You mean Ethan. His name is *Ethan*."

"Sorry, force of habit." Dan shook his head and smiled. "He does look a little like Connor. Would you like to see pictures?"

"I'd love to." She set down the empty water glass.

Dan collected a few of the photos from the shelf and then pulled an album out of the bookcase.

He sat down and passed photos to her.

"Here's Connor at about two months." A photo of a chubby baby, lying in a woman's arms, as she sat at a picnic table, a deer-in-the-headlights look in his big blue eyes. Which, she had to admit, did look a little like Ethan's.

"He's adorable, Dan."

"Look at this one. It was all about trucks at that age." Dan grinned, his voice growing soft. Em looked at the little boy with a head of soft curls, hunched over a big yellow truck, guiding it with both hands across the carpet.

He passed her a photo of a larger boy, slimmed down and stretched out, confidently straddling a bicycle on a dirt trail in the woods.

"So grown up all of a sudden." Em looked over to see the proud look in Dan's eyes. "How old is he here—five?"

Dan nodded slowly, not taking his eyes off the photo.

"You know he learned in one day? I took him out on the trail, and he just did it. He didn't even need training wheels."

"You're such a good dad. When do you get to see him?" Em turned Ethan over on his stomach and stroked his back. She stifled a yawn. She should go soon.

Dan frowned and looked down at his hands. He placed one hand over the other, and Em realized he was trying to keep them from shaking.

"The thing is, I don't, Em. I *don't*." He stacked the photos neatly on the table and turned to her. "And all the money they gave me in the settlement won't bring him back."

"What? But I thought—Didn't your wife leave—"

When she first started looking at the photos, her eyes had felt heavy—about right for midmorning. Now, she was having a hard time staying focused on what he was saying. But she knew now. Connor was dead.

"You're looking sleepy, Em." Dan's voice sounded soft, solicitous. He smiled at her and looked at the baby on her lap.

She didn't like the way Dan was looking at her or Ethan. Something wasn't right. Dan's son was dead, and somebody had given him money. She blinked and forced herself to keep her eyes open. An alarm beeped in her brain, and it sounded like the doorbell alarm. Maybe it had happened yesterday afternoon. Maybe it was happening now.

"It's time to go—" Em clutched Ethan to her and and tried to stand. Her legs felt rubbery. She couldn't lift herself all the way off the seat, and she landed back down with a thud. Startled by the jolt, Ethan's wide eyes locked onto hers.

"The medicine I put in the water won't hurt you, Em. It's a strong antihistamine. It'll make you sleep." Dan reached over and lifted Ethan off her lap. "Get some rest. I'll take good care of Connor."

Ethan let out a shaky cry. The more he cried, the farther away the cry sounded. The last thing she heard was Dan's voice.

"Don't cry, Connor. We'll go for a drive like we used to. Drives always make you sleepy."

* * * *

Em woke up on a low-backed, midcentury sofa, a soft blanket laid over her. Her full breasts reminded her she was a mom. *Ethan.* Fear came over her in a way she'd never felt before. It churned in her stomach. It gripped her shoulder like a claw.

She raised herself off the sofa and ran to the table for her phone. It was gone. She looked in the kitchen, then the master bedroom. No landline.

The clock on the nightstand read 10:45 am. They had left for their walk at 9. She felt like she'd lived days since then.

There were photos all over the bedroom, on the dresser, on the walls.

A blond woman with curly hair holding Connor, a stand of giant redwoods behind them. Connor laughing in front of a tent, his fingers splayed out, sticky with marshmallow.

A knock on the door drifted into her consciousness. It grew louder, more insistent.

She ran toward the front door, her mouth dry, her head groggy, and pressed her eye to the peephole.

A policeman.

"Emily Carter? Officer Santos, Los Gatos Police Department."

Em twisted the deadbolt and opened the door, her voice hoarse as she barked the words out.

"The man who lives here took my son."

There was another man with the officer. Familiar, yet Em could not remember who he was. Armpit sweat stainedhis rumpled shirt.

"You met me the other day, Emily. I'm Margie Derosio's son, Stan."

Em was confused. Why was he here? A warm, numb haze drifted down over her. Her breasts were leaking into her sweatshirt.

Matt met them at home, straight from work, his face pale, as took his place on the couch next to her. Officer Santos was taking notes. Stan Derosio sat in the recliner chair, fiddling with its buttons. When the foot rest suddenly swung up, he jumped.

"Mr. Derosio noticed that Mr. Robertson had a baby with him and was buckling him into a car seat in his vehicle. He recognized the baby as yours. He had spoken with Mr. Robertson earlier that day and was concerned about some of the things he was saying. After the man left and Stan saw your stroller was still there, he called 911."

"Thank you, Stan." Em nodded at him weakly.

The man turned pink.

"I knew something wasn't right, hon."

"We've put out the Amber Alert." Officer Santos continued. "Gray 2016 Honda Accord and a description of Mr. Robertson and your son. Emily, I know this is difficult for you, but I need you to tell me everything you can remember about Mr. Robertson. Anything he might have said to you."

Em told him how Dan had paid special attention to Ethan from the first morning they'd met. How he'd confused Ethan for Connor twice. She told him about the spiked water and how Dan had taken Ethan from her lap.

"Officer, is Ethan in danger?" Matt leaned forward on the couch. His hands were folded neatly on his knee, like he was in a budget meeting at work. How could he be so calm? But then, he cleared his throat, and Em heard him choke on his words. "Does this man have a record of violence?"

"Mr. Robertson has no criminal record."

Emily took apart every bit of her conversations with Dan. She told Santos about the pictures he'd shown of Connor. Places he'd taken Connor as a stay-at-home dad. After a while, she could no longer remember his words. She wanted to forget the sound of his voice.

That night, she and Matt lay side by side in bed. A night of quiet instead of Ethan's insistent cries for feedings. She never slept. Worry thrummed through her body like an electric current. Every few hours, Matt put his hand over hers. Neither of them spoke.

At 6 am, the sun rose pink and grey outside the window. Em couldn't lie there any longer. She went to the couch and pumped, the machine's mechanical wheeze reminding her that this was food for a child who was not there, might never be there again. Every news article about missing children she'd ever read flashed through her mind. Ones that ended happily, ones that ended in dumpsters.

Ethan. Be alive.

She took a drink from her water bottle. The SUV stroller sat in the hall, ready for the morning walk. She thought about the photos Dan had shown her. Something seemed the same in the pictures. A clearing in a forest. A certain angle of light filtering through the trees. Memories came back to her from a camping trip years ago with a church youth group.

Em paced the kitchen. Then, she called Officer Santos and woke him up.

"I have an idea," she said, fighting against her fears of dashed hope. "I think I know where they might be."

* * * *

Mist drifted through the redwood trees overhead, as Santos drove them on highway 9 through the Santa Cruz mountains. A patrol car followed them. They took a turn onto highway 236 toward Big Basin.

The gray Honda was parked at the far end of the empty lot, barely visible in the mist. After Officer Santos parked, she, Matt, and Santos headed uphill toward the walk-in campsites.

The dark green tent was small, partially obscured by trees. Smoke curled up from a wood fire nearby.

The backup officers dispersed among the brush along the trail. The morning's cold dampness sank into her bones, and Em shivered. She prayed Ethan was warm.

She heard the music first. Dan Robertson paced back and forth near the tent, singing and humming, as he carried Ethan in a Baby Bjorn carrier over his chest.

When he saw the three of them, Dan stopped singing and stared, confused at this intrusion. He stood near the fire, his feet planted apart, one arm cradling the back of the carrier.

After a few minutes, Santos edged away from them and slowly made his way through the brush, around the back of the tent. When Dan saw him, he let out a harsh, animal wail that echoed through the clearing. Birds in the trees shrieked in response and fluttered upward.

Santos approached Dan and laid a hand gently on his arm. Em couldn't hear what they were saying.

A few minutes later, Ethan was in the arms of Santos, and the backup officers were walking Dan back down the trail to the patrol car.

Once Santos laid him in Em's arms, Ethan straightened his head. He turned his gaze on her in a look of perfect calm.

Em broke into hard, shuddering sobs.

* * * *

The next week, the story broke of LegiPro CEO Rick Whalley's million-dollar settlement with Dan Robertson over the death of his wife and son, due to reckless driving. He'd veered into their lane on 101, as Gina and Connor drove home from an afternoon playdate. The day after the story appeared, Melissa called and told her Rick had stepped down as CEO.

Not long afterwards, on a crisp clear day, Em packed Ethan into his car seat. She'd packed the diaper bag and car the night before, realizing that the planning she'd done as a marketing manager paled in comparison to the preparation required for leaving the house with a baby.

They drove to the convalescent home to see Mrs. Derosio. Em had missed her opinions.

The sparsely furnished room smelled of medicine and soup. Mrs. D lay in the hospital bed. Pale and tired, but obviously thrilled to have the company. She smiled and reached out a bony arm.

"Bring that sweetie over to me, will you, Em?"

Em lifted Ethan up to Mrs. D, who played peekaboo with him, until he lowered his chin into his neck and let out a wet gurgling noise.

Mrs. D lay her head back on her pillow and laughed.

"Thank God that son of mine was watching out for Ethan. Stan's always been the kid I had to shake my head at. In and out of trouble like you wouldn't believe." Mrs. D's face relaxed into a thoughtful smile. "But he was there when we needed him."

It was a small valley. Em knew this from the many times she'd run into new coworkers she known from previous jobs. Paths in Silicon Valley often crossed, like the network of freeways that twisted through the valley, merging and dividing. The lives of Dan and her boss—complete strangers—had been linked forever by a careless lane change during rush hour.

A man using a walker stopped and waved at Mrs. D from the hallway. Mrs. D groaned and rolled her eyes like a teenager. "This place is filled with too many damn old people. Please tell me you're going to come back and see me."

Em bounced Ethan on her lap and smiled.

"Of course, we will, Margie."

Em looked down to see Ethan's mouth slowly opening and closing as he examined his fist and considered eating it. Fully in the moment, Ethan seemed oblivious to all that had happened last week.

Em hoped it would stay that way.

Based in Silicon Valley, Victoria Kazarian is a former marketing professional who writes short stories and is hard at work on her second novel. When she isn't writing, she's teaching high school English and doing publicity for her local Sisters in Crime chapter, SinC Coastal Cruisers.

STRESS KILLS

CHERYL MARCEAU

"You'll love Joe. He has a gift." That's what my friend Beth said, when I asked about the massage therapist she'd recently discovered. I'd been suffering from miserable upper-back pain for a while, and my doctor wasn't too happy with the way my heart was functioning. After a barrage of testing, she'd chalked up the heart problems to stress. My work was challenging, at the best of times. I had recently moved out of the condo I'd shared with the man I once thought I'd marry, and my parents were going through their own health issues. A massage might help with some of the stress, or at least un-knot those back muscles screaming for attention.

Peaceful Escape Massage was on the first floor of an imposing office building next to the Cambridge reservoir, just off Interstate 95, "America's Technology Highway" outside Boston. The most prominent tenant in the building, announced by a blazing red sign visible across the reservoir, was Synyrgys, a darling of the biotech industry with a reputation for a workaholic culture that made most of its industry peers seem like slacker havens. Nearby was an outpost of a Silicon Valley software company known for its punishing hours and cutthroat competitiveness. Venture-capital firms flourished like weeds in this office park. Start-up tech companies sat alongside Fortune 500 headquarters. A massage office here, catering to the compulsively overworked? It didn't seem like Beth's style. While she had enough family money to afford weekly massages, she was a painter and longtime Zen Buddhist, who had a strong negative reaction to anything that seemed corporate. We'd met in a qigong class and had become friends, in spite of my career in finance. I wondered how she'd ever found a massage practitioner in this setting.

I fought evening rush-hour traffic to reach the exit ramp and sped around the reservoir until I got to the Synyrgys building, then screeched to a stop in the first visitor parking space I spotted. As I climbed out, I noticed a guy in the next car. Longish brown hair, nerdy-hip black glasses, plaid shirt buttoned to the top. I grabbed my purse as I rushed inside, through a lavish atrium and past a sign pointing me to the hallway on the right, arriving at my appointment out of breath. I opened the door, announced by a sound like a temple gong, and nearly bumped into a woman leaving the office, wearing a beatific smile. Joe the massage therapist must be a genius with his hands.

The waiting room was softly lit. New-age flute music floated from a sound system on the bookcase. The Asian art scrolls on the walls looked original. I was calmer already.

A man came out of one of the rooms facing the waiting area. "Sara? I'm Joe." He smiled and pulled the door closed behind him as he came toward me. "I'll be with you in just a moment. Please fill out this questionnaire while you wait." He handed me a clipboard and went to a small office that also opened onto the waiting room.

Beth said he was talented, but she didn't mention that he was gorgeous. Just what I didn't need. Now, I'd spend my entire appointment stressing about whether I was too flabby, instead of relaxing and letting him work his magic. I wouldn't be able to cancel without paying, or I might have faked some kind of sudden illness.

I tried to focus on the client-intake form in front of me, but all I could think about was how awkward this session was going to be. For me. Joe would surely be just fine.

It was one of the most conflicted hours of my life, alternating between anxiety over my out-of-shape body and bliss, as Joe worked through knots I didn't even know I had. Way before I was ready, the massage was over, and I had the treatment room to myself. I dressed as quickly as I could, tugging my clothes over oily skin, and walked into the office where Joe typed on his computer. "How are you feeling?" he asked as he looked up.

Did I actually have to go home, or could I curl up on the table and stay for another massage tomorrow? "Um, good, I feel really…good."

"Your upper back was incredibly tight. Do you spend much time on a computer?"

"If twelve hours a day counts as a lot, then yeah. You probably see that in a lot of clients."

"That's what keeps me in business." He laughed, a self-deprecating kind of laugh. "Would you like to schedule another appointment?"

"Do you have anything next week?" Did I sound too eager?

"I just got a cancellation. Thursday, 6:45 p.m.?"

"I'll take it."

I floated out of the building to my car, then stopped, suddenly aware that I wasn't alone. The guy in the next car was still there. As a woman living and working near a big city, I'd developed certain instincts about dark parking lots and other potentially risky places. This guy made me nervous. I unlocked my car, threw myself behind the wheel, and locked the doors as fast as I could. My muscles knotted themselves right back to where they'd been. Breathing heavily, I fumbled with the key until I got it into the ignition, then hit the gas. All the way home, I watched my rearview mirror, feeling anxious but also a little silly. I knew I was overreacting. Maybe it was time for a nice long vacation.

My purse buzzed when I set it on the kitchen table. I pulled out my phone and read a text from Beth.

hope u like david

David? Beth must have been tired. As bad as I was with names, I'd never get Joe's name wrong. But then, it was like her to forget things.

* * * *

Work consumed me the following week, preparing charts for my company's quarterly earnings call with investment analysts. After the Thursday morning call, which mercifully went without a hitch, I finally had time to get lunch and catch up on my email.

"Increase in Stress Behind Executive Deaths," blared the *Boston Globe* email alert. I opened the article about a recent uptick in serious health issues, including stress-induced deaths at several area firms. My company wasn't listed, so I moved on. Death by overworking wasn't a new phenomenon. Years earlier, a well-loved manager, where I'd worked at the time, had dropped dead in the cafeteria line. I just hoped the pressure wouldn't catch up to me that way.

* * * *

"Give me a few minutes to prepare the room," Joe said when I arrived for my appointment that evening. I hovered nearby, while he carefully cleaned the face cradle. He took a small glass bottle from a nearby table, sprinkled something on a fresh cover for the face cradle, and put the cover in place. His exercise pants caressed his backside as he leaned across the table and smoothed out crisp sheets.

He caught me staring. "Um, I was wondering what that stuff was that you put on the face thing?" I blurted. The face thing? I couldn't believe I'd just said that.

"You mean the face cradle? Eucalyptus oil. Clears your sinuses, makes it easier to breathe."

I pointed at an array of bottles on a shelf. "What are all those?"

"I create special aromatherapy oils for some of my clients. At some point, when the time is right, we can talk about what would be best for you."

Aromatherapy wasn't even close to what would be best for me at that moment, but he didn't need to know that.

As much as I wanted to sink onto the table and let go of every last knot in my shoulders, I found myself resisting the sublime sensation of Joe's large strong hands, kneading my neck and shoulder blades. What would I do if the weird guy waited by my car again tonight?

On the way out, I thought I saw someone not far from the building entrance and immediately tensed. I peered into the dusk, as I hurried to my car, looking for anyone who might be lingering, once again checking the rearview mirror as I drove.

My phone pinged. I glanced at a text from Beth when I pulled into my driveway.

Hope u r ok. Working 2 much! Call when u get time.

She was worried about me. I owed her a phone call and a thanks for the referral. When Beth didn't pick up my call, I sent her a quick reply. *Thx so much fr new man in my life, I owe u.*

* * * *

The following Thursday afternoon, I flew out of the office to make sure I got to Joe's on time. It had been only a week since my last appointment—and just two weeks since the first one—but I was frantic with impatience. Traffic on I-95 was unusually heavy. I flipped to the traffic report on the radio and caught the end of the news, some story about an executive at Synyrgys found dead in his office of an apparent heart attack, the third death at the company's Waltham headquarters in three months.

The buzz on the street about Synyrgys was that the hours were long, and it wasn't for everyone, but I'd never heard anything unusually brutal about the culture. A couple of old B-school friends worked there, and neither of them talked about the pressure. Although, truth be told, the company could have been a sweat shop, and those two would never admit it.

I got a stitch in my side, running through the parking lot and down the long hall at Joe's building. Seven minutes late. I looked up and nearly tripped on my own feet. There was the guy with the glasses, coming out of a treatment room. He shook Joe's hand. "Thanks for fitting me in on short notice. I really needed that. Can I schedule another appointment?"

Joe waved me into the other treatment room where the table was already set up. I'd been worried about that guy for nothing, apparently. He was here for the same reason I was. I started to apologize about the traffic, but Joe stopped me. "Nothing to worry about," he said, his voice gentle. "You're here now. Go ahead and get changed. We'll start with you face down." The tension drained from my body. I stretched out on the table in happy anticipation, thinking about what kind of special aromatherapy oil I'd ask Joe to make for me.

* * * *

I became more obsessive about my massage appointments as I felt less pain. Joe was a healer, his massages the only thing keeping me going. If I were completely honest with myself, though, it wasn't just Joe's healing powers that drew me back again and again.

At the beginning of my fourth week seeing Joe, my boss scheduled a mandatory team meeting for that Thursday. I'd have to miss my massage. I called Joe in a panic as soon as I read the email invitation. "I have a cancellation this afternoon," he said, "but it might be a little early for you."

"I'll be there." I'd have to sneak out of the office, but it was worth it. "Doctor's office, they just had a cancellation," I said to my assistant on the way out. She looked surprised but didn't say anything. She'd never seen me nearly giddy about a doctor's appointment.

As I pulled into the parking lot by Joe's office, I caught something on the radio about another Synyrgys executive found dead, this time at her home. Note to self: Do not take a job at that company.

* * * *

I was on the table, face down, fidgeting with the face cradle. Joe's hands slid over my shoulders, down my back, working on knots that resisted the usual level of pressure.

"Your muscles are seriously tight this afternoon," Joe said. "How's this?" He dug his elbow deeper into my left shoulder blade.

"Ummph," I answered. "It's a little much."

"You're tightening as I work. I'll back off, and you try some deep breaths."

"Sure. Hey, I'm curious." Silence, as Joe kneaded my lumbar spine. "What's going on at Synyrgys, anyway? You must have a lot of their employees as clients."

"I don't talk about my clients."

The pause that followed was ominous. I feared I'd overstepped in a big way and damaged our budding…what?

Then, he added, "I haven't heard anything much about them, although I sure see a lot of Maseratis in the parking lot." He chuckled softly and continued working.

"That guy who came in the other night, with the black glasses, is he a new client?"

Joe stopped kneading. "Are we going to talk, or am I going to work on your back? It must hurt, all this tension you're carrying."

"Sorry. Please, massage away."

Fifty-five minutes later, I drifted out to my car.

My stomach lurched. The guy was there. Parked where I would have to walk directly past him. No way he just happened to have an appointment today. Had he been following me? How else would he know when I'd show up? If he'd tracked me unnoticed, there must be some reason he wanted me to see him now, to know he was capable of finding me. It might have been my paranoia working overtime, but I was sure I saw a smirk below those heavy black glasses.

I sprinted past his car and ducked into mine, trembling. If he was playing some kind of sick game with me, home would not be safe. I could go to the nearest police station, but of course, they'd be unable to do anything, even if they got a look at the man or his car.

Why was he after me? Was it random or personal? I couldn't think of anyone who'd want to harm me. I remembered mystery stories I'd read, horror films I'd watched. Was it someone I'd turned down for a job, cut off in traffic, ignored at a party? It was unimaginable that I could have angered a stranger that much. One thing seemed certain. If he was working this hard to track me, his motives could not be good.

I sensed movement and watched his car glide past mine, slowly and deliberately. Did he stare right at me as he passed? I watched as he turned out of the parking lot. He'd know where I lived if he'd been following me, but maybe I could get home and pack a few things before he resumed the chase. I'd stay in a hotel somewhere, cancel my massage appointments, lie low. I could take that vacation I obviously needed.

This was nuts. I was spinning out of control. Time to stop reading those psychological thrillers.

A text alert buzzed, and I jumped, irrationally terrified for a moment that he'd found my phone number.

Any news? Have 2 talk!

I wanted to call Beth, but if I did, she'd know instantly that something was wrong and would demand to help fix it. This was something she couldn't fix, and I couldn't drag her into.

I shrugged off the text and headed home, watching for the weird guy's car. He had a nondescript small dark sedan that could have been any of a dozen makes and models. Every other car on the road seemed to match. By the time I got to my front door, I was exhausted, unable to do much more than check under the bed and inside the closets after ensuring the doors and windows were locked.

During an endless night with no sleep, I thought hard about what to do. I'd get myself a dog, for my safety, as well as for the company. And I was going to keep my massage appointments, even if it meant running into the man I'd come to think of as my stalker. I refused to stop seeing Joe, and not just because my back pain was so much better.

* * * *

Beth finally caught me on the phone the next day. "Has he called you yet?" she asked.

"Hunh? I've had a few appointments with Joe, if that's who you mean. He's a real find—just as good as you promised."

"I *know* who Joe is. I meant my brother. I gave him your number and made him promise to call. It's time you started dating again."

"Sorry to break it to you, but he hasn't so much as texted a hello. Guess it isn't meant to be."

"I'll work on him. You'd really hit it off, I'm sure."

I hoped she'd forget about the whole thing. I hated dating under the best of circumstances, making small talk with a stranger and trying to impress, while wondering whether there was any future, at all. A blind date with the brother of a dear friend was about as far from the best circumstances as I could imagine. Nothing good was likely ever to come from it. Besides, there was Joe. Magic hands, serene personality, no demands. He was the only man I needed in my life right now.

* * * *

I drove to Peaceful Escape Massage with some trepidation the following Thursday, nervous that the weird stalker guy might be there. It was just dark enough that a lot of the cars could have been his, but none of them were occupied. Clutching my keys in the weapon-like grip described in self-defense articles, I slammed my door and marched into the building. If the stalker was waiting for me, I'd be ready.

My arrival in Joe's office was uneventful. I stretched on the massage table, breathing deeply and letting the new-age music wash over me. The door closed, and I heard Joe shaking massage oil out of a bottle.

"We haven't talked about aromatherapy oils again," I said, as he started rubbing my lower back. Did I imagine his hand lingering a little longer than necessary?

"Something relaxing maybe? You might do well with lavender oil. I'll have to think about a very special blend for you," he said. I sensed flirtation in his tone. "Right now, we should focus on these knots."

The gong for the outer door resonated softly. Multiple pairs of feet scuffled in the waiting room. Joe's hands gripped my shoulders in a painful vise, then released. I sensed him moving away from the massage table and craned my neck, watching him throw aromatherapy oil bottles into a big satchel.

The door crashed open. The stalker rushed in, tackling Joe.

I jumped off the table. "N-O-O-O-O!"

Joe and the stalker wrestled on the floor, staggered up, shoved each other around the treatment room. Joe broke free and grabbed his satchel, heading for the door. The stalker jumped on him, pulling him to the ground. They pummeled and grunted, a tangled knot of arms and legs flailing in a small space.

I had to save Joe from this maniac. I grabbed a carved stone buddha figure from a shelf and swung it at the weird guy, grazing his head. He sagged on top of Joe, who shoved him off. I backed up and lifted the statue, ready to swing if the stalker assaulted Joe again.

Joe sprinted out, taking the satchel with him.

"Stop!" the weird guy yelled. "I'm a cop! That man is a murder suspect!" He rubbed his head where I'd bashed it.

The buddha shook violently, as I held it over my shoulder, prepared to strike. I wouldn't go down without a fight. "You've been following me like some pervert. Why should I believe you?"

"He killed the Synyrgys people," the stalker went on, chest heaving from exertion. "Those oils…poisoned his victims…face cradle. Don't hit me with that thing again!"

Three cops ran into the room. And stopped, mouths agape. Not only was I holding a buddha as a weapon, I was completely naked.

"He was stalking me," I said, pointing at the weird guy, realizing how crazy I must sound as the words left my mouth. The whole situation was mortifying.

"I've got this. Go after him!" the guy yelled to the cops. He clambered to his feet and gave me a long, slow, appraising look, as he handed me the top sheet from the massage table. I tore it out of his grasp and clutched it in front of me, still holding the buddha.

"Who are you?" I asked.

He flashed a badge as he pulled the door shut on his way out. "Police. Come outside when you're dressed. Leave that," he said, nodding at the statue, "in here."

He was with a group of uniformed cops when I emerged to a chaotic scene in the hall. It was hard to know for sure, but I sensed Joe might have slipped past them. The weird guy said something to one of the other cops, who intercepted me before I could head to my car. "We need to ask you a few questions about this massage operation." He said. "Don't leave."

"It isn't one of those massage parlors, if that's what you're thinking. Joe was always completely professional."

Did they suspect I'd been here to buy sex? Or…worse? Ohhh, please tell me they hadn't installed cameras in the treatment rooms, like at the Florida spa where the football owner got caught. I didn't ask the question, unable to bear the thought of anyone watching videos of my naked body. I'd had enough embarrassment for one day.

* * * *

The reality of the last hour hit me as finally I drove home, shaking, after the police finished questioning me. Joe—gentle, kind, caring Joe—had poisoned people using the face cradle on his massage table. The same face cradle I'd used.

He'd killed his victims with those very special aromatherapy treatments we'd discussed, one of which could have been Beth's. Or mine. I'd assaulted a cop and possibly aided and abetted the escape of a murder suspect.

I'd narrowly escaped from a serial killer who'd managed to elude the cops. He could be anywhere, waiting to kill again. And he knew where I lived.

Even so, I was already missing those massages. I'd loved the sensation of Joe's warm, firm hands all over my body. I was probably lucky to be alive, but really upset that I'd have to find another massage therapist that skilled. One who wasn't a serial killer.

And damn it, I'd have to find a man in my life. Was there any chance Beth's brother was good at backrubs?

Cheryl Marceau is the author of eight published short stories, including "The Mask," in *Malice Domestic 15: Mystery Most Theatrical*. Her other stories have appeared in several Level Best Books anthologies as well as in *Fish or Cut Bait*, a Guppy anthology. She is also working on a historical mystery set in New England. Cheryl is a former human resources executive who worked primarily in the aerospace and defense industries. If she told you more about her past life, she'd have to kill you. She and her husband live in the Boston area.

GRANDDAD'S BLOOD BAIT

GENE GARRISON

Granddad's blood bait was downright revered in our hometown. It drew catfish like flies. No, more like magic. Unfortunately, it drew Cletus, too.

I'm old, too old. It's hard to get around. My eyes and ears have let me down. Most worrisome, my short-term memory is shot to hell. But I can remember each and every detail of that long ago day and night. In the normal course of events, I would be writing this to your daddy, but we lost him—and your mom—way too soon. He never should have taken the job in Riyadh, and never should have taken you and your mother halfway around the world with him—hazard pay or not.

All oil fields are death traps…just like the one that killed my own father—your great-grandfather. Granddad always said the rig explosion in the panhandle that killed my daddy was the end result of nothing but callous disregard for the most basic of safety issues. Gram just said her boy was a lost soul after my mother died—and he took foolish risks. Nonetheless, they took me in. The way I took you in when you lost your folks. And I daren't go to my grave without telling you the whole story….

The Great Depression hung around longer in the prairie than it did elsewhere, thanks to the droughts and windstorms of the Dust Bowl. In those years when even farmers could barely feed their families, every man, woman, and child fished in whatever mudhole they could find. No one was too proud to eat any living thing they could pull out. Mostly chub, suckers, or carp—junk fish they'd have used for bait in more plentiful times.

Once the Depression eased a bit and life went back to normal, folks got more particular about which fish they bothered with. In our neck of the woods it was catfish—channels, blues, and flathead—that mostly ended up on Saturday night dinner plates. Once in a while, we'd catch-and-keep a mess of, say, smallmouth bass or crappie. They made a nice change from the scrawny chicken, too worn out to give eggs…or the tough old jackrabbit, raiding the herb garden. But for sheer eating pleasure, nothing could beat pan-fried channel cat. If the prize was fresh-cooked by the bank of the river where it was outsmarted, why, it tasted all the better.

This is where Cletus comes in. Our neighbor Cletus coveted Granddad's secret blood bait recipe. When Granddad went out for catfish, he always took two big ice chests. He caught the biggest and best cats every single time. Cletus took note of that. He knew there was something different about the bait Granddad used for himself. Now, the blood bait we sold was far and away better than anybody else's. No doubt about it. But, when Cletus was "between jobs," he spent a fair amount of time with Granddad. He must have figured out that the tiny X scratched into the bottom of Granddad's jars was significant. The Xs ensured that the really good stuff stayed in the immediate family.

Not too long after one of their biggest hauls, something changed; the very air between them was so charged that, even as a kid, I noticed it. Granddad refused to tell Gram what was going on, but muttered under his breath that ole Clete was so sharp he'd cut himself one day.

Despite the coolness between them, Cletus would pop over to the house at all hours with far-fetched excuses. Granddad made little time for him, busying himself with vague chores. He cut down on his trips, affecting disinterest, until Gram complained that our boxes of salted fish were running low.

Cletus surely did try everything he could think of to get hold of the recipe, or failing that, to appropriate one of the jars marked with an X. Granddad knew what the man was doing and pretended to get a good laugh out of it. Cletus even sent his wife over to see if she couldn't talk or trick Gram into letting slip a hint or two. For a while there, Marva was in our house nearly every day, never sitting still for long. She'd hop up to get a spoon from the drawer, or go twitch the curtains over the sink, or stand at Gram's elbow while she was fixing supper.

One day, Gram ran out to the service porch to get a jar of blackberry preserves. She stepped back into the kitchen, just in time to find Marva rooting around in the larder, her hand on a small wooden box. Of course, they both knew what she was up to—as if Granddad's secret would be filed with Gram's food recipes! Let me tell you, it was some months before the two of them were back on speaking terms, and still longer before they became friendly again. After that awkwardness, whenever Marva dropped by to visit, Gram made a point of setting out the Dr. Pepper and pound cake on the low table in the front room. Marva was no longer welcome in the kitchen.

Cletus had been a fairly successful traveling salesman in the twenties, Gram told me, and he and his wife had lived high on the hog. Not long after the '29 Crash, his routes dried up and he couldn't pay the bills. He was lucky to be taken on right away in the oil fields, but it was backbreaking work, and he wasn't the strongest or youngest man on any of the crews. He didn't last long. In fact, he was let go just before the first of the wildcatters went missing. I recollect they used to drive past our place on the way to town to bank their pay.

Granddad was a bit older than Cletus, but they were friends of sorts. Granddad felt sorry for him. Gave him a couple bucks here and there and the occasional jar of blood bait—X-less—to put some food on the table for him and Marva. To make ends meet, Cletus took to selling things. He'd drive his rusty Ford pickup all over Kay County and beyond, rummaging through abandoned homesteads and barns for anything saleable. Sometimes he'd rumble past our house with a load of lumber (mostly barnwood, which for some reason is real popular today.) Other times he'd fill the truck bed with cut-rate bales of hay and tie a couple more to the roof of the cab. His old rattletrap had no springs left. At every dip or bump, those bales would shed a bit and litter the road with mucky, dried grass. Once, Cletus hauled a crooked, paint-chipped outhouse all the way to Wichita to sell to some gullible soul. Granddad said he wouldn't be surprised if there was a copper still hidden inside it. I don't think Granddad was joking. Remember now, Oklahoma was dry in those days.

Cletus tried to sign up when it began to look like war was brewing again over in Europe. He was sorely shamed when they classified him 4-F. Gram wasn't all that sympathetic; he was too old for the army anyway, she said. Gram reckoned he wanted to join up as much to get three squares a day as to do his patriotic duty. She also hinted he might be hoping to put some distance between himself and Marva (who had never really adjusted to having to pinch pennies—and didn't hesitate to let Cletus know it.)

His unfitness for military duty turned to his advantage in the end. A goodly number of our local boys had gone to Canada to join the war effort before FDR got us into the fray officially, so Cletus picked up a lot of odd jobs from their wives and mothers. What with most of the remaining able-bodied men toiling away in the oil fields for weeks at a time, he had a purt' near full-time job as the town handyman. Soon he had his "slickness' back (Gram's word); he looked to be getting prosperous again. He bought himself a newer truck, one with a decent suspension and hardly any dents. When, one Sunday, Marva wore a new hat to church, she set the whole pew to fluttering.

Yet, Cletus became more and more fixated on the blood bait. At the snooker parlor, he spread it around that anyone who could name Granddad's secret ingredient stood to make some ready cash. Granddad pooh-poohed to all and sundry the very idea of a secret ingredient, but he now avoided Cletus like the plague.

Now, you know as well as I do that anglers love catfish for their cunning—and for the fight they put up when hooked. What's more, they love to brag that their own bait or lure is sure-fire guaranteed to tempt the wiliest ones up from their hidey-holes. In truth, most anglers find out the hard way that catfish have exceptional senses of taste, sight, hearing, and smell—and they adjust their technique to that understanding. Granddad swore by the sensitive 'nose' of a catfish. He was convinced that any cat could pick out the scent of a tasty crushed leopard frog over a more boring nightcrawler better than any fish in the world. The size of Granddad's catches proved over and over that the right blood scent could entice the shrewdest channel cat from his deep hole and tempt him to the surface. That's why our bait—the non-X, customer version—sold far and wide for a tidy sum. Little did I know, 'til later, that Granddad was also selling his X version—at a much stiffer price—to a few highly select, very discreet cronies and well-vetted out-of-staters.

In Granddad's day, most of the blood in folks' bait came from chickens…or roadkill, if it was fresh enough. Whatever was handiest. Granddad wouldn't ever tell me what kind of blood he used. He'd say I wasn't old enough yet. He had a sturdy shed tucked in a cottonwood grove down by the river that ran along the back of our property, well away from the acreage. After each hunting trip, he'd carry his kill, hidden in an oiled canvas sack, to the shed and lock it up tight. He had two locks on the door and one on the window, and each piece of framing was reinforced.

Early next morning, while the air was still cool, he'd be back inside the shed, where he drained the blood from the dead critters into a heavy-duty mop bucket. Then he'd pour in the other ingredients. Flour, probably. Or, corn meal? Brown sugar, for sure; Gram always bought extras boxes of it and kept them on hand at all times for Granddad. I always suspected garlic, too. Gram grew an awful lot of garlic in her vegetable patch beyond the clothesline poles, but we never put garlic in our food. Nobody we knew admitted to using the stuff. It was felt that garlic was too 'foreign.'

Guess it doesn't matter what I thought then, based on sneaked glimpses now and again. I soon learned what was really in the recipes. Anyway, once Granddad measured the ingredients, added them to the bucket, and put the unmarked cannisters back on the shelf, he'd call me into the shed and let me watch the mesmerizing part of the process. If I'd been real good, he'd allow me to give the mixture a couple stirs with a long wooden paddle. Then, he'd take over. Sitting on a low stool, he'd reach both hands deep into the bucket to pull up the mixture from the bottom. Over and over again, he worked the liquid until it became silky and cascaded slowly through his fingers until, eventually, it hung suspended in folds…like heavy drapes. At that point, he poured and spread it with a trowel onto a screen fixed over a 3 x 5 wood frame. By then, it resembled black icing, shiny and thick. After a couple days, it was strong enough to be cut into strips and folded into empty Miracle Whip jars. The smell could knock you down, if you didn't leave the shed door ajar.

One Saturday after the matinee (I favored the serials, especially Flash Gordon, more than the westerns), I saw Granddad standing on the sidewalk at the far corner of the snooker parlor. Usually, he played pool there with his friends for most of the afternoon, while I was at the movies.

I think he used that place like an office—the way people today use Starbucks. Everybody in town knew they could find him there on Saturdays. Early in the day, he'd load up the Hudson's trunk with jars of his blood bait and give me a ride to the theater, the jars clinking a little, if he drove too fast. Rarely was there a sound from back there on the way home.

This day, he was alone and off to the side of the building (kind of lurking, really.) He kept looking back and forth, as if waiting for someone. My first instinct was to call to him, but something in the way he held himself stopped me. Just then, a big, rough-looking man I'd never seen before joined him. They edged into the alley and talked awhile. Then, Granddad gave the man a brown paper sack, as the man slipped him what looked like a thick wad of bills. They shook hands and took off in opposite directions, without another word.

At the time, I didn't understand what I was seeing. I decided to walk home by myself, taking a different route, so Granddad wouldn't see me. I was thinking so hard I forgot to buy my favorite Abba Zabba candy bar from Killian's Market on the way.

Later that same summer evening, Gram and Granddad sat out on the front porch after supper—ham hock 'n beans with cornbread (the only dish Gram cooked that you didn't need bicarbonate with) and strawberry shortcake for dessert. I helped clear the table, then told Gram I was going to my room to read the brand new Superman comic I'd gotten for my tenth birthday. She teased me that reading it so often would soon wear the ink right off the paper.

I lied. Instead, I crept in darkness through the house, until I could hear their voices through the open window. Inside, I crouched down to listen. Gram was knitting—I could hear the needles click—and doing most of the talking. Why did Cletus care so much about the blood bait recipe? Was he that hungry for catfish five or six nights a week? Did he think he could catch enough fish to put on ice and sell them out of the back of his truck? Granddad chuckled here and there, but didn't bother to reply.

"I had an interesting conversation with Marva earlier today." When Gram had a juicy piece of gossip, she didn't let a lack of interest deter her. "Yep, she overheard Cletus on their phone talking to someone about your blood bait, along the lines of analyzing something or other. He said 'it could be worth a lot to the right person.'" Silence from Granddad.

"Cletus has been getting more and more squirrely about your recipe,

Dad. Marva finally lost her composure and lit into him. She'd had enough and said so in pretty bald terms—'It's me or the blood bait!'" Finally, Granddad responded. He opined that he had expected her to do it sooner.

Gram pulled out the big guns. "Marva came cryin' to me 'cause Cletus'd slapped her hard on the cheek and stormed out of the house." Granddad ventured that a man ought never do that—not without real good cause.

"Hmph!" Satisfied she had his full attention, Gram switched gears. "Marva told me she saw Cletus downtown the other day, talking to his old boss from the oil fields. She's got it into her head that the man might give Cletus an indoors job, because afterward, all Cletus could talk about was 'the lab' this and 'the lab' that." Granddad hmm'd.

"Oh, and by the way," Gram said, "another wildcatter's gone missing."

"Lotsa wildcatters go missin'...dangerous work," murmured Granddad.

A few minutes later, he said "good night" and came into the house. He didn't see me because he didn't turn the lights on as he moved through to his and Gram's bedroom. That, for sure, saved me a hiding.

I couldn't understand how Cletus's analyzing the problem was going to help him get the recipe. He'd obsessed over this for a good long time, to no effect. He couldn't even steal the recipe, because Granddad told everyone he kept it in his head (that was a fib!)

Another thing didn't make sense to me. How could Marva think that this oil man would give Cletus a job indoors? She boasted to everyone who'd listen that she was the one who'd organized his sales receipts and travel expenses, and even written his sales reports when he came in off the road. Said he hated paperwork. So, it wasn't likely he'd want a job in an office.

And finally, what was all that stuff about a lab? Did Marva think maybe Cletus could work in a laboratory? I supposed he could be some kind of assistant, like Fritz in the Frankenstein movie I'd seen a few weeks back.

While I pondered, I saw Granddad ease out the back, closing the screen door softly so it wouldn't bang. I followed him, just as quietly.

There was a full moon that night, so it was easy to keep my eye on Granddad from a distance. Almost immediately, I spied a shadow following him. I hung back and watched the shadow glide into the shed, literally on Granddad's heels. I reached the shed in time to hear the snick of a door lock and see thin blades of light outline the tightly closed shutters. At first, there was a low buzz of conversation. Then, one raised voice yelled indecipherable words. I inched closer and nearly stumbled over a milk crate. By upending the crate under the window, I could stand on tiptoe and peek through a tiny crack in the lower left corner of the wooden shutter. I dug my nails into the outside sill for purchase. When I pressed my ear against the gap, I could hear every word. If I shifted my eye to the slit, I could see pretty well, too.

It was Cletus in there, saying he just wanted to borrow a jar of blood bait for a fishing trip over to the Salt Fork. He hoped to hook some large-mouth bass and maybe a few blues. Granddad wasn't buying it. He told Cletus he'd always given him a jar whenever he asked.

"Nope! You been spyin' on me, trying to get yourself into my work-room. Well, you're here now. Did you think to persuade me into giving you one of my 'special' jars?" Granddad eyed the knife in Cletus's right fist. "Or mebbee just finally get proof of what critter I use for the prime stuff."

Cletus could hardly deny it, as he looked greedily at the canvas sack open on the table, its inside edge lined with longish brown hairs sticky with blood. His left hand involuntarily crushed a sheet of waxed paper. He was dying to take a scraping. Suddenly, he pounced on the salient point. He was vindicated.

"I knew you had two different versions!" As his grip on the knife tight-ened, it slowly angled toward Granddad's midsection like a dowsing rod. The canvas sack fell away. "And I want the one with an X on the bottom."

Granddad taunted him, saying he was crazy—and stupid! "You think you and your oil field buddy can analyze my bait, figure out the ingredients, and then go into competition with me? Why, after this, I wouldn't give you a jar of baby food let alone my.... Huh! You best get right on home. Go on.... Git!"

Enraged, his shoulders shaking, Cletus thrust his knife forward a cou-ple times, trying to back Granddad away. That shed space was close, and at first, Granddad didn't budge. Cletus waved the knife again. Shifting his weight, Granddad's foot knocked into something on the floor. He froze. Cletus looked down. Under the worktable, beneath an old green army tarp, he spotted a sunburned arm, flopped palm up. Lifting his eyes, he recog-nized that Granddad wasn't a bit shocked. In that split second, he flung the sack at Granddad, who waved it aside. Cletus made for the door. He fumbled with the upper safety bolt, finally throwing it free. As he franti-cally wrestled with the second door lock, Granddad grabbed a boning knife from the rack and swung it in a wide arc. Blood spurted from the jugular as Cletus slid to his knees, still holding onto the doorknob.

I gasped. Granddad must have realized it was me. He reached over and released the door lock. I ran inside and found him propping a startled, life-less Cletus onto a stool in the corner by the door. He pointed to the coiled tubing hanging from a metal coatrack. I handed it to him, and he quickly hooked up Cletus to the contraption. I watched the blood stutter from the rubber tubing into the big bucket. It made a funny pinging sound as it hit the galvanized metal.

By dawn the next morning, Cletus—and that other fellow with the brown hair and deep tan—were safely buried in six different holes in the dense timber stand topping the bluff above our section of the river, far from the shed and our house. For better or worse, we also had ourselves a fresh batch of bait X. The image of Granddad hovering over the bucket, glossy dark ribbons slipping through his fingers, visited me less often over the decades. But its vividness never faded.

"Marva says Cletus still ain't home," Gram announced over Cream of Wheat the next morning.

"Lotsa crazed people out there. Can't trust nobody these days," hissed Granddad.

Cletus had indeed planned to steal one of Granddad's special, X-marks-the-spot bait jars to have the contents assayed. He'd also (correctly) believed the recipe was written down somewhere and hoped to unearth it in the fortified shed. He and his old boss would then sell it to a manufacturer and split the profits…but someone had loose lips. Cletus was unpopular with the old-timers; he wasn't considered 'sound' at snooker (I took that to mean they thought he cheated, but couldn't prove it.) Word got back to Granddad, who readily concluded it was only a matter of time before Cletus broke into the shed. He'd been keeping an eagle eye out for him.

Instead, Granddad went into business with the very man I'd seen talking to him in the alleyway that Saturday—a Mr. Redding. He was an out-of-town businessman, whose only daughter lived here and had just made him a grandfather for the first time. He'd been visiting the family, but liked to play pool when he wasn't dandling the baby on his knee. He heard about Granddad's blood bait there in the snooker hall and was impressed by the word of mouth. Soon the two men were in confab (and discreetly sharing a pocket flask, I suspect, based on subsequent encounters with the jolly Mr. Redding.) The wad of bills I'd watched being passed was earnest money to seal the deal. The bag Granddad had given Mr. Redding held a jar of the regular bait he sold out of the back of his car most Saturdays. Mr. Redding wanted it, so that his people could analyze and standardize the formula.

Granddad bought out Mr. Redding a few years down the road, but they continued to play pool together whenever the big man came back to town. He carefully sold off the remainder of his 'special' formula, including the impromptu batch I always think of as the "Saturday night special." He never made another X version. Our town was once again safe for wildcatters. Much as Granddad despised all oil men, he wouldn't risk what was now the family legacy.

Except for the very last 'Saturday' jar. He kept that for himself, high on the top shelf of the shed. After Granddad died, I took the dusty container down from its perch and drove to the edge of town where, late on a starless night, I emptied the contents into the Chikaskia River.

* * * *

Well, now you know everything. Almost. When I die, and you come into your inheritance, the lawyers will hand you a sealed packet, containing Granddad's original handwritten recipe. Had Marva thought to look in our family bible, she'd have found it in the Book of Revelations. When you reach the final ingredient, you'll see the name of the animal whose blood is so enticing to catfish. Then, you'll know it all.

One more thing. No matter how cautious Granddad was about who he offered it to, word spread fast of the record catches from the 'custom' batch we spawned that infamous Saturday night. It was so good he just couldn't resist exacting a premium (read 'staggering') price for the stuff. We still get the occasional inquiry about that near legendary, super special batch of blood bait.

Well, you need to understand that was a one-time windfall. If anyone asks, just say you don't have any idea what they're talking about.

All the big-name outdoorsman retailers carry us. Internet sales have remained strong. This latest downturn in the market hasn't hurt our bottom line one bit. "Granddad's Blood Bait" has been good to our family. It sent me to college and you to law school. Most of all, it paid for a life that didn't involve working a piece of land 'til you died in your tracks. You'll pass the family business to your own children one day, with my blessing. Though I plan to be around a few more years yet.

Every family has secrets. Ours is in the blood.

Gene Garrison has been a member of Sisters in Crime since the early 1990s—and currently belongs to the Chesapeake, the Citrus Crime Writers, and the Guppy Chapters.

THE LEGEND OF BAHAMA BOBBY

MELINDA LOOMIS

Davey's Bar was stuffy and sparsely populated; the crowds would come later. The bartender was smoking hot and probably a decade my junior, but I was still tempted to flirt with him like crazy—after all, it was Key West, and although it was my first trip there, I'd read enough to know it was not small-town America. Think weird, kind of like if Las Vegas had a remote, oceanfront sibling.

But that's not what I was there for. What I'd come to see was hanging on the wall behind the bar, the now infamous painting of a run-down RV park, surrounded by palm trees and backed by a beautiful sunset. For some odd reason, the artist had placed Key West's iconic Southernmost Point buoy among the aged vehicles. Just to establish location, I supposed, in case anyone didn't twig to it on their own.

But by the time I arrived in Key West, everyone knew better than to dismiss the painting's shabby setting. We all knew not only what had gone down there but also why the artist, surrounded by the tropical beauty of his island surroundings, had opted for such a decrepit site in the midst of paradise.

One of the rusty RVs in the painting had a tiny white cross on the door. You wouldn't have noticed it, if you weren't looking for it. At least, not before everyone discovered why it was there in the first place.

It said a lot for the artist that, as I gazed upon the painting, I almost forgot about the bartender. It was really well done; the artist had real talent. I was lost in it, until Aaron, as his name tag identified him, came over to take my order.

I nodded at the painting, and Aaron stiffened up and gave me a hostile look. "It was a gift," he snipped. I wasn't surprised that he might be tired of being asked about it. The story had brought looky-loos in droves, wanting to see for themselves the exotic locale that the now legendary Bahama Bobby had briefly called home.

I ordered a margarita and continued to inspect the painting. Aaron brought my drink, and then, nodded at a man at a nearby table. "Davey," he called out, "Another one of those reporters."

I wasn't sure what had given Aaron the impression I was with the press. It had been a couple months since they had come and gone. Maybe it was the notebook at the ready. Rather than correcting him, I decided to wait and see if it was something that could work to my advantage. Besides, it sounded so much more impressive than "ambitious, crime-obsessed blogger, hoping for a book deal." Plus, I had a theory, and I needed to see Davey to confirm it.

I followed Aaron's gaze to the weather-beaten gentleman he had called to. Probably in his late forties and not a bad-looking guy twenty years ago. He had that permanent tan, indicative of people who lived their lives out in the elements. I wasn't sure what the protocol was, if should I invite myself over, or wait and see if he would join me at the bar. I was a fish out of water with enough sense to know I was in their world and would have to play by their rules.

Then, Davey gave me a weary but friendly smile and waved me over. Okay, his table then. I gathered up my backpack, notebook and margarita, which was easier said than done, as I had only two hands and three items to carry. But I made it without dropping or spilling anything and clumsily deposited myself at Davey's table.

He extended his hand and introduced himself as "Davey, as in Davey's Bar." "Mandy Parker," I responded. I offered no affiliation, and he asked for none.

Davey struck me as a proverbial old salt, or at least on his way to becoming one. I was kind of disappointed he didn't come complete with the obligatory parrot on his shoulder, but I figured I could always add it to the story later, if I wanted.

"You know how to make friends in Key West?" he asked, and I was relieved that I'd done my homework. Hoping it would open the floodgates of conversation, I gave him my biggest smile and chirped, "Buy a round!" I waved at Aaron, who nodded.

As we waited for Davey's next round, I tried to scope him out without seeming rude. He had an air of genuine kindness, and I took an instant liking to him. There was a gentle quality to him that I wasn't expecting in a party town, especially after the media horde had descended on the place when the story first broke. I hadn't expected much of a welcome, at all, especially since I didn't have any actual credentials.

"I know what you want," Davey observed. "You want to hear all about the legend of Bahama Bobby." Not accusatory; more of an observation. "Well, you came to the right place."

"I've heard what everyone else has heard," I told him. "What I want to know, what I want to try and figure out, is his backstory. I want to know what made him tick. What made him do the things he did."

Davey smiled sadly. "Don't we all." It wasn't a question.

Aaron appeared, and then, disappeared in a flash, leaving Davey's drink in his wake. We raised our glasses and sipped in silence.

"Well," he finally asked, "where do you want to start?"

"The beginning seems as good a place as any," I offered.

He nodded. "Bobby arrived here about a year ago. He just showed up one day up in this big, beat-up RV. Drove into town and parked it in one of the lesser local RV parks, and that's where it stayed, until he left. In that respect, he blended right in pretty quickly."

"He arrived with his paintings, art supplies, the clothes on his back, and not much else," Davey continued. "He said he wanted a fresh start and a change of scenery and picked Key West, because it sounded interesting. Have to say, it was a good choice. We get all types here, and all are welcome."

I was pleased by how much Davey was willing to talk. He looked so much like a man of few words. I scribbled notes and nodded encouragingly, while he talked.

"There's a bunch of art galleries around town. He tried to get them to carry his artwork."

I'd biked past the galleries earlier. None of them carried Bobby's work, although some of the tourist-oriented gift shops were offering copies of the RV park painting on mugs, postcards, shirts and anything else they could slap it on. But the only original Bahama Bobby in town was the one in Davey's bar. I bet the galleries regretted rejecting him now.

"You know why they didn't want his paintings?" Davey asked.

"Because they weren't seascapes or beach scenes," I answered.

"Bobby told us he came from Colorado. Lived in a little cabin up in the mountains. He'd always painted mountains and forests. So much greenery."

I leaned forward. "Did you see the Colorado paintings?" I asked. "Did you think they were any good?"

Davey nodded. "Oh yes, they were beautiful. They were like looking at photographs. They were so good, but Rocky Mountain scenes don't sell in Key West. I don't know why he brought them down here."

"Maybe, he didn't want to leave any more traces of himself back there."

Davey smiled and nodded. We were on the same page. "The point is, galleries in Key West don't carry paintings of mountains or forests, no matter how good they are."

"You seem to have liked him, at least as an artist," I observed.

He sighed. "I did. I really did. He needed a friend. He seemed kinda beat up by life. He was this mousy, quiet little guy, and I don't think he'd ever really fitted in anywhere."

Davey finished off the last of his drink, and I waved at Aaron to hit us again.

"He adjusted to island life over time," he continued. "Started wearing shorts, and his pasty white legs started getting some color. I finally talked him into wearing a wide-brim hat, after he got a nasty sunburn. And somewhere along the line, someone tagged him with that ridiculous nickname. Bahama Bobby. They might have been poking fun at his Hawaiian shirts, but he loved it, and it stuck."

Davey's voice had softened, as if he had wandered off into a daydream. "Bobby was never gonna be mistaken for a Conch, but he seemed to be settling into life here. He was a little on the strange side, but not as batshit crazy as some people who land here. Just a good soul who had never been able to win at life. I thought this would be a good place for him. And he was painting, but he was still doing mountain scenes."

Aaron showed up with our drinks, and after wetting his whistle, Davey continued. "I kept telling him to paint local stuff. Boats, the Hemingway House, pelicans, tropical scenes. But he just kept painting forests."

"Except that one," I said, nodding at the painting behind Davey's bar.

"Yep," he said. "That one was a surprise. I didn't know he was doing it, until he brought it in and gave it to me. It was right before he left, though I didn't know, at the time, that he would be going."

"Do you think he knew he was leaving?" I asked.

Davey shrugged. "I don't know if he did or not, at that point. Though the way things turned out, he probably did."

"When you looked at his Colorado paintings, did you see the crosses?"

He sighed. "Not at the time. But my eyes have seen better days, not to mention they were pretty well hidden." He rubbed his eyes, as if for effect. "But toward the end, he showed me the crosses in his paintings."

Now, we were making progress. "Crosses, like you'd find marking a grave." I wasn't asking. I didn't have to.

He nodded. "Bobby always had a little cross hidden in each of his paintings."

"Did he tell you why?"

"He told me that it was because these places were so beautiful that it made him feel closer to God."

"Which begs the question of why he would leave Colorado in the first place, if he loved it there so much," I pointed out.

Davey nodded again. "Yeah, but to me, who wouldn't want to live here? Ask anyone in town. Every last person will tell you we live in the best place on earth. Like I said, he told me he wanted a change of scenery. I didn't read anything into it."

"So, it didn't make you suspicious, at all?"

"Bobby was a sensitive guy," he explained. "He didn't talk much about himself or his life before Key West, and when you asked, it was like you were digging at a scab. I'm not a nosy person. If people want to keep their secrets, I try to respect that."

"And then, one day, he just wasn't here anymore," I said.

Davey sighed. "I don't know how he knew to move on. Just drove off one day, not too long after he brought me the painting, and never came back. I'd started worrying about him, when all hell broke loose."

"When they found his RV abandoned in Florida City," I prompted. That's what had led the authorities to the Keys. Florida City is the last stop coming or going on US 1, the highway that runs from the mainland through all the Keys. It's the only way in or out by car. I'd stayed at the Best Western there before embarking on the final leg of my journey to Davey and his bar.

"Yep. And after they found the RV, it was like an invasion. Feds, sheriffs, local cops, just swarmed the town. And they were all looking for Bobby."

Turns out, they'd been looking for him for a while.

Back in Colorado, several people had vanished from the vicinity of a small mountain town, but it didn't send up too many red flags at the time. One was a chronically homeless alcoholic, and they figured he'd met his inevitable end via freezing winter weather. Then, a couple of tourists went into the mountains and never came back, but you know what happens when city people go out into the wilderness and don't know what they're doing. The local attitude was that they were either wildlife chow, in which case nothing could be done, or they would turn up eventually, dead or alive.

While Bobby hadn't had any luck with galleries in Key West, he'd sold almost a dozen of his paintings around town, while still in the Rockies. And when hunters and fishermen started stumbling across human remains, eventually, someone made a connection between where they were being found and the locations in a couple of Bobby's paintings, playing a hunch that paid off in spades. When they looked even closer, they found those white crosses, so tiny and unobtrusive you'd never have noticed them, if you hadn't been looking for them, and it was then that they realized where the mild-mannered loner with the artistic touch had found the inspiration for his paintings. After that, finding more of Bobby's victims was easy. They just checked the other paintings, and the crosses marked the spots. The manhunt was on, but by then, Bobby had long since departed for parts unknown.

"The scenes he painted were where he buried the bodies of the people he killed," I said to Davey. "The crosses marked their graves."

"And they weren't happy that they missed him again." Davey shook his head. "We tried to tell them he was gone. It was like the cops thought we were hiding him. They really gave us some grief before they finally left."

"But they only tracked him as far as Florida City," I pointed out. "How did they know to look for him here? He could have stopped there, snagged another car, and gone anywhere. In fact, how did they know about Florida City?"

He observed me kindly. "Because, honey, Key West isn't Las Vegas. We don't care if you got secrets you'd rather not share, but we're not going to keep them for you. Key West is a good place, if you want to get lost, but not if you're trying to hide."

"Someone ratted him out for the reward?" I was kind of shocked, mainly because I hadn't heard anything about that. And granted, Bobby was a serial killer, but that didn't seem to fall into line with his adopted town's live-and-let-live philosophy.

Davey shook his head, vigorously, indicating that I was way off-base. "No," he said, "Nothing like that. Haven't you noticed all the webcams around town?"

"Not particularly, but I guess I hadn't really thought about it." I mean, I knew they were around, but I hadn't considered it important.

"Well, they're everywhere. All over Duval. They're at hotels and resorts and marinas, and especially at bars. In fact, most bars have multiple cams. Stage cams, bar cams, crowd cams. And the bar cam over at Sloppy Joe's, not only does it pan the crowd, but the picture is really clear. Not fuzzy, like some webcams you see. What happens in Vegas may or may not stay in Vegas, but what happens in Key West gets broadcast all over the internet."

"Someone saw him on a webcam?"

"He liked to bar hop on the weekends, and someone spotted him," Davey explained. "That's why they were headed here. I don't know how he knew it was time to get the hell out of Dodge, but they were on their way when they found the RV. But by then, he was just gone."

"And you haven't heard from him since?" I asked.

He looked down into his glass, no longer making eye contact. "Nope. No one has as far as I know."

I motioned to the painting. "Did they ever find the guy who lived in that RV, the one he painted the cross on?" Bahama Bobby's one and only Key West victim, at least as far as anyone knew.

"No," he sighed. "And I don't know if they will. But more than one spot opened up in that park by the time Bobby left."

With that, Davey polished off his drink and exhaled. It was like watching the curtain fall on a performance.

"You guys seem like you were pretty good friends," I observed, hoping it would keep him talking.

"Bobby didn't really let people get close to him." Davey rubbed his stubbled face. "I was probably as good a friend as he had."

"You were the only one who got a painting."

He smiled sadly. "Only because the galleries wouldn't take his stuff." He shook his head. "I think he was very misunderstood. I think things might have been very different for him, if he'd felt accepted by the world."

"It can be a tough place," I sympathized.

He nodded, but he was no longer engaged. Those kind eyes, so much like Bobby's, were a million miles away. I closed my notebook. "Thank you for your time," I said. Davey nodded vaguely and answered, "You're welcome, Mandy." And I knew that I'd gotten all I was going to get from him.

I believed that Davey not only cared about Bobby, but might even be protecting him from the authorities. And I was pretty sure I knew why, and that was my theory about their familial resemblance. Seeing him in person had driven it home.

I had never seen anyone who looked less like a serial killer than Bobby. That's one of the things that sucked me into his story. He was the least-threatening person I'd ever seen. In every picture I saw of him, he had kind eyes and a passive expression. I couldn't see him swatting a fly, much less taking a human life. But his trail of paintings and victims, as well as his flight from authorities, said otherwise. That's what had gotten my attention and fueled my interest in Bahama Bobby, America's newest famous serial killer and my current obsession.

Davey, as the recipient of Bobby's painting, had been all over the media for some time. His bar had been inundated with media. I don't think he was happy about it, but he seemed to need to explain to the world that he'd barely known Bobby and had no idea where he could have gone. He was on my TV, and when he looked into those cameras, the light bulb went off.

Maybe not brothers—the police would probably have twigged to that—but somehow related. If I couldn't be the first person to notice it, I could be the first person to go on record with it. Book deal, here I come.

I didn't think Bobby was being hidden in Key West, nor would he come anywhere near it. He seemed more comfortable in the mountains. Fewer people, easier to hide. Winters in the mountains would provide much better coverage than the bright sun of Key West. Eric Rudolph, the Atlanta Olympic bomber, eluded authorities for five years in the Appalachian Mountains. Forests are better cover than beach towns.

Hopefully, he'll stay on the run long enough for me to write his story. The longer he evades the authorities, the better the story will be. The Legend of Bahama Bobby.

Melinda Loomis was born and raised in Southern California. She has at times been an office drone (working in everything from insurance to post production), culinary student, and unemployed bum. Her work has appeared in anthologies from the Los Angeles and San Diego Chapters of Sisters in Crime. Melinda lives in Los Angeles with her extremely photogenic cat Sophie. Visit her online at www.melindaloomis.com.

RELEASING LIVES

P. A. DE VOE

The vibrant bamboo pit viper slithered from side to side as it moved up the man's bone-thin arm. As if suddenly aware of the approaching danger, his eyes bulged. Flailing madly, he screamed: "Aiee! Aiee!"

In response to the sudden movement and noise, the snake struck. In a flash, its long, needle-sharp fangs sank into the man's flesh. Streaks of blood rolled down his arm.

The circle of men and women surrounding him gasped. Young children hid their heads in their mothers' skirts, peeking out only when safe within their fabrics' folds.

Instead of writhing in fear and pain, however, the snake's victim stared at the blood with a slight grimace. Then, eyes on the viper, he slowly grabbed hold of its head and extracted its teeth while the blood continued to flow. Once free, he allowed the snake to remain wriggling on his arm. Mesmerized, the onlookers held their breath, waiting for the next attack.

Turning toward his audience, the snake handler called out, "Do not worry, my friends. I cannot be hurt by this snake's evil poison! I am Shen Cong, master of its spirit."

At that moment, a slender girl wearing heavily mended clothing stepped out from the crowd. She handed Cong a bamboo stick, which he took in his free hand. With a deft touch, he removed the viper, transferring it to the rod. He held it up to show the gathering before kicking open the lid of one of two bamboo baskets at his feet. With an experienced move, he placed the emerald green snake inside its woven container. After closing the lid, he lifted the carrier in one hand while gently waving his bloodied arm back and forth high above his head.

The crowd cheered.

"Don't be shy. Jun is here to take your tokens of respect." He swept a hand toward the girl who had handed him the stick. She went among the audience with a money bowl, thrusting it toward each person and pausing just long enough for them to drop in a coin or two before moving on. When she came to a young woman carrying a large bag, however, she looked up and paused. A smile transformed her face.

The woman smiled back. "Good show."

"It's an honor to see you here, Sister Xiang-hua," Jun said, using the honorific "Sister" for the young women's doctor. She bowed to Xiang-hua before moving away without requesting money for the show.

Xiang-hua, however, already had a copper in hand and released it into the bowl.

Jun stared down at the coin, back up at Xiang-hua, and then over at her father, who was in the midst of a soliloquy on giving alms to build merit for the givers themselves as protection against the evil the venomous snakes represented. His audience appeared to be both mesmerized and scared. Some purposefully stood behind others, as if making sure there was someone between them and Cong. Jun seemed uncertain as to what to do about taking money from the doctor who had cared for her when she was sick.

"Accept my token of appreciation for your father's performance," Xiang-hua said to Jun, who ducked her head. Her mop of tangled hair fell forward as she did so, partially hiding her expression.

The nearby Buddhist temple was holding the popular festival of Releasing Lives. During this time, the pious released captured animals in order to gain merit. And, while Xiang-hua was certain Cong would make a few coppers selling harmless snakes to worshipers, she also knew he struggled to make ends meet. Selling snakes for the ritual and snake-related medicines gave him a paltry living, at best. She often saw him out on the streets with his snakes, Jun at his side, engaged in what Cong called street entertainment. Some, less generous souls, called his performances a scam to squeeze money from the gullible. Others saw him as a true master of the snakes he handled.

Jun was one of the last patients Xiang-hua had treated as an apprentice to her grandmother, a famous women's physician, before her grandmother's reputation had come to the Emperor's attention, and he appointed her doctor-in-residence for the empress and other women of the palace. The absence of her beloved teacher thrust Xiang-hua into the position of being the only professionally trained women's doctor in town.

Watching the child now, she was happy to see how well Jun had recovered. Thoughtful, hardworking, and smart, she had been one of Xiang-hua's favorite patients.

Xiang-hua adjusted her hold on the medicine bag, clutched it to her chest, and turned to leave. As she did so, a cry went up. "Get him! Grab him!"

Two brawny men pushed through the circle of onlookers and rushed toward the snake charmer.

"Run!" Cong yelled to Jun.

Xiang-hua watched as Jun fled into an alley.

Not as lucky, Cong found himself held in his attackers' grip.

"Hey, careful! What're you doing? Watch my baskets!" he bellowed, struggling in vain against the attackers' grip.

As the assailants held him, a short, rotund man swaggered up and smirked. "Well, Snake Man, you're about to get yours." He smacked Cong across the face.

The thugs' hold kept Cong from collapsing as the assailant struck him again, but, even from a distance, Xiang-hua could see him crumple within their grasp.

Xiang-hua's pulse raced. A buzzing filled her ears. She stepped forward. "Gao Li-dao, why are you attacking this man? You are an important person; he is a simple street entertainer. Why bully him?"

Li-dao glared in her direction. Spying the young woman, he pressed his lips into a hard line. "Mind your own business. This is a private affair."

Xiang-hua glimpsed Jun peeking out from the alley, staring at her father, eyes wide with fear. Looking back at Li-dao, the doctor met his gaze, challenging him.

Although Xiang-hua was a physician, she was still young and a woman. Li-dao, on the other hand, was not only older and a man, but the notorious second-in-command of a powerful local gang. If Xiang-hua wanted him to take her seriously, she could not show weakness.

"Cong is my client. I demand to know what's going on."

Li-dao snorted. "Your client? Not likely. Unless, he's more woman than man." He guffawed, and his henchmen joined in.

It was true that, as a women's doctor, she could never treat a man. Nevertheless, she refused to back down, even as her blood pounded a relentless rhythm in her temples. "I treat his family. They are under my care."

Turning fully toward her, he pointed to Cong. "This villain poisoned my wife Ma-fan He. Will. Pay."

"No. No, I never," Cong said, struggling to stand against the men holding him. "I make a living with my snakes. For medicine. For rituals. For entertainment."

"And what about your pit viper? What about being 'the Master of the Snake's Spirit?'"

He shrugged. "I've never hurt anyone."

"Liar. You're evil, and I will avenge my wife." He spun back to face Cong and raised his hand to strike him again.

"Wait. How do you know Cong poisoned her?" Xiang-hua said.

"She's home, dying," Li-dao said. "What more is there to know?"

"Why do you think she's been poisoned?" Xiang-hua asked.

Li-dao faced her again. "She told me. This monster's poisonous snake bit her, and now she's dying."

Xiang-hua looked at Cong. "Is this true?"

Cong coughed. "It's possible I threw a snake which accidently landed on his wife. But it wasn't poisonous." He tried to twist out of his arm prison. The goons just tightened their grip, crushing Cong's bony frame.

"A lie! There's the proof." Li-dao kicked at one of the bamboo baskets lying on its side. The lid popped open, and a bright green snake slithered out.

The circle of people that had been watching this new entertainment, jumped back, pushing against those standing behind them. A couple of men fell and immediately scrambled away in the dirt. Others snickered, while keeping a cautious distance between themselves and the snake.

"Jun! Daughter!" Cong called.

With concern, Xiang-hua watched Jun break away from the protection of the alley and sprint over. Once within the circle, she reached toward the snake and, with a practiced calm, carefully scooped it up, returning it to the carrying case and locking the lid in place.

The audience let out a long "Ahh!"

Xiang-hua caught the girl's attention and motioned for her to come to her side. Jun glanced at her trussed-up father and did as Xiang-hua indicated.

"See. I told you. Harmless. Your wife was afraid of a harmless snake. That's not my fault." Unfortunately, Cong's mocking tone was unmistakable.

Li-dao turned sharply and socked him on the jaw. He pointed to the second covered basket. "Are you going to tell me the snake in there is harmless, too? You know what you did. Ma-fan is dying, and it's your fault."

Xiang-hua held up her hand. "Why don't you let me examine your wife? She may be poisoned, but she may have another illness. It's possible I could help. If her condition is caused by snake poison, you can take Cong to court. I'll even support you in your case."

Crinkling his forehead in thought, Li-dao looked from Xiang-hua to Cong.

"What have you got to lose? If you kill Cong, you'll surely be executed for murder. If he's guilty, let the court handle his punishment," Xiang-hua said. "Take me to Ma-fan."

* * * *

The opulence of Ma-fan's women's quarters impressed Xiang-hua. Highly polished, dark wood shelves filled with blue-and-white, celadon, and multi-colored pottery ranged against one wall; long, horizontal paintings of women in gardens or playing stringed instruments covered another wall. Between them, a mounded coverlet lay on a kang outlined by an elaborately carved, ebony frame. A table set nearby held a tea pot, cup, and an assortment of dishes, each filled with various foods. All apparently untouched.

The elaborate trappings of the room told Xiang-hua that its occupant relished conspicuous luxuries, as well as comfort.

"My wife," Li-dao announced to Xiang-hua as they approached the kang.

At the sound of his voice, the coverlet stirred, its brilliant, silk colors slowly undulating under the weak light filtering in from a paper-covered, latticed window.

Ma-fan attempted to sit. Her maids rushed forward to assist. She relaxed into their arms, allowing them to hold her up. As they did so, she raised her hand to her mouth. She coughed until her face turned a dark red, her long sleeve trembling against her heaving chest.

Li-dao thrust a hand out toward his wife. "What are you waiting for? Help her, you lazy fools."

A maid tried to hold the cup to her lips, but Ma-fan pushed it aside. Gradually, her cough subsided. She glanced at Xiang-hua, ignored her, and looked over at her husband. "Did you find that snake man and punish him?"

"He's here," Li-dao said.

"Here?" She coughed delicately into her sleeve. "You didn't need to bring him here. I don't ever want to see him again. He's dangerous. Being poisoned once by his snakes is enough."

"My lady." Hoping to break Ma-fan's apparent single-minded desire to penalize Cong, Xiang-hua stepped forward. "I have come to see if I can be of service to you."

"This is Sister Xiang-hua," Li-dao hurriedly said. "She'd like to examine you. Perhaps she may be able to cure you."

Ma-fan scowled. "I know who she is. I don't need another doctor. Bell doctor Shu has already been here and given me a tonic." She listlessly pointed to the tea pot.

"I'm sure Shu has done all that he can. However, he's a bell doctor and has only limited knowledge. I believe their training is too haphazard," her husband said. "Sister Xiang-hua has studied for years under her renowned grandmother. Her training is much broader and in-depth. There is no comparison."

"I have complete trust in the bell doctor's abilities," Ma-fan said. She sniffed and, raising her chin, glanced in Xiang-hua's direction.

"My lady, I'm not here to question your trust in bell doctor Shu's diagnosis. However, I understand you are not better. If you'll allow me to check your pulse, I may be able to discover more about your condition," Xiang-hua said.

Ma-fan shook her head. "That Cong is a thief, plain and simple. He can't deny what he did." She trembled with anger. "How many times do I have to tell you?" Her eyes darkened as she glared at her husband. "When I walked past his ridiculous act, he threw that vicious snake, and it landed on me. I cried and begged him to remove it, but he didn't. Not until I gave him all the money I had." She began to cough, more violently this time. One of her maids quickly grabbed the medicine and tried to get Ma-fan to drink. She turned her head aside.

Finally, glaring at her husband, she said: "You must revenge me before I die."

As if stung, Li-dao spun around and started to march out of the room.

Listening to Ma-fan, Xiang-hua was more convinced that she had to examine her. She couldn't let Li-dao leave before she had permission to examine his wife. She quickly intervened. "Sir, did the bell doctor actually examine your wife and take her pulse?"

He halted. "No, of course not. It wasn't his place. It would be improper for a woman of my wife's standing to be touched by a strange man. Any strange man."

"Then, may I ask on what he based his opinion?"

"Don't be so bold," Ma-fan scolded. "Shu has years of experience. He doesn't need to fondle me."

Xiang-hua ignored the implication that she had no right to question the bell doctor. Silently, she thought that Li-dao's wife was aptly named. Ma-fan. While an auspicious name for a woman, suggesting both domesticity and reproduction, Ma-fan also sounded like the word for troublesome. Biting back her irritation, she bowed politely toward the patient, then said to Li-dao, "I mean no disrespect, but as a women's doctor, I can do a much more detailed examination of your wife to determine the cause of her suffering, be it snake poison or something else. Will you give me permission to examine her?"

Normally, Xiang-hua tried to include both her patient and her patient's family in all conversations; however, in this case, she purposefully ignored Ma-fan and spoke only to her husband. She didn't understand why Ma-fan was so adamant that she not be examined, but Xiang-hua felt she had not only a responsibility as a physician to fulfill her mission but also a commitment to Jun's family. For that, she would ignore Ma-fan's wishes and speak only to Li-dao. No one would dispute her doing so. No one would challenge the husband's right and, indeed, responsibility, to make all decisions concerning his wife's treatment.

But such was not the case in this household.

"I will not have a neophyte replace Shu. I place my full confidence in him and his care. If I don't die, it's only because he was able to save me from Cong's wicked bullying and his dangerous and embarrassing snake trick."

As Ma-fan spoke, her torso went rigid and her voice hardened. Observing this, Xiang-hua began to see how this proud woman interpreted Cong's snake trick: not as a time-worn way to extract more alms from someone in his audience, but rather as an unforgiveable public humiliation. As a loss of face.

"You will live long and well, my wife." Li-dao cast an irritated glance toward Xiang-hua. "I'll take care of that scoundrel."

Ma-fan leaned back onto her pillows. "I put my confidence in you," she said, coughing into her sleeve.

Her maids looked plaintively toward Li-dao, as if pleading for him to let their mistress rest.

As if noticing their silent request, he said to his wife, "Don't concern yourself. I'll take care of it." Addressing her servants, he gave orders for them to care for her and to be sure she took her medicine, or they would certainly suffer the consequences.

All this time, the most Xiang-hua could do was carefully watch Ma-fan, evaluating her complexion, her breathing, her overall strength. Even though she couldn't take the woman's pulse—the gold standard in any medical examination—her grandmother had also taught her how to read other signs of stress and health. From what she observed, she was certain the woman had not been poisoned. But she needed to do a proper examination to convince her enraged husband.

Hustling a reluctant Xiang-hua out of the room, Li-dao led her to his front courtyard where Jun stood next to her father, still bound and slumped on the ground. Li-dao kicked Cong and ordered his guards to haul the entertainer to his feet.

"Please, Sister Xiang-hua, help my father," Jun pleaded. "He didn't hurt Madam."

Li-dao sneered. "Didn't hurt her. Didn't hurt her! His viper bit her. She's dying! He'll pay for this, and it won't be a quick death, either."

"No. I didn't. It wouldn't," Cong said, his voice rough with emotion.

"Are you denying you threw your snake on my wife?" Li-dao yelled.

"I admit I threw a snake, but it was a harmless grass snake, not the viper."

"A likely story. How do you explain my wife's condition?"

Cong dropped his head, then looked up. "I don't know, but it wasn't because of me or my viper. I promise. I only threw the grass snake."

Xiang-hua had seen his street show many times as she walked through the town to visit patients. She frequently watched Cong throw a green snake onto well-dressed pedestrians as they passed. They inevitably panicked and begged him to retrieve it. Most believed it to be the viper he used in his act. Before rescuing the victim, he always exacted what he called a donation. While the gambit was one of his most profitable money-making ploys, it nevertheless made her nervous. One day, she was sure he would go too far. This was that day.

"Ha! Grass snake. A likely story. Lying won't do you any good." He peered at his brawny guards. "These fellows are going to beat you to a pulp. It's up to the gods whether or not you survive."

Jun began crying.

"What proof do you have that Cong threw the pit viper and not a green snake?" Xiang-hua asked.

He pointed his booted foot toward the woven bamboo baskets lying next to Cong. "There. The one may have a green snake in it, but the other has the viper. Today, he miscalculated and threw the viper. My wife's bad fate. His bad fate."

Xiang-hua walked to the baskets and opened a lid. The green snake gazed up at her. She closed the lid and went to the second basket.

As she reached out to open its lid, Li-dao stopped her. "Don't. He may have magic powers over it, but we don't. Leave it be."

Xiang-hua opened the lid. An emerald snake with a series of small white dots running down its side, raised its head and flicked its tongue. The pit viper.

Li-dao and his guards stepped back, away from her and the carrying case.

Cong leaned forward.

"I told you it was a viper," Li-dao said.

"But harmless," Xiang-hua said.

The gang leader guffawed. "A harmless pit viper. That's a new one." He squinted over at Cong's daughter. "Jun, reach in and take that snake," he ordered. He smirked, then added: "If it's so harmless, she'll be fine."

His guards cast nervous glances at each other and back at their boss.

Xiang-hua pushed back on her heels, never taking her eyes off the young girl.

Cong seemed frozen in place.

Jun strode over to the basket and knelt next to it. With a slow and steady motion, she placed her hand on its rim. The viper raised itself higher and, flicking its tongue, moved its head rhythmically back and forth.

Slowly, Jun turned her hand up and stretched toward the viper.

The snake seemed to be as entranced by the slowly unfolding scene with Jun as they were. It was as if they were all held suspended in time.

"Another sorcerer!" Li-dao's roar startled the viper. The alarmed snake attacked, biting down hard on the small hand extended toward it. Blood gushed over Jun's palm, between her fingers, and onto the ground.

With an anguished cry, she jerked her hand away; a bright green ribbon flew with it. She rose, stumbling toward Xiang-hua.

"Aiee," the guards said as one, lurching backward.

"Oh, Jun," Cong moaned, his face drained of color.

"Ha," Li-dao crowed.

Xiang-hua grabbed for a small stick and thrust it as best she could between the snake's upper and lower jaw, trying to force it to open further, allowing her to release its grip. As she worked, Jun wept softly, holding her pain in check as much as possible.

Finally, Jun's hand was free. Xiang-hua did not stem the blood flow immediately, allowing it to continue oozing over her palm.

Li-dao watched, a satisfied look on his face. He glanced at Cong. "Fate. Your viper poisoned Ma-fan. Now, it's poisoned your daughter."

"It didn't poison Jun." Cong shook his head, although he kept his eyes on Xiang-hua and Jun.

"Pitiful." Li-dao smirked. "Being in denial won't help your daughter. If she dies, it'll be your fault."

"She won't. She's hurt, yes, but she won't die."

Xiang-hua, with one arm around Jun's shoulders, reached into her medicine bag and pulled out a bundle of cloth and a bottle. "He's right. The viper didn't poison her."

Li-dao shook his head. "Look at her hand." The blood continued to flow. "Letting her wound bleed won't keep the poison from spreading throughout her body."

"It was a dry bite," Cong said. "There was no poison."

The gangster looked from Cong to Xiang-hua, confused.

"A pit viper can have a dangerous, poisonous bite. But Cong drains its poison, collecting it for the medicines he sells. So, while the viper can still bite, it doesn't have deadly toxins to inject into its victim."

"But my wife is deathly ill. And his snake caused it," Li-dao sputtered.

"Let me examine her," Xiang-hua said as she spread a salve over Jun's wounds before wrapping them in a bandage. "If she's truly been poisoned, I can diagnose it and cure her." She spoke with a conviction she didn't feel. However, she knew that anything less than a full-throated statement of certainty would not persuade Li-dao to let her personally attend to Ma-fan—especially with his wife's refusal of her treatment.

Li-dao furrowed his brow and chewed his lower lip.

Xiang-hua quickly added: "I believe you want to save your wife. If so, you must let me care for her. You know my grandmother's reputation and that I've trained my whole life under her. I'd never let her down. I'll not let you down, either."

He rubbed a pudgy hand over his jowls and cast a long look back toward his wife's room.

Xiang-hua was about to lose heart when Li-dao drew in a deep breath and finally relented.

"But if you find she's been poisoned, he will be punished, and my wife avenged."

* * * *

They walked to the women's quarters together. At his wife's door, Li-dao ordered the guards to remain just outside with Cong and Jun.

Seeing Xiang-hua enter behind her husband, a scowl passed over Ma-fan's face, but she said nothing.

"Sister Xiang-hua has my permission to examine you as she thinks necessary," Li-dao said.

"It isn't necessary," Ma-fan asserted as before. "Bell doctor Shu…."

"I've decided," Li-dao snapped.

Xiang-hua stepped up to the kang and reached for Ma-fan's wrist. The woman started to resist, but a glance at her husband's face suppressed the desire.

Closing her eyes, the young doctor concentrated on Ma-fan's pulse. She wasn't surprised by its strong rhythm. She also examined her face, neck, shoulders, and arms. Before giving her diagnosis, Xiang-hua inspected the pot containing the bell doctor's medicine.

"Are you taking any other medicines besides this infusion?"

Ma-fan looked away. "That's all Shu prescribed," she replied in a low voice.

"Well? How is she?" Li-dao badgered.

Xiang-hua met his gaze. "She has a slight scratch on her shoulder. Her pulse is strong."

"Due no doubt to the medicine the good bell doctor prescribed." Li-dao interrupted with a nod toward the pot she had just inspected.

She shook her head. "That is chrysanthemum tea. While good for many things, it isn't a remedy for snake bite or any other poison."

"What are you saying? That she's only drinking herbal tea and hasn't been poisoned by that viper?" Li-dao stared at his wife. She averted her eyes and pulled the brightly colored comforter to her chin.

"She shows no signs of poisoning. Further, there are no indications of a snake bite." Xiang-hua didn't belabor the point. She merely said what was true.

"Ma-fan?" Li-dao roared, his neck and cheeks turning a furious red.

Trembling within her silk cocoon, she peeked out at him.

"What have you done?"

"He did throw a snake, and it did land on me. He did it just so I'd give him money."

"And for that, that, you wanted me to beat him to death?"

Pouting, Ma-fan sat up. "You know how I hate snakes. Maybe it was the grass snake and not the viper. How would I know? They look the same. I was terrified. I yelled. I begged him to take it away. He didn't. He let it crawl over me. I thought I would faint. And then…and then…people started laughing. Laughing. He purposefully humiliated me in public." She paused. "I was mortified for you," she said, a simper edging into her tone. "I'm your wife, and he was making fun of me." She pouted and peered toward the door where Cong could be seen standing between the two guards. "Even if I wasn't bitten, I couldn't let him insult you like that."

Xiang-hua looked back and forth between the husband and wife as Ma-fan spun her tale. The young doctor didn't want to do anything to ignite Li-dao's violent temper, which could easily be directed either at Cong or Ma-fan, depending on with which he became most aggrieved.

Unfortunately, it looked like Ma-fan's story was beginning to twist her husband around again. Given another well-placed remark or two, Xiang-hua was afraid Ma-fan could once more manipulate him into viewing Cong as a problem to be dispensed with. A target for her misplaced sense of pride.

"Indeed, you are right, my lady," Xiang-hua said with a nod, as if in agreement with her.

Ma-fan cast her a questioning look.

"Before your husband sets Cong free," Xiang-hua said, making a claim for Cong's freedom that neither husband nor wife had spoken about, much less agreed to, "he should apologize to you for his careless use of his snake lassoing trick and embarrassing you in public."

Confused by these comments, Ma-fan wrinkled her brow and pursed her lips as she stared at Xiang-hua. Li-dao stood, glowering and arms crossed, but he listened.

Taking advantage of their silence, Xiang-hua quickly continued. "You know the local temple is holding its sacred ritual of Releasing Lives. Cong will free his snakes and assign the merit gained at releasing them to you, Ma-fan, thereby building your karma."

Although Ma-fan's pout amply announced her uncertainty at Xiang-hua's suggestions, her husband nodded. "Perfect. The Releasing Lives festival it is." He stared at Xiang-hua. "Just one thing. You must personally accompany Cong to make sure the captured snakes are released."

Xiang-hua bowed deeply toward Li-dao and Ma-fan, saying she would carry out their desires. As she did, the young physician glanced toward the doorway and saw Jun throw her arms around her father, while he bent his head in a small bow.

P. A. De Voe, an anthropologist and Asian specialist, writes contemporary cozy mysteries, as well as historical mysteries and crime stories immersed in the life and times of Imperial China.

A Silver Falchion award winner and an Agatha and Silver Falchion award finalist, she is a member of Sisters in Crime National and Guppy Chapter, the Short Mystery Fiction Society, St. Louis Writer's Guild, Saturday Writers, the Historical Novel Society, and Mystery Writers of America/MWA Midwest. Find her at padevoe.com.

KILLER'S CRUISE

JOSEPH S. WALKER

The *Majestic* made its stately way across the Pacific, and from the balcony of his portside state room, Dent watched the watery world go by.

On the table at his elbow rested a book from the ship's library, a small notepad and pen, an almost depleted bottle of Jack Daniels, and a glass. At his feet was a cooler filled with ice and cans of Coca-Cola. Periodically, he refreshed the glass with soda or whiskey to keep the mixture where he liked it. Sometimes, he picked up the book and read a few pages. For the most part, he simply stared out at the empty ocean. He felt the engines thrumming along and the great bulk of the ship rolling slowly beneath him and, beyond that, the infinitely greater force of the water itself, gently rocking one of the largest cruise ships in the world as casually as a bathtub toy.

Shortly after Dent first boarded the *Majestic*, almost two years ago, he met a scientist who told him that, from a planetary perspective, the ocean was simply the lowest layer of Earth's atmosphere. Since then, Dent has been acutely aware of the void yawning beneath him. The ship was a day and a half out from Honolulu and still three days from Bora Bora, skimming along a few miles above a landscape no human would ever see.

The idea of a life perpetually suspended over the abyss suited Dent.

The shadow of the boat stretched far out over the ocean in front of him by the time he tipped the last of the whiskey into his glass. Almost sunset. The starboard side of the boat would be crowded with most of the passengers, shading their eyes to try to catch the moment the sun slipped over the horizon, hoping for the green flash of nautical lore, getting geared up for the promised party tonight. Dent set the empty bottle down on the table and picked up the pen and pad. He took a long pull from the glass, rubbed the back of his neck, and began writing.

In 1997, I killed a man named Edgar Facinelli in Atlanta, Georgia. I was paid $100,000 and told to make it look like a burglary gone bad. I made Facinelli give me another $50,000 from his safe and then hit him behind the ear with a souvenir Hank Aaron baseball bat displayed over his desk. I only had to hit him once.

He tore the sheet from the notepad, rolled it into a tight tube, and stuck it into the empty bottle, using his little finger to push it in past the neck. In the wide part of the bottle, the paper unrolled a little, and brown spots appeared as it picked up the remaining traces of the whiskey. Dent screwed the cap on tight and stood to lean over the railing. There was nobody on any of the other nearby balconies and, looking up, he saw no heads peering over from the main deck. A chaotic wake was unfolding continuously from the ship's waterline, six stories down. He dropped the bottle and watched it spin twice before disappearing into the churning water.

There was a good chance the bottle would be dragged under the boat and shattered by the massive propellers. There was an excellent chance that he was the last person who would ever lay eyes on it. Dent didn't know where his impulse toward confession came from. For a man who'd managed to safely slip away from a career of murder and mayhem, it was an urge so stupid as to be suicidal, but one he could not shake. He was just pleased to have found a way to scratch the itch.

He turned from the balcony. There was work to be done.

* * * *

The *Majestic* was scheduled to cross the equator shortly before midnight, ship's time. In keeping with centuries of tradition, there would be a lavish party featuring boisterous, bawdy performances by members of the ship's crew, with special attention to the humiliation of those making their first crossing. In keeping with a modern age of omnipresent video and aggressive lawsuits, the explicit torture and sexual assault that had often marked the ceremony in past centuries would be considerably softened.

Dent drifted around the edges of the thronged main ballroom. Half of the space was open to the darkening sky, the other half tucked under the ship's towering superstructure. The total area would have covered most of a football field. The *Majestic* could accommodate more than 3,500 passengers, and many of them were here, eating, drinking, and dancing to the pounding rhythms of the rock band occupying the main stage. In front of the band, a group of young male crew members were wearing grass skirts and, with widely varying degrees of enthusiasm and ability, attempting the hula.

Dent paid no attention. The *Majestic* crossed the equator six times on every trip around the world, so he'd been through this party a dozen times before. Of course, he wasn't on this trip for the parties. He was here because a luxury ship in perpetual motion, spending weeks on end in the most isolated parts of the planet, seemed the ideal hiding place if you were seeking to avoid very serious men who didn't give much thought to tourism, apart from occasionally exploiting it for smuggling. Dent knew he could never, for the rest of his life, think of any home as secure, but the *Majestic* was not a home. It was simply a completely transitory place where he could be invisible.

It was working fine. Until today.

While the party held little interest for him, he was counting on the spectacle being a draw for the newest passengers, the ones who had come aboard in Hawaii. Only a small portion of the ship's travelers ponied up for the full circumnavigation; most were here only for a leg or two, and at every port there was a significant turnover. Dent let his gaze float across the crowd, looking for the faces that hadn't become familiar between San Francisco and Honolulu, looking for the one face that had given him a nasty twist this morning after breakfast.

Alex Brock.

Dent had been walking back toward his cabin when Brock had gotten off an escalator just in front of him and walked past, almost brushing Dent's shoulder as he went by. Only Dent's long experience had allowed him to pass with no sign of recognition or surprise. He hadn't seen Brock in five years, but there was no doubt in his mind of the man's identity.

And now here he was again, leaning against a bar table thirty feet away, wearing a gaudy Hawaiian shirt and yellow shorts, tipping back a bottle of beer. Dent's face again showed no flicker of response. He found a seat at another bar where he could watch Brock in the mirror out of the corner of his eye, while seeming to watch the workmen at the stern of the boat preparing a fireworks display for the moment of the crossing.

The band had shifted into a ballad, and the rookie crew members were slow dancing with each other, to the rehearsed jeers of the more experienced hands. Brock was paying no attention to this, seeming entirely occupied with something on his smartphone. Within twenty minutes, though, Dent was fairly sure that Brock was actually keeping tabs on a group at a small table near the edge of the dance floor: a middle-aged woman with red hair, and two teenaged boys doing their best to look completely uninterested in everything happening around them. At one point, the three of them stood up, and Brock straightened from his own table, tucking away his phone and casually brushing back his hair, but it turned out that they were simply changing seats to give the woman a better view of the dancers. Brock resumed his former position. Dent mentally shook his head; Brock hadn't lost some of his bad habits. He almost felt an urge to walk over and berate the younger man for being sloppy.

For Dent's current purposes, though, Brock's carelessness was good news. Satisfied that Brock would be at the party for as long as his target remained, Dent walked casually to the nearest elevator and took it down four levels. Down here, away from the luxury and spectacle of the ship, were the services passengers might need but wouldn't be taking pictures of: a small drugstore and first-aid station, a row of ATMs, an hour laundromat, and Dent's goal, a business center with computers and printers. Since most of the well-heeled passengers brought their own laptops and tablets, Dent had the place, as he almost always did, to himself. He used the login code he'd quietly paid a deckhand five hundred dollars for the year before and began scanning the list of new passengers.

He found the name he was looking for almost immediately, and this time he allowed himself a small smile. Brock really should have broken some of his bad habits by now.

* * * *

Four hours later, Alex Brock walked down the corridor to his state room, frustrated but not surprised at the way his night had gone. The woman and her kids had stayed at the party right up through the fireworks, cheering with everyone else as the boat crossed over to the southern half of the globe, and then lingered another half hour. There had never been a point where the woman was alone and vulnerable. Brock had entertained brief fantasies of her standing by an isolated spot at the railing, half in the tank. One quick nudge, and the job could be over and done with. There were too many people around to risk such a thing, though, and anyway, she had never gone near the edge of the deck. Three days left. He would have his chances.

He used his key card to open the door of his room. He walked inside, his hands busy putting the card back in his wallet, his mind occupied with plans and possibilities for the next day, and he realized his mistake only when he felt the cool metal touching the base of his skull.

"Inside," said a quiet voice behind him. A hand came to rest on his back, lightly, guiding him quickly forward.

Brock dropped his wallet and held his hands at shoulder height in front of himself. The hand alarmed him, because it meant this guy knew what he was doing. "You're the boss," he said. They moved together into the main part of the room.

"On the bed," the voice said, calmly, volume just above a whisper. Something about it tugged at Brock's memory. "Face down. Fingers laced behind your neck. Move."

Brock moved. He was half expecting handcuffs, but instead the gun stayed pressed firmly against his neck, while the man's other hand moved across him in a quick, efficient search.

"I don't have a gun," Brock said. He didn't expect to be believed, but establishing a conversation had to be the immediate goal.

"You mean aside from this one here?" the voice asked, and the gun tapped his neck, causing him to flinch more than he wanted to. "I found it taped to the underside of your bed, complete with silencer. Very handy."

Brock cursed to himself. Rolling to the floor and going for the gun had been his emergency plan here, and now he needed a new one fast.

"Now hold still," the voice said. The gun moved away, and Brock tensed, waiting for the shot, but instead a hand grasped the waistband of his shorts and yanked them down to just below his knees.

Brock yelped in surprise. "What the hell, man?"

"Relax," said the voice. Brock was certain now that he'd heard it before. "Just making it a little harder for you to jump me." The man moved across the carpet and sat in the chair in the corner of the room, just to the right of the sliding doors that let onto the balcony and about eight feet from the bed. A light clicked on. "Okay," said the voice. "Moving very slowly, put your hands out spread eagle and flat on the mattress. Then, you can turn your head."

Brock followed the instructions. He blinked against the dim light in the room, trying to get his eyes to adjust as quickly as possible. The man in the corner had turned the lampshade so that almost all the light from the reading lamp next to the chair fell on the bed. He was a mere outline in the shadow beyond, his legs crossed, the hand with the gun resting casually on his knee. He wanted Brock to see it and know that he would have all the time in the world to shoot if Brock tried something.

"I'll tell you the code for the safe, mister," Brock said. "You take what's there, and I swear I won't say a damn thing before the next port."

"I'm not here for the safe, Brock," the man said.

Brock knew he didn't completely cover his shock at that, but he had to try. "You've got the wrong man, mister. My name's Tommy Herr. I'm just a car salesman on vacation."

"Your name is Alex Brock," the shadow said. "You're a hit man. Unless something has changed in the last five years, you work primarily for a syndicate out of Miami, with occasional freelance gigs. And you've never learned that using the names of old St. Louis Cardinals is a really stupid way to choose an alias."

Brock's eyes narrowed. "Who the hell are you?"

"Come on, kid." The amusement in the voice was obvious. "Who would know all that shit, except your old partner?"

For the first time in his life Brock felt his jaw actually fall open. "Dent?" He started to push himself up from the mattress, but a quick waggle of the gun reminded him to stay where he was. "That's impossible. You're fucking dead."

"Not dead," Dent said. "Retired."

"Retired," Brock said. "Who the hell retires?"

"You should consider it," Dent said. "This job you're on now, for example. Seems like it could be bad for your health."

Brock turned his head back to the pillow and closed his eyes. Dent knew he was trying to acclimate to the dim room more quickly, but let him do it. Preferable to having him think about an immediate move. "I'm not on the job," Brock said. "Just a vacation."

"I was watching you on deck. I saw the target."

"Bull," said Brock. "Think I wouldn't have recognized you?"

"Plastic surgery." After the deliberately broken nose, the days wrapped in bandages in an off-the-books clinic outside Toronto, Dent still wasn't completely used to the face in the mirror, which always looked a little more tired than he felt. "You walked right past me on your way to breakfast this morning."

Brock turned his head carefully back and tried to look past the bulb. "Let me get a look at you."

"No. Tell me about the target."

Brock shrugged as best he could in his awkward position. "Janet Weinstein. Lives in Hawaii, has real estate and business interests all over the South Pacific. She's afraid to fly, though."

"Who'd she piss off?"

"She's got an uncle about to die of cancer in Connecticut. Somebody wants her out of the will. I'm supposed to drop the hammer before we get to Bora Bora."

"For which you're getting…"

"Fifty K."

"Interesting. I took a hundred in bearer bonds out of your safe, and I assume that's just the up-front."

Brock dropped his head and groaned into the pillow. "Fuck. Since when are you a safecracker?"

Dent snorted. "I've been on this boat two years. Think I wasted all that time? I've got passkeys for every door and the master code for every safe." The cruise company's website boasted about their state-of-the-art security. What it neglected to mention was the incredibly high turnover among the crew, many of whom were just using the ship to get around the world for their own purposes. All it took was finding one or two a year willing to share what they knew in exchange for a little extra severance package.

"So, you really are just a thief. Intravia said you hit the Miami office for a million in gold coins before you vanished."

It was two million, but there was no reason Brock needed to know that. "He also the one told you I was dead?"

Brock spoke more slowly, reliving it. "Yeah. They told us that nobody got away with that kind of thing and that you were gator food."

"Quite the cautionary tale."

"Yeah," said Brock. "Well, fuck, Dent, I'm not gonna tell anybody anything. I see why you braced me. You had to be sure the boys weren't onto you. I get that. But if you slipped their net, I say way to go. You just stay out of my way, and I'll stay out of yours. You can even keep half the Weinstein fee."

Dent shook his head, even though Brock couldn't really see him. "Sorry, Brock. You're going in the water."

He'd been watching Brock's body slowly relaxing as he'd gotten absorbed in their conversation. Now it tensed, so visibly that Dent almost shot him from pure reflex. "Fuck that! Don't you think killing me is going to foul up whatever little scam you've got going here? You think whatever name you're using is going to stand up if the cops really start looking?"

"What cops?" Dent asked. "We're in international waters. You got any idea how many people die or go missing on these boats every year? They get drunk and fall overboard. They eat like pigs and have heart attacks. Hell, there have been two suicides on this tub in the last four months. You think the company wants cops crawling all over the place? YouTube videos with customers complaining that they spent their vacation being interrogated?"

Brock's breathing was getting shallow. "They can't just ignore a shooting."

"I didn't say I was going to shoot you. I said you were going in the water." Dent stood up and, keeping the gun on Brock, walked over to slide open the door to the balcony. Cool, salty air flooded the room and the thin curtains billowed around him. "Besides, you just told me you're supposed to kill the Weinstein woman on the boat. If I'm sweating a body either way, I'll take the option where I don't also have to worry about you sneaking up behind me with a shrimp fork." He took a half step onto the balcony and risked a quick look both ways. Nobody around. It was the wee hours of the morning, and the *Majestic* was dozing.

He stepped back into the room and crossed quickly to the wall by the TV, leaving a clear path from the bed to the balcony. "Get up, Brock. Time to go swimming."

"Fuck you." Brock's voice was muffled by the pillow. His hands were clenched in the sheets. "You're gonna have to shoot me, you son of a bitch."

"You think I won't?" Dent asked. "How many people have you watched me kill?"

"You didn't know them." Brock's voice was rising, with a clear note of panic. Time to give him something else to think about.

"You think that helps you?" Dent said. "Let me ask you something, Brock. You remember our last job together? The husband and wife in Seattle?"

Silence for a second as Brock flipped through his memory bank. "Yeah. Big fucking house on the water. What about it?"

"You killed the dog," Dent said. "It wasn't a dangerous dog, and it wasn't part of the job. There was no reason in the world for that but meanness. I damn near shot you then."

"Well, you can shoot me now, you bastard."

"Turn over, Brock. Look at me."

There was a long pause. Slowly, Brock released his grip on the bedding and rolled onto his side. The light from the lamp fell on Dent's face now, and Brock did remember walking past him earlier in the day. He never would have pegged the man as Dent. The new face was harsher, more angular, the nose pronounced. The once brown hair was now an iron-gray buzz cut. But if he really looked, the eyes were the same, sharp and black and focused, and as steady as the gun in the right hand.

"I can shoot you," Dent said. "You yell or move an inch toward me or don't get up, and I will shoot you. And then, I'll wipe my prints and put the gun in your hand and take my chances, and yeah, it's a little riskier and a little more work for me, but you'll surely be one hundred percent dead."

He held up a finger. "Or," he said, "you get up and walk over to the balcony and go over the rail. And maybe somebody sees you, and they bring the boat around, or maybe you manage to catch on to something, or, hell, maybe you last until morning and get picked up by another ship. I'm not going to lie to you, Brock. It's a one in a hundred chance. But I'm giving it to you to make things a little easier for me."

He raised the gun and pointed it straight at Brock's forehead. "Your call," he said. "Make it right the fuck now."

Glaring, Brock rolled to get his feet on the floor and stood, reaching down awkwardly to pull his shorts back up to his waist without breaking his eye contact with Dent. Breathing through his nose, he kicked off his shoes. Then, he just stood for a moment, and Dent could see the thoughts like they were printed on his forehead, calculating the distance, how fast he could move, how Dent was holding the gun, and the times he'd seen Dent use guns before. Dent watched Brock think his way through it and come to the answer they both knew he would, and then, he waggled the gun minutely toward the balcony.

Brock moved. He took the first few steps painfully slowly, and then he did what Dent had been waiting for, what he himself would have done in Brock's place, the only slim possibility there was. He burst into sudden action, sprinting for the balcony door, aiming to vault the side railing and jump for the neighboring balcony, about twelve feet away. Dent waited until Brock began his leap, his hand stretching out for the railing and his whole body silhouetted in the starlight, and then shot him once in the head, seeing the spurt of blood that marked the hit clearly. Brock's momentum and the force of the bullet carried him up and over, and he was gone.

Dent stood still, waiting for a cry of alarm or terror. It had been a long time since he'd fired a gun and, even with the silencer, the sound echoing in the small cabin had seemed loud enough to wake the entire ship. It was why he'd only allowed himself one shot, trusting that the reflexes he'd spent years honing would still be there. One loud noise could be anything. A box dropped on a tile floor. A leftover firework from the party. People would wake, blink into the darkness for a minute, trying to figure what had happened, then roll over and forget about it.

When five minutes had passed, with no shouts from above and no pounding steps in the corridor, Dent went to the balcony and looked. Nobody on any of the other balconies. No curious heads above. No cries of man overboard, no lifeboats dropping on their lines. Just a spatter of blood on the railing. He went back into the room and found a clean t-shirt in Brock's closet. He got it wet under the bathroom faucet and used it to clean up. Then he wiped the gun, wrapped it in the shirt, and dropped it over the side. It could join Brock and all the rest of Dent's confessions, falling forever into the void as the *Majestic* skimmed away.

* * * *

Fourteen hours later, Dent was back on his own balcony with a fresh cooler of soda and a brand-new bottle of whiskey. It would be several days before the bottle would be ready to go overboard, but he'd also salvaged an empty from a recycling bin that would serve his purpose.

He was showered and well-rested and feeling, as he always had after killing, a need for company in bed tonight. It was a need easily met on a ship filled with vacationing women in the mood for a fling and accommodating young crew members in the mood for a sizable tip. He'd had several idle thoughts, over the course of the day, about the Weinstein woman, who was not at all bad looking for a woman with teenaged sons. Dent liked rich women. They knew what they wanted and didn't bother with hints. In a little while, he would go see if she was dining in the main ballroom again. In the meantime, there was a task to be done.

He had to wait for the sea to empty. There was a cargo ship passing by about a half mile to the *Majestic*'s port, a monstrous thing with boxcar-sized containers stacked six high above its deck. Not a soul could be seen on her, but a number of people were on this side of his ship, watching it glide by and waving as though there was somebody waving back. Soon enough, the ship would be gone, and the sunset would once again draw people to the opposite rail.

There had been a bad moment last night, when Brock had opened the door from the hallway, and the noise had startled Dent, dozing in the room's small closet, awake. He'd recovered quickly, but falling asleep in such a situation could have easily resulted in him, not Brock, floating down into the crushing nothingness. It wasn't the kind of mistake he would have made a few years ago. Maybe two years on the boat was making him soft in ways he couldn't afford to be.

Maybe he needed to think about ways to change that.

On the other hand, he passed the little test he set for himself, making a clean, accurate kill shot in the near dark, with a gun he'd never handled before, at a moment when a miss would have been disaster. Whatever that was, it wasn't soft. He wasn't quite a civilian yet.

The lights of the cargo ship were fading in the gathering twilight.

Dent picked up his pen.

Joseph S. Walker is a college literature teacher living in Indiana and an active member of the Mystery Writers of America. He began writing fiction in his forties. His stories have appeared in *Alfred Hitchcock Mystery Magazine* and a number of anthologies, including the recent *Life Is Short and Then You Die*, edited by Kelley Armstrong. He roots for the St. Louis Cardinals, plays chess very poorly, and has become a cat person against his better judgment. Follow him on Twitter (@JSWalkerAuthor) and visit his website at https://jsw47408.wixsite.com/website.

BOOK DROP

SARAH A. BRESNIKER

Stealing books from libraries is not an uncommon thing. You may have even done it, or at least thought about it. But stealing books for a library? Not so common.

Sure, there have probably been desperate librarians with shrunken budgets who have slipped a book or two or fifty off the shelf of the local Barnes & Noble. But whatever it was that started happening last month at my library was different.

The first time it happened, I was at the front desk. We're a modern library with self-checkout machines that read a tag inside every book. Staff is usually only involved when something goes wrong. One of our regulars, a mom with four young kids, was checking out a big pile of books and one of them wasn't triggering the sensor. I went over to help. When I took the book, I saw that it was a small volume, covered in faded green fabric. Before I could say anything, the mom, grabbing one child by the hood of his sweatshirt and trying to get another to put his legs into the stroller, said "Never mind, we have plenty of books. I don't even know where that one came from."

"I found it in with the Roald Dahl books," Emily, her second grader, said. "I thought it looked weird. It doesn't even have one of your labels. But you can keep it."

I thanked Emily and held onto the book. It was definitely not a Roald Dahl book. I'm not an expert on old books, but I am a librarian, and it appeared to be a first edition of Walt Whitman's *Leaves of Grass*.

When Sal, our local history librarian, came to relieve me on the desk, I showed her the book and told her what had happened. She immediately pulled the sleeve of her sweater down over her hand and grabbed the book from me with the covered hand.

"That shouldn't be on our shelf! You shouldn't even be touching it!" she said.

I knew that, plus I thought I deserved some credit for rescuing it from Emily and her little brothers. Sal held the book and sat down at the desk, so I went back to my office and stayed there until my next shift on the desk. When I came out, Sal was wearing the white cotton gloves she uses to handle historical documents and there were two other old books, piled on top of the first one. "Something strange is going on," was all Sal said.

We decided to go check the stacks, looking for books that didn't belong. Within 15 minutes, we found five more books that weren't ours. A quick internet search showed that most titles had gone at auction for over $1,000 recently. Some for quite a bit more. "I think we need to talk to Nora," I said.

Nora is our boss, the head librarian of the Pacific Grove Public Library. She is the smartest person I have ever met. And the largest. And the laziest. She is well over six feet tall, and half that wide. She reads constantly and seems to retain it all. She's a great librarian, but she's also much more, because we are not like other libraries. Yes, you can check out books and use the public computers. But you can also have any question answered, no questions asked. Was your grandma really your grandpa's first wife? Where did your sister disappear to? Who murdered your next-door neighbor? We've answered all of those reference questions and more.

But that's a story for another time. Suffice it to say, Sal and I are used to finding answers. It's what we do. And like Nora, we have skills. Sal never forgets a face, and she can tail a person for weeks without being noticed. She's a woman of average height, average weight, indeterminate age. Her hair is somewhere between dishwater blonde and mousy brown, and her clothes tend to match her hair. People underestimate her, or don't even notice her, and she uses that to her advantage.

Me? My hair is blonde, usually in a ponytail. My eyes are blue and not hidden behind glasses. I'm not much for sitting still, and though I can't match names and faces the way Sal does, I can generally repeat back anything I hear. I've worked for Nora for a while now. I even live in her house, in my own suite of rooms. That comes with some downsides, but rents here are high, and the upside is that Mitzie, Nora's chef, is in charge of my meals.

When Sal and I entered Nora's office, she was sitting behind her old oak desk in her custom-made leather chair, reading Toni Morrison's *Beloved.* Sal set down the pile of books we had found on Nora's desk. Nora's eyes moved slowly over the bindings. "You found these on our shelves," she said.

Of course she already knew. Even though she rarely leaves her office, she always somehow knows exactly what is going on. "What should we do?" I asked.

Nora set her book down and closed her eyes, saying nothing for a full ten seconds. "Has anyone made an inquiry regarding these books?"

"No," I replied. "But they're not our books. Someone is sneaking them onto our shelves. It's weird."

"It may be 'weird,' but it is not a question for us to answer at this time. Arlie, put them in the safe for now, and if you find any others, store them there, as well."

I unlocked the safe and placed the books on the top shelf. Nora had gone back to reading, so we left her office and went back to work without saying a word. But I was pretty sure that Sal was as bothered as I was.

We were busy, but we kept finding books that weren't ours. The rest of our week got even busier. Along with our usual book clubs and story times, our biggest fundraising event of the year was coming up on Saturday and the volunteers were descending.

The Picnic in the Grove has been an annual event for at least 50 years. Originally, it was held in the Butterfly Grove, with tables heaped with homemade casseroles and jello salads. The current Picnic in the Grove is not a picnic, and not in a grove. It is a fully catered, five-course meal held in the library, complete with elaborate decorations, live music, and costumes. The theme this year was Bedtime Stories, and each table had a different book as its theme. Our regulars like to get creative with their ideas.

The next chance Sal and I had to talk was Friday morning. When I went into the break room, Sal was there, going back and forth between typing furiously into her phone and scribbling on a legal pad.

"There are at least 40 rare book collectors between Big Sur and Seaside. Including, of course, Nora," she said, before I could even sit down. "Plus, the Henry Miller Library, the Carmel Heritage Society, and our Pacific Grove Historical Society. They also have rare books in their collections."

"Anything reported stolen?"

"Not that I could find."

"Okay, so our suspects are basically anyone who walks into the library," I replied. She nodded, and I sat down next to her to enjoy my coffee with an almond croissant that Mitzie had made. "Could it be one collector getting back at another?" I asked. "Some kind of rare book beef?"

"Hmm. They can get competitive. Some will go to extraordinary lengths to keep a book out of another collector's hands. But I haven't seen any of them here lately."

"Maybe we're on a library-themed reality show!" This was from Adam, one of our part-time staff, who was walking past. "Have you seen anyone wearing glasses that could have a hidden camera in them?"

At least it was an idea, but Sal ignored him. "What are we supposed to do with these books?" she asked. "They're valuable. What if they were stolen? It makes me nervous to be responsible for them. Especially the ones that could just be sitting on the shelves, waiting for a two-year old to chew on!"

Sal is usually a calm, unflappable rock. But she's very protective of books. The rest of that day passed quickly with two school tours and volunteers for the gala streaming in and out. I imagined that everyone who came in with a backpack or bag was a suspect, but no one actually did anything suspicious.

On Saturday, the library was closed to prepare for the event that evening. After breakfast, I took the opportunity to go for a long run. As I finished, I wound back through town and stopped in at Olde Tyme Sweets for a scoop of Swedish fish, my usual reward after a long workout. Tim, the owner, was handing out samples of Zotz. When there was a momentary lull, Tim's perpetual smile drooped. "I expect kids to be brats sometimes," he said, "but for some reason, I'm still surprised when it's the adults. A gang came in wearing their fancy golf gear, demanding whiskey. 'That's our kind of candy,' one of them said, at least four times. Even his friends didn't really laugh. Then, the women were debating the BMI of a three-year-old. What is wrong with people?"

"That sounds like the same group that came into the library yesterday. All too beautiful to be natural? Young?"

He nodded, and I continued.

"They came in because one of the women wanted me to charge her phone. To keep it safe behind the desk and text her husband if it rang. When I refused, she actually pouted. On their way out, her husband kept pulling books off shelves, saying 'Dude! People still read books! Like, why?' It took everything I had not to punch him."

Tim grimaced. "Yeah, that sounds like the same group, all right. If they're that awful in a candy store or a library, I can't imagine what they're like in private."

When I got home, it was time to prepare for the gala. Our table's theme was *Alice's Adventures in Wonderland*, and I was assigned the role of Alice. I do have blonde hair and tend to go down the rabbit hole, so I guess the costume fit. Nora was the Queen of Hearts, Sal the Mad Hatter, and the part-time staff who completed our table were card soldiers. Sitting down to dinner was going to be interesting for them.

It's always fun to see the library transformed for the gala. We entered through an arch covered in giant flowers made from the pages of old books, and huge star lanterns hung from the ceiling. Each table was unique. Ours, of course, was a mad hatter's tea party, with a giant centerpiece made of topsy-turvy teacups in gloriously clashing patterns.

I mingled and charmed, knowing that was my job for the evening. Sal isn't big on small talk, and Nora prefers to sit and let people come to her. She really did look like a queen with her Elizabethan gown and a ruffled collar surrounding her giant head, sitting in the elevated reading nook that held the bar. From there, she could see everything, and everyone could see her.

Some costumes were obvious, but others I couldn't figure out until Nora rang a bell and everyone sorted into their perspective tables. Individually, our book sale volunteers made almost no impact. Each wore a simple monochromatic outfit in a neutral color. Once they went to their table, I got the joke. Fifty Shades of Gray! From nearly black to almost white, they made a colorless rainbow. And looking closer, they each had a different implement of torture. Handcuffs, a whip, a blindfold, other items I was afraid to google. There were smirks and gasps of recognition when they gathered around their table.

I knew already that Lyle Rowan would be there. That Lyle Rowan. Trust fund baby, former Navy SEAL, guy TMZ likes to showcase from time to time. He grew up here and comes back whenever the mood strikes. He had texted me the day before, but he wouldn't tell me his costume.

I scanned the tables trying to guess which one was his. Before I could narrow it down, laughter from the entrance made me turn my head. A broad-shouldered man in a white terrycloth hooded sleeper topped with pointy ears and a crooked crown marched in, waving a silver scepter. He was followed by a parade of round-headed monsters, dancing and roaring. *Where the Wild Things Are*, of course. That was Lyle. And for some of his family members, their costumes weren't much of a stretch either.

As they wound past our table, Lyle gave me a wink. We have a long history together, most of it good. Pacific Grove is a pretty quiet place, but I always know something interesting will happen when Lyle's in town. On the surface, well, on the surface he's gorgeous, but also rich, spoiled, and privileged. Usually a bad combination, but he's surprised me often enough that I keep coming back.

Once Lyle and his family of monsters found their seats, Nora gave a quick speech and the meal was served. Lively chatter floated up from the tables, and the photographer had everyone hamming it up as their characters. Even Nora nearly smiled when he asked her to yell "Off with their heads!" for the camera.

Amidst the revelry, I saw a guy in sweats trying to get through the front door. He held what were clearly McDonald's bags! I went over to help Milly, the volunteer who was on door duty.

"What's up, Milly?" I asked.

"This gentleman claims to be some kind of 'dasher'? And says someone from this address ordered McDonald's to be delivered?" she said, as though the words didn't quite make sense. Milly doesn't have a smart phone. She prefers to use the library's public computers to check her emails and print out the photos her family posts on Facebook.

Just as I was about to question the man, a short, stocky guy in a brown track suit with reindeer horns on his head ran up. "Dominic?" he asked the delivery guy. "That's our order. Did you remember ketchup?"

The reindeer grabbed the bags before the dasher could answer and waved them over his head as he made his way back to his table. Milly just stared. I looked to see where he had come from. He was one of eight people in the lamest reindeer costumes possible, four men in track suits like his, four women in tiny brown shorts and tank tops, all with plastic reindeer horns on their heads. The other two members of his party were a tall skinny guy in a red tracksuit with a cheap felt Santa hat on his head and a gorgeous young redhead in the tiniest flannel nightie I had ever seen, with a matching green flannel triangle tied around her hair.

"*The Night Before Christmas*," Sal said to me as I sat down.

"Drunk Santa, Hot Ma in her Kerchief, and the eight Douchey Reindeer," I said, nodding. "Who are they? They seem kind of familiar."

"Do you remember Mr. Willowby? The one who died last fall? He lived in that big house behind the butterfly grove."

"I think I know the house, but I don't remember the name. Did he come to the library?" I left most of that history stuff to Sal. She's much better at it than I am and enjoys it more.

"No, he hadn't really left the house much in the last decade or so. But he always bought a table for this event and had the principal at the high school offer it to teachers who promised to be creative with their costumes."

"That gang doesn't look like they're trying very hard," I said, confused.

"No, those aren't teachers," Sal replied. "Mr. Willowby had already paid for the table before he passed away. I think that's his grandson and his friends. I know Milly had tried to reach him to let him know about the tradition, but she never heard back. I guess he decided to use the tickets himself."

As she was finishing her sentence, I felt a fuzzy arm wrap around my shoulders from behind. "Can I have the first dance?" Lyle whispered in my ear.

Of course he could. I leaned back into his wide, firm chest for a moment. As I did, I saw Nora beckoning to him. Lyle's contribution to the event every year was to find a band or DJ to provide the music. We never knew who it would be in advance, but they were always good, sometimes famous, and the mystery helped sell tickets.

Lyle hopped up onto the stage and motioned for everyone to quiet down. With his usual wit and charm, he introduced one of the hottest DJs in Miami, whom none of our guests had ever heard of. A small young man walked out to sit behind various types of electronic gadgets and turntables.

He looked up for a moment, nodded to the crowd, and dropped the needle on the first record. From that point on, he didn't stop moving and the library vibrated with sound. Even Nora's head bobbed slightly to the rhythm, and I'd swear I saw her foot tap once or twice.

Lyle pulled me onto the dance floor and we bounced like Wild Things. I forgot about everything else for a moment, until a crash that could be heard over the music brought me back to my surroundings. Drunk Santa was wrapping the tablecloth from his table around his shoulders like a cape. Of course, his cape had, moments before, been covered in dishes, wine glasses, and empty McDonalds wrappers. The crash we heard was all of these items (well, not the wrappers) hitting the floor and shattering into tiny pieces. Hot Ma screamed and the DJ stopped abruptly. Ma was covered in red wine, and possibly blood.

Lyle rushed to the table and grabbed Drunk Santa. Nora rolled out of her chair and followed him at an impressive pace. I went over to Hot Ma and convinced her to follow me in the opposite direction. The reindeer all scurried toward the exit.

Once I had gotten her into the employee restroom, Hot Ma stopped screaming. "Are you okay?" I asked.

She looked herself over. "Mostly just drowned in wine," she said. "But I think my knee is bleeding."

I looked closer. Her knee had been cut, probably by broken glass. I handed her some toilet paper and she held it to her cut. "This is why I can't have nice things," she said, more to herself than to me.

I looked at her questioningly. "My husband," she said. "Santa. He thinks shocking people is the same thing as being clever. It really isn't."

I smiled. "I'm just glad you're okay. I'm Arlie, by the way. I'm a librarian."

"Thank you. I'm Avi. Well, Avonlea, actually. My husband thinks my real name sounds like I was named after cheap perfume, so he calls me Avi."

"From *Anne of Green Gables*," I said. "One of my favorites."

"My parents too," she said. "They were librarians. It's the reason I convinced everyone to come tonight, when I saw the invitation at the house. I'm sorry. I should have known it was a bad idea. This library is so beautiful, though. I just had to see it all done up."

"You don't need to apologize. You're the one who took the hit. I have some emergency clothes in my office. Would you like to borrow them?"

She agreed, so I grabbed the leggings and sweatshirt from my desk. She cleaned up in the restroom and came out scrubbed and dry, looking like a different person with her hair pulled back and her makeup rinsed off. "I'm so embarrassed," she said. "I can't even look at myself in the mirror."

When we returned to the party, the mood had changed. The DJ was playing what sounded like whale calls, combined with a pan flute, doing what he could to calm everyone down. The lights were up and caution tape had been strung around Santa's table to keep anyone from stepping on the shards of glass. Santa and the reindeer were nowhere to be seen.

Lyle came over and asked Avonlea if she needed a ride home. "Or somewhere else," he added. "I have a driver, and Asilomar can always find a room for me, if I need one. Your husband and friends already left in an Uber."

"Thanks," she said. "I'll take you up on the driver, but I'd better get home. He isn't always like this. He just gets carried away in front of his friends sometimes."

I purposely kept from making eye contact with Lyle. This was a story we'd heard before, but we needed to respect her decision.

"Thank you, really. This whole event was just lovely, and I'm sorry we messed it up."

Sal was deep in conversation with Millie in the lobby. As we walked by, I saw her pause and stare at Avonlea, like she was matching her face with something in her memory bank. Lyle had texted his driver, who arrived within minutes. Avonlea waved to us as she got into the car, and we made our way back to the remnants of the gala.

"I remember her husband from grade school," Lyle said after she had left. "He was a jerk even then. Third generation wealth. It truly brings out the worst in people."

I looked at him, quizzically. "As you would know, rich boy," I said.

"Oh, but I'm fifth generation wealthy," he said with a grin. "Completely different."

I rolled my eyes at him as we went over to talk to Nora. She was back in her chair, drinking a root beer straight from the bottle with her eyes closed.

"So," I said to her, "What now?"

"What do you mean, what now? Has our assistance been requested?"

As usual, she was right. Avonlea had specifically refused any help. It just drove me crazy to see someone like Drunk Santa get away with ruining the night for everyone.

"Luckily," Nora said, "There are no refunds on tickets. No matter what."

With that, she slowly got up from her chair and went out the front door. I swear, sometimes all she seems to care about is money. I went over to Sal and Millie, who were cleaning up the registration table. "She's been here before," Sal said.

"What? Yeah, I think they were the ones who wanted to charge their phone. But they left as soon as I said no," I replied.

"No, before that. In the 300s. The legal section. But when I asked if she needed help, she just shook her head and scurried away. That happens from time to time. People are embarrassed to admit that they need legal help. And now that I think about it, we did find a first-edition Steinbeck in with the statistics books the next day. That's in the same row."

Could it be her? Mystery solved? But why? And where did she get the books? I was feeling my adrenaline crash, and my mind felt hazy. Lyle and I helped clean up, and then we went back to Nora's so I could get out of my Alice dress. It felt good to get into some sweats. Lyle insisted that his Max onesie was the most comfortable thing he owned and kept it on. Even in those ridiculous pjs, he was hot.

Mitzie, Nora's chef, was still up, so we filled her in on the events of the evening, while she pulled together a minor feast. I told both of them about the mystery of the books. Before long, Mitzie went up to bed, and Lyle and I sat in silence.

"I blame you," I finally said. "Nothing ever happens here, until you show up."

He looked at me through his thick, dark lashes. He knew they were my weakness. "I've heard the stories," he said. "You manage to find plenty of action, even when I'm not around. You're just frustrated because Nora has been holding you back."

He was right, and there was nothing I could do about it tonight. "I can't help you with that, but I'm willing to sacrifice my body to provide you with a distraction…." he offered.

"Always the martyr." I grinned as he tiptoed up the two sets of stairs to my rooms, and I raced to follow.

I knew, before I opened my eyes in the morning that he was gone. Nora would prefer to think that men rarely entered her house, and Lyle likes to indulge her fantasy. He had left a note on the pillow that said he was on his way to the opening of the Invictus Games with Prince Harry. I grabbed my phone, texted "Say hi to Meghan for me," and then got up.

Mitzie was in the kitchen with a video playing on the iPad she keeps on the counter. She shushed me and pointed to the screen as I came in. A man I recognized as Drunk Santa was leaning back on a sofa with a glass of whiskey sloshing in his hand, mumbling. It was hard to make out what he was saying at first.

"They're all idiots, honey! All of them. They think they're so smart, but I've sold that same piece of property to 50 different people! Even dear old Grandpa couldn't come up with such a brilliant idea."

He went on like this for a while, detailing all of the people he'd fooled, until he appeared to pass out, his drink spilling down the front of his t-shirt. Then, a reporter came on. "This video was released anonymously to Instagram early this morning, along with scans of documents, detailing what appears to be one of the largest pyramid schemes since Madoff. The man in the video is Max Willowby III, grandson and sole heir of Pacific Grove philanthropist and developer Maxwell Willowby, who passed away last year."

"Apparently, the police went to the house to arrest him this morning," Mitzie said. "He was still passed out on the couch, and there was no one else there. The place was a wreck. Antiques and fancy rugs trashed beyond saving. Poor Mr. Willowby! It's a blessing he's not alive to see this. He was a kind soul, but he had a weakness for that nasty grandson of his."

"He was a collector?" I asked.

"Oh yes, and a good friend of Nora's, back when he still left the house. They shared many interests."

At that moment, there was a knock on the door. I opened it and Sal burst in. "I just left the library," she said. "I was getting notifications that the book drop wasn't working. When I got there, the book-drop room was overloaded. With even more rare books! So many it jammed up the system, and there were more just sitting out front. It took me five trips with a book cart to get them all inside."

Mitzie replayed the video for Sal and we all watched in silence. Just as it finished, Nora came in, looking surprisingly refreshed after the events of last night.

"Sal, I hear we've received some amazing donations," she said. "Combined with everything we've received this week, I'm sure they'll more than make up for the money we lost out on last night, when everyone left before the silent auction."

So, all of this was Avonlea? But last night she seemed resigned to her marriage. What had changed? Nora acted as though all of this was business as usual and sat down to her breakfast, which began with eggs benedict and continued through two cheese Danishes, hash browns, strawberries and cream, and three cups of coffee, two lumps of sugar each.

As the weeks went on, the story unfolded. Drunk Santa was a young Bernie Madoff, just not as smart. Once the feds started looking, the paper trail was more like a neon arrow pointing to his guilt. Avonlea, however, was nowhere to be seen. She had divorce papers served on him the day after the gala, and she hadn't been seen or heard from since.

Mr. Willowby's house and what was left of his collections were sold, and the profits went to his grandson's victims. Nora had me sell most of the books we had received. Although she would never admit to the connection, the full amount, minus our usual take for the silent auction, went to the GoFundMe that had been set up for the victims. I'm in charge of the accounts, so I knew this, and she knew that I knew, but we never talked about it.

A few weeks later, a courier showed up at the library with a box for me with no return address. Back in the breakroom, I opened it up. Inside were the leggings and sweatshirt that I had given Avonlea. A postcard fell to the floor as I shook them out. It was a photograph of a sunset over a beautiful, windswept beach. Somewhere tropical? No, I turned it over to see it was from Prince Edward Island. The note on the back said, "Thank you so much for lending me your clothes and providing me with the right words at the right time. With love, Anne."

I stared at the card. I didn't remember giving her any advice. I had consciously bit my tongue to keep from giving her advice. Then I looked at the sweatshirt I had lent her. It was from our summer reading challenge the year before. "Read Better, Be Better," it said on the front.

Sarah A. Bresniker is a former librarian and paralegal who lives in Northern California. A lifelong lover of mysteries, she is finally taking the time to write her own.

THE LAST LAUGH

LORI ROBERTS HERBST

When we found Spanky curled in a fetal position in the back seat of his yellow clown car, Paloma and I assumed he was sleeping off another bender. Wouldn't have been the first time. There was a reason Spanky didn't need to wear a plastic red nose like the rest of the clowns.

I tugged at the end of my lime-green tie and took a deep breath, inhaling the familiar odor of elephant dung. I opened the car door, stuck my foot inside, and prodded Spanky with my floppy blue shoe. Not a whimper or a moan. I squeezed through the door and shook Spanky's shoulder.

"Up and at 'em, pal. Gotta get ready for tonight's show."

No response. A purple hue radiated beneath his white makeup. His thick tongue protruded through painted lips. I slid my finger under his nose. No air puffed from his nostrils.

Guess Spanky hadn't passed out, after all.

I wriggled out of the car and turned to Paloma in her sequined costume, auburn hair piled atop her head. She lifted a well-plucked eyebrow and raked a set of purple fingernails across her neatly trimmed beard.

"Is he—?"

"Can't be sure. Gonna need some help getting him outta the car."

I clutched Spanky's armpits. Paloma hurried around the front of the vehicle and opened the opposite door. She wedged her hands against Spanky's nether regions, shoving as I tugged, until we dislodged his six-foot frame.

Once Spanky lay prone on the sawdust-covered arena floor, I dropped to one tweed-covered knee and dragged a finger across the greasepaint that covered his neck. When I located his carotid artery, its stillness confirmed what I had already deduced. We had a dead clown on our hands.

I wiped white goo from my finger onto the back of my tie and leaned closer. A jagged smear across his jugular interrupted the smooth makeup on his neck. I dabbed at the smeared line with my floral hanky, uncovering an angry red ligature mark.

Spanky the Clown had been strangled.

Sitting back on my heels, I spotted a length of tightrope snaking from beneath the clown car. The murder weapon, I presumed.

An oft-told circus joke popped into my head. How do you kill a clown? Go for the juggler. Ba da boom.

I chastised myself. How could I think such things when a man was dead? Was I in shock? Or had I simply developed a sense of humor as sour as the frown painted onto my face?

Rain pinged against the tin roof covering the arena. I shut my eyes and listened to the rhythmic sound, glad it wasn't sleet. Sleet would keep the crowds away, and our paychecks depended on crowds.

Pickles & Peanuts Traveling Circus was preparing for the final show of our annual three-day gig at the Sunflower Fairgrounds in Hazard, Kansas. And now my partner, the only other clown in our act, was dead. I'd have to carry the comic load on my own tonight. Not an easy task, especially since I was the sad clown in our duo.

Paloma's shadow fell across Spanky's body, and I struggled to my feet.

"Dead," I told her, pointing at Spanky's neck. "Murdered."

She nodded and hugged her arms across her body, causing generous breasts to bulge over the seam of her low-cut costume. I squirmed, and the plastic daisy affixed to my lapel squirted an embarrassing trickle of water.

Lifting my gaze back to Paloma's face, I was surprised to see tears in her eyes. I hadn't pegged Paloma as the emotional type.

"How well did you know Spanky?"

She averted her eyes and shrugged. "Not well. Just in the...you know... biblical sense."

"You've been sleeping with him?"

She rolled her eyes. "Of course. He's a clown. Everyone knows about clowns. Just look at his big feet. You know what they say—"

I cut her off, the heat rising in my face. "I'm a clown. How come you and I never...?"

She glanced down at my feet. Despite the oversized shoes, they measured a mere size eight, the low end of average.

"Oh," I said. My lips curved downward, mirroring the painted red arc surrounding my mouth.

Paloma placed a gentle hand on my shoulder. "Besides, Buster, you're a sad clown. No woman wants to look up during her moment of passion and see a frown. It kills the mood."

The word "kill" brought me back to reality. I fished the phone from the pocket of my baggy pants and dialed 9-1-1. When I told the dispatcher Spanky was dead, she said she'd send in the cavalry.

Even so, I didn't hold high hopes anyone would expend much effort toward solving Spanky's murder. Circus folks fell on the low end of society's hierarchy. After a cursory investigation, the police would dump Spanky's death into the unsolved files. The circus would pack up and move to our next stop, hire another clown, and forget all about poor Spanky.

Word spreads fast through a tight-knit community, so I wasn't surprised to see the circus family gathered near the clown car, silent and respectful. Paloma regularly assumed the role of caretaker, so now she went to each of them. Jeffrey the Juggler took her hand solemnly in his nimble fingers. Our newest crew member, a skinny guy named Jimmy, dropped his eyes when Paloma approached, no doubt reluctant to display his emotions, but his hand rested on Paloma's bare shoulder a few seconds too long for my liking. Twin acrobats, the Winged Wagners, pulled Paloma into a three-way embrace. The animal trainer, the ticket seller, the concessionaire—Paloma graced each of them with words of comfort.

My nature was more cynical than compassionate. As I studied the faces of the assemblage, it occurred to me that one of them might actually be Spanky's killer. Years of watching *Dateline* had taught me that the people closest to the victim were the most likely suspects. Had some circus family squabble resulted in the clown's death? I lifted my phone and shot a surreptitious photo of the small congregation. Just in case.

Our manager, a squatty bald man who called himself Tiger, plowed through the door and stomped across the sawdust, stopping beside me. He chewed on the cigar butt clenched between his teeth and glared at the dead clown. "We got a performance in three hours," he said to the group. "Show must go on, right? Spanky woulda wanted it that way. That's all I got for a pep talk. Now scram."

* * * *

That night, I honored Spanky by painting an extra tear onto my sad face. The show indeed went on, followed by a hundred others in dozens of cities over the course of a year. At first, I hounded the police for weekly updates, then monthly. After half a year, the cops stopped taking my calls. As I had predicted, the case grew cold, and Paloma and I resigned ourselves to the fact that Spanky's killer had gotten away with murder.

For a while, we went through replacement clowns like popcorn. First was Pasty, who lasted three weeks before deciding that even a romp in Paloma's RV didn't compensate for the stress of life in a traveling circus. The next hire, Beanbag, made it two months before dumping us in Omaha for a mascot gig with a minor league baseball team. A couple of others followed, until finally, we got lucky—or should I say Paloma got lucky—when we stumbled onto Tickles, a happy clown with a resume as impressive as his huge feet. Despite simmering jealousy over the nightly rocking of Paloma's RV, I liked Tickles. His wide grin and goofy antics caused children—and even adults—to squeal in laughter. He became the yin to my yang, and we developed a top-notch act. Months passed, and Spanky's memory faded.

But I never again felt comfortable inside that yellow clown car.

Now, a year after his murder, Pickles & Peanuts Traveling Circus had landed back at the Sunflower Fairgrounds for our annual Christmas extravaganza, complete with reindeer and a rented Santa, who reeked of whiskey.

And, as if it were a bad movie sequel, I'd stumbled across another dead clown.

This one hadn't been strangled. In fact, with his painted grin unmarred and his pointy, pom-topped hat snugly in place, I thought at first he might simply be resting. On the floor of the cage. But the bloody gash gouged into Tickles's torso told a different story. A low growl drew my attention to Old Nelly, our circus lion, now poised atop his red and yellow platform. He casually licked a paw, as he watched me through narrowed eyes.

What was the lion thinking? That clown sure tasted funny. Ba da boom.

I tugged on the cage door. Locked. Then, I spotted the key in the sawdust, several feet outside the bars.

Poor Tickles. He hadn't stood a chance.

A door slammed behind me, and Paloma entered the arena. I hurried toward her, spreading my arms to block the grisly scene.

She peeked around me, eyes wide. "Is that—?"

"'Fraid so." I maneuvered her toward the exit and away from the bloody crime scene. Behind us, the big cat emitted a satisfied roar. Paloma shuddered.

I led her out of the dimly lit arena and into the bright sunshine of the winter afternoon. A few circus workers milled about the grounds, their pace unhurried, since the day's only performance was still four hours away. Paloma shuffled forward like a bearded zombie. When one of the mechanics happened by, I grabbed his arm and whispered in his ear. "Freddo, call the police. Then, stand guard in front of the arena door. Nobody goes in."

"What's goin' on?" Though the turnover rate was high in a traveling circus, Freddo was a Pickles & Peanuts veteran with a long memory. I saw suspicion cross his face.

"Tickles is dead," I said. "Lion cage. I wanna get Paloma back to her RV. Can you handle this?"

He nodded, wiping his hands on a work towel. "Go on, then. I got it under control."

I prodded Paloma forward, my floppy shoes slapping against the dirt, as we headed toward the housing quarters. One of the Winged Wagners—I wasn't sure which one—pedaled by on a unicycle, raising her hand in greeting. A black and white circus cat scampered across our path. As we passed the wooden ticket booth at the fairground's outskirts, I noticed the local rent-a-Santa we'd hired, slouched in a rusty folding chair, slurping from a mug. I doubted he was drinking coffee.

"Hey, buddy." I glanced at him as we passed. "If anyone comes looking for us, we'll be in Paloma's trailer."

"I bet you will," he said with a smirk. "Ho. Ho. HO."

Paloma froze. "Did he just call me a Ho?"

I tightened my arm around her shoulder and propelled her toward the RV. "He's Santa. It's a traditional greeting. Don't be paranoid."

She took a deep breath. I felt the muscles in her shoulders relax. Still, when I looked back at the leer on Santa's face, I knew he'd meant every single Ho.

* * * *

Despite our year-long friendship, Paloma had never invited me into her love nest. While she washed up, I stood in the living room, noting the beat-up floral loveseat, stacks of empty pizza boxes, and beer cans scattered everywhere. A rumpled queen-sized bed dominated the left side of the trailer. Images of Paloma flailing about with her big-footed companions flooded my brain. I pushed them aside. This was no time to indulge my green monster.

To my right sat a kitchenette, complete with a small coffee maker. I filled the carafe with water and spooned grounds into the filter. While the coffee brewed, I sat on the loveseat and picked up a book that lay open on the rickety coffee table. Victor Hugo's *Les Misérables*. In French. Paloma was a multi-faceted creature.

She emerged from the bathroom, her beard dewy with water droplets. Squeezing onto the loveseat, she leaned in to me. "You're sure it was Tickles?" I nodded. "Damn." She sighed. "He was okay."

I glanced at the bed. "Yeah. I didn't know him like you did, but he was a good guy. A friend. Knew how to make people laugh."

"Could it have been an accident?"

I raised my eyebrows. "You mean, did he wander into the lion cage by mistake? The door was locked, Paloma. The key had been tossed out of reach. I doubt Tickles did that himself."

"I suppose not." She pursed her lips. "He was murdered then. Just like Spanky."

The coffee maker beeped. I filled two mugs and handed one to Paloma. We sipped and contemplated the fate of the two clowns, until a knock rattled the RV door. I opened it to find two men in dark suits and sunglasses. Both looked to be twelve. Either they were rookie detectives or late trick-or-treaters dressed up as the Men in Black.

The one on my left held up his credentials. "Detective Bronson," he said. "And this is Officer Walker."

"Buster," I said. Paloma moved in behind me, and I tilted my head toward her. "Paloma."

Bronson looked me up and down, settling his gaze on my nose. "You always dress this way?"

"Show today," I said. "I get ready early, in case any kiddos come on-site. Kind of like Santa. Don't want to ruin the magic." I glanced toward the ticket booth, but our drunk Santa had disappeared. Off to get a refill, I expected.

"You found the body, right?" I nodded. "Mind if we talk? Just take a minute."

"Sure. Want to come in?"

He looked past me at the RV's grimy interior and wrinkled his nose. "Why don't you and your…lady friend…step outside?"

I moved back to let Paloma precede me. The four of us stood in a circle. The sunshine reflected off the sequins sewn across Paloma's skimpy costume. Bronson's sunglasses paused on her beard, fell to her ample cleavage, and rose again to the beard. I sighed and waited. Every man who met Paloma passed through the same steps. I knew from experience there was no use trying to converse before the process had run its course.

Bronson eventually lifted his gaze to me. "Just wanted to let you know where we stand on the dead clown."

"Tickles," Paloma said, glaring at the cop. "He had a name. Show some respect."

Bushy eyebrows rose above his sunglasses. "Sorry, ma'am. Tickles."

"Thank you. He was a real person—" Her voice caught, and she wrapped her arms around herself, amplifying her bosom. The detective's eyes darted downward again.

He shifted from one foot to the other. "Anyhow, our initial findings lead us to conclude this was an accident. A tragic, gruesome accident."

I shook my head so hard my wig jiggled. "You're kidding. Are you saying Tickles accidentally got eaten by a lion?"

He nodded. "No sign of a struggle. Maybe he entered the cage to feed the big guy. Maybe he was just screwing around. Either way, we think the clown…." He glanced at Paloma. "Tickles…entered the cage on his own. Then…well…"

"Did you see the key a couple of yards away? How could the door accidentally lock and the key accidentally fly out of reach?"

Bronson shot a sidelong look at his partner and shrugged. "Suicide, then. Locked himself in and tossed the key to keep from backing out."

"Suicide by lion?" Paloma said through gritted teeth. "Ridiculous. You just don't want to waste your time on a clown in a traveling circus." She looked at me, eyes blazing. "It's just like Spanky. They're not going to do anything at all."

I narrowed my eyes and turned to the detectives. "You know about Spanky, right? Murdered right here one year ago. Never solved. Does that seem like a coincidence to you?"

I could see by the flex of his jaw that he was unaccustomed to being challenged. "We know about the other clown. And yes, in spite of what you see on TV detective shows, coincidences do happen. But just so you know, we're only talking to you as a courtesy. Now, we're done. If the crime scene tech finds evidence to the contrary, we'll let you know."

He swung on dusty black wingtips and started to leave. After a brief pause, he turned back and faced Paloma. "Off the subject, but are you a guy or a gal?" He pointed from her beard to her chest. "Is that fake, or are those?"

I caught Paloma's wrist as she reared back to swing at the detective. When he turned his gaze to me, the image in his sunglasses showed a sad clown's frown beneath a menacing glare. Horror movie fodder. Walker smirked and loped off after his partner.

"By the way," Paloma called after them, "they're real—the beard and the boobs. And they're spectacular."

* * * *

Back inside, Paloma paced the small confines of the RV. "Two dead clowns. Same circus, same town. Is it some local who just doesn't like freaks and geeks? Or have we stumbled across a serial clown killer?"

I shrugged. "It's definitely more than a coincidence."

She mused for a moment, then gasped. "Buster, you could be in danger."

"Nah, I doubt I'd be a target."

"Why not?"

I hesitated. I had a hypothesis, but I didn't want to make her feel bad. Still, the cops clearly weren't going to investigate, so it was up to us. "Don't take this wrong, but what do the two dead guys have in common?"

She blinked slowly, like I was a nitwit. "They're clowns."

"What else?"

She considered, and then, her eyes widened in comprehension. "I slept with both of them." Her voice cracked. "You think I got them killed? Because I had a few rolls in the hay with them?"

More than a few, I reflected. "Not exactly. Hear me out. What are the usual motives for murder?" I held up a finger. "Number one: money. But circus clowns rarely qualify as members of the one percent. Two: power. Not many people vying to be top clown at the Pickles & Peanuts Traveling Circus. That leaves number three. Love. Or at least lust. Is it possible you've left a jilted lover in your wake? That, for some sad sack out there, you're the one that got away?"

Her face paled, and her hand flew to her chest. Despite my best intentions, my eyes followed it and lingered longer than they should have. My phone buzzed with a text, dragging me from my momentary reverie. As I reached into my pocket to retrieve it, Paloma's phone beeped from across the room. We both had the same message: Asshole cops cancelled tonight's show. Pack your stuff. Rolling out at 6 a.m.

The clock on my phone read 4:57 p.m. That gave us just thirteen hours to nab this killer.

But if my suspicions proved true, it wouldn't even take that long.

I scrolled through the photos on my phone and showed Paloma the shot taken a year ago of the circus family gathered together, following Spanky's death. "Did you go out with any of these men? Even a casual date?"

She concentrated on one face, then the next, shaking her head at each. When she reached the end of the row, she bit her bottom lip and pointed at the screen. "This guy… Jimmy, I think. One of the floor crew, right?" I looked at the man. Just who I had expected. "I didn't go out with him—not a clown, you know, and way too scrawny—but he hounded me for at least a month. I finally told him I'd hooked up with Spanky, that we were exclusive." She looked up at me, her blue eyes round and shining. "Jimmy quit the circus after that show. I never saw him again."

"But you have seen him again, several times over the past couple of days. In fact, we passed him on the way back to your RV this afternoon."

She blinked a few times as the wheels spun. Then, recognition dawned in her eyes. "Santa? But he's fat. Jimmy was so skinny. And he looks so much older."

"A year of boozing it up can do that to a guy. I didn't recognize him at first, either."

She shook a finger at me. "You said he wasn't calling me a ho."

I rose to my feet and extended my hand. "I was wrong. And I think I know where he is. Let's go shove that ho ho ho back down his throat."

* * * *

The Salty Pig was the only bar in Hazard, so I laid odds that's where we'd find drunk Santa. We'd borrowed the rusty Peanuts and Pickles service truck and parked in front of a row of faded brick storefronts. I spotted our reflection in a shop window as we walked toward the bar at the corner—a clown in full makeup and a bearded lady in a tight spangled bodysuit. Probably not a sight they saw every day in this one-horse town. I ushered Paloma through the paint-chipped door, pausing to let our eyes adjust to the dim lighting.

The interior looked as tired as the exterior. Peeling leather stools surrounded old whiskey barrels. Strings of dingy globe lights dangled from the ceiling. A vintage jukebox in the corner warbled an ironic tune: *Tears of a Clown*.

But the scene stealer appeared mounted above the bar: the back end of an enormous pink plastic pig, its curly tail spinning beneath a spotlight.

Happy hour had commenced, and a smattering of old timers guzzled longnecks. Paloma pointed toward the oak bar against the back wall. I followed her finger to see Jimmy slumped onto a stool, still wearing his red plush Santa suit. His synthetic beard, tinted yellow from cigarette smoke, lay piled beneath his chin. As we approached, he gave Paloma a sidelong look, took a long drag on his Marlboro Light, and returned his gaze to the whiskey in front of him.

Paloma slid onto the stool next to him. I stood beside her, resting my elbow on the bar. The bartender, a big white-haired country boy, whose craggy nose spoke of a bronco-busting, bull-riding past, looked up from the glass he was polishing. "Santa Claus, a bearded lady, and a clown walk into a bar…," he deadpanned. The three of us stared at him. "C'mon, that was funny. What can I get y'all?"

Paloma and I ordered beer. The bartender filled two glasses and slid them in front of us. Then, he picked up a rag and began wiping the bar, feigning disinterest.

Paloma gestured toward Jimmy. "Is this what you've come to? Some boozed-up strip-mall Santa Claus, smelling of wet diapers? Promising whiny brats crap they'll never get?"

He blew a trail of smoke from his nostrils and mashed his butt into the plastic ashtray. "I'm much more ambitious than you imagine. In the spring, I become a boozed-up strip-mall Easter bunny."

She shook her head. "That's so sad. I remember you were actually pretty good-looking, once upon a time."

"And you're probably halfway decent underneath that facial hair."

I held up my hands. "Hey, now. Let's not resort to insults."

He tilted his chin toward me. "You bangin' this clown already? Tickles ain't even cold yet."

Paloma's hand flew across Jimmy's face so fast I couldn't stop it this time. Her fingernails scored a trio of welts into his cheek. I glanced at the bartender, who leaned against the bar, close to the shotgun he surely kept there.

Rage flickered in Jimmy's eyes, followed by mournful resignation. "You're a firecracker. Always liked that about you. We coulda been good together."

The rage had evaporated from Paloma, as well, and she touched his forearm. Her voice was soft. "Is that why you killed them? Jealousy?"

Tears welled in his eyes. "I loved you, Paloma. Still do. After Spanky died…I thought, if I quit the circus, let you get away, I'd get over you. Didn't happen. I still think of you every day." He fumbled around the pocket of his Santa pants and produced his wallet, flipping to a miniature advertisement featuring Pickles & Peanuts' Famous Bearded Lady.

He folded the wallet and took a swig of whiskey. Paloma leaned toward him. "I had no idea, Jimmy. I thought it was just a crush. You killed Spanky because of me?"

Jimmy didn't speak. Didn't even move.

"And Tickles?" she prodded.

The atmosphere changed in an instant, electric and dangerous. Jimmy leapt to his feet, and the motion sent his stool clattering to the ground. Paloma squealed as he grabbed her shoulders. I stiffened and leaned forward, ready to jump to her defense, but she caught my eye and gave her head a little shake. The bartender made a move, but I held up my hand. "Wait," I whispered.

Jimmy's lips were tight, his face red. "Do you know what it was like to see you escort him into that stupid RV? To see it rocking on its tires and to imagine…." He blew out a breath and cocked his head toward me. "At least I know this guy gets it."

I glanced at Jimmy's small feet, feeling a sudden kinship with the man. Paloma put her hand on his cheek. "Did you kill him?" she whispered. "Did you lock him in that lion's cage—" Her voice choked.

He stared into her eyes and nodded. "I acted like I was going in myself. Told him I wanted to end it all. He tried to stop me. I shoved him inside and locked the door. Didn't take but a minute for Old Nelly to realize he was getting a clown burger for lunch." His lips curved into a manic grin. "Spanky was even easier. Passed out in the clown car, the old souse. Barely came to when the rope tightened around his neck."

"Oh, Jimmy. How could you?"

"Those clowns weren't good enough for you. I woulda made you happy. Still can. I just gotta make you give me a chance."

He unzipped his Santa coat, reached beneath a padded fake belly, and pulled out a black snub-nosed gun. Then, he spun Paloma around, flinging his arm across her chest. "I don't wanna hurt anybody," he said, his eyes darting from me to the bartender. "But she's coming with me."

He moved backward toward the door, dragging Paloma with him. In a moment of theatrical instinct, I stuck my floppy shoe in his path. He tripped over it and pinwheeled to the floor, the gun bouncing from his hand and skittering away. Paloma landed on top of him and rolled off, thudding onto the dirty wooden planks.

Jimmy scrambled to his feet, wild-eyed, and darted for the door. The bartender rushed around the bar, cradling his shotgun. I lifted Paloma to her feet, brushing peanut shells and cigarette butts from her sequins. "Are you okay? Did he hurt you?"

She fluffed her hair and smoothed her beard with a steady hand. "I'm fine." The woman had ice water in her veins.

The bartender returned, breathing hard. "Santa's got some zip in his gitalong," he muttered. "Couldn't catch him. I'll call the cops." The bar's patrons, unfazed by the excitement, turned back to their beers.

Paloma looked at me, red lips curving into a knee-weakening smile. She wrapped her arms around my waist and pulled me close. "My hero."

"But I let him get away," I said. "Again. A real hero would've made him pay for Spanky and Tickles."

"Cops'll catch him."

"They didn't last time—"

She put a finger to my lips. "Maybe they won't. Either way, his clown-killing days are over. And that's because of you."

She kissed me, a deep, wet kiss that made my flower squirt. Her breasts heaved against my chest, and I stroked the soft down of her beard. Definitely real. The boobs and the beard.

"Let's go back to my RV," she said, her voice husky.

"Does that mean…?"

She nodded. "Buster, I'm about to turn your frown upside down."

Lori Roberts Herbst spent thirty years as a journalism teacher and counselor in the Dallas area. She recently published her debut novel, Suitable for Framing, the first in the Callie Cassidy Cozy Mystery series. Lori is secretary of the North Dallas chapter of Sisters in Crime, as well as a member of the national chapter and the Guppies. Visit her at www.lorirobertsherbst.com.

THE CANINE CAPER

MICHELE BAZAN REED

"I tell you, Art, this is somebody's idea of a sick joke." I slammed the letter down onto the polished oak, wetting the paper with the ring from my glass. "And it's all because of that ad."

Business had been slow lately, so I'd used some of my reward money from the case of the Lady in Black to purchase an ad in the local rag. Two inches on page 14 of the *Syracuse Herald*, touting the services of Harry Jerome, Private Investigator.

"Missing relative? Purloined pearls? Precious cargo need guarding? Call 'The Hound' at JEfferson 3828. Harry Jerome, P.I., is on the case." I included the address of my fourth-floor walk-up on the city's main drag.

Back when I was on the force, I'd earned the nickname "The Hound," as the best tracker in four states. It was a well-deserved moniker: I could find anyone or anything. That was no joke.

But when I got an official-looking letter offering me a case at the State Fair Dog Show, I was sure someone was pulling my leg.

That's what I was telling Art down at the speakeasy the day after the postman slid the letter through the slot in the door of my less-than-posh digs.

"Do you believe this, Art? What some people won't do for a few laughs!" I waved the letter at him as he swabbed down the bar.

He glanced over at the deckled sheet with the gold-trimmed seal of the Empire State Kennel Club.

"How do you know it's fake, Harry?" Art asked with a raised eyebrow. "I heard the dog show at the 1921 State Fair was going to be the biggest and best ever—dogs coming from all over the US and across the Atlantic. There's even some police dog who's a champion over in Germany."

Art had been keeping me in bootleg booze ever since I tipped him off to the approach of Federal agents on a mission to enforce the Volstead Act. We'd grown to be friends. But that didn't mean he wasn't a little too gullible sometimes. That's what I told him that day.

"No, Harry, I mean it. Look here." He flung down a copy of the *Herald* on the bar. A story on Page 3 touted the upcoming show as "Brilliant,

Attracting Well-Known Prize Winners from Most Famous American Kennels."

"Didn't know you were so partial to the puppies, Art." I had to tease him. "Except maybe a nice dog slathered in mustard from Heid's." We were both fond of the new local hot dog stand, which had attracted quite a following for their Coneys.

"Well, it says here, the judge for the Airedale group will be the fella that bred Laddie Boy, President Harding's dog. That's attracted a nice field of those black-and-tan terriers, and you can imagine there will be a lot of interest in winning a ribbon given by such a famous breeder."

I'd heard of Laddie Boy. Who hadn't? It was impossible to pick up a newspaper in America and not read all about the President's favorite "advisor." Harding interrupted a cabinet meeting the day after his inauguration, when the breeder brought the new puppy to the White House. Even I laughed at the newsreels when Laddie made an appearance at the Easter-egg roll on the White House lawn and travelled in style in the president's limo. Harding even had a special chair made for the cabinet room, so his pup could sit in on meetings.

Laddie Boy almost vied with Mary Pickford as America's Sweetheart, and I could well believe his breeder would draw an enthusiastic crowd of exhibitors, as well as the adoring public. Plus, show dog owners were rich. Their fee would probably fetch me lots of Coneys.

* * * *

My assumption was confirmed the next day, when I visited the kennel club director, a Mr. Reynolds, at his offices on James Street. "Call me Charles," he said, coming around his carved walnut desk to shake my hand. My gaze took in the leather chairs, thick Oriental carpet, and flocked wallpaper of the offices in the former mansion on one of the city's wealthiest blocks.

Reynolds was a tall drink of water, elegantly slim, with a head of thick, black hair, slicked back in the style of Rudolph Valentino. He was dressed in a blazer with the crest of the kennel club and a pair of linen pants. I half-expected to see an ascot around his neck, but he'd settled for a tie with the discreet seal of an Ivy League school. I hadn't guessed wrong about the money attached to this club of dog lovers.

"I'm glad you came by, Mr. Jerome," Reynolds said. "As you can imagine, we have some very valuable dogs coming for the State Fair show, and we want to ensure the show goes off without a hitch."

I told him I'd read about the event in the paper and that I knew the breeder of Laddie Boy was attracting a nice field of Airedales, an attention to background which he seemed to appreciate.

"Yes. And there are plenty of valuable hounds, pointers, shepherds, and bulldogs, as well." He sniffed, and I figured either he must not be a terrier man or was used to being diplomatic around his membership.

"But you're right about the Airedales. They've been a very popular breed, and not only because of Laddie Boy." He gestured to a photo on the wall of a man with two terriers wearing gas masks and saddlebags. "Many of them are war heroes. That's Lt. Col. Richardson with one of the many Airedales he trained for the British Army. During the Great War, they carried messages and medical supplies, fearlessly running through enemy fire and continuing on, despite serious wounds. Dozens have been honored for their service."

Reynolds went on to explain that the field of dogs at this year's State Fair show was bigger than ever, and the audience was expected to be huge as well, because of the fame of Laddie Boy's breeder and the reputations of several championship dogs.

"All that attention brings its own problems. You would be surprised at the lengths some people will go to influence the judging. At a show in Des Moines, one overly enthusiastic owner tried to lure a rival Pomeranian out of the ring with a sausage, foiling the dog's chances at a ribbon."

I scowled. Now, I would be guarding sausages? I waited for him to continue.

"But not only that, the 'hardware,' as we affectionately call it—engraved silver platters and bowls for the top prize winners, along with blue ribbons for the dogs and medallions for the kennels—are worth a lot of money. Who knows what opportunistic scoundrel may get the idea to make off with a valuable loving cup?" He shuddered a bit at the thought. "And our dog owners are always nervous about the safety of their precious charges. These dogs are worth hundreds, in some cases, thousands of dollars."

"How can I help?" I tried to remain noncommittal, but I had to admit the idea of the dog show intrigued me.

"Well, this year's show is at the northern edge of the fair, and we need you to patrol the grounds, keep an eye on the grooming areas, and have a presence among the spectators. Of course, you will accompany the judge into the ring for the proceedings, to keep an eye on the silver." I fidgeted as he looked me up and down. I'd worn my best suit and fedora, but it was a 1918 model, bought with my last paycheck from the force. Not exactly the latest Brooks Brothers style from New York City.

"We have a closet full of EKC blazers for guest judges who aren't members of our club to borrow. I'm sure we'll find something suitable for you there." There was that sniff again. "Consider it an undercover disguise."

Before I had a chance to be offended by his tone, he quoted the fee he was offering. I managed to stifle a whistle at the last moment and, instead, stuck out my hand to shake on the deal, trying to exude as much savoir faire as my new client.

* * * *

On Tuesday, I headed out to the fairgrounds to have a look around in preparation for Wednesday's big event. The dog show was so large this year, a whole building was devoted to it, with a grand ring taking up the bulk of the space. The sides of the building were roll-up canvas panels, which, owing to the heat of the day, were in the upright position. A low fence separated the show ring from the bleachers where spectators could cheer on their favorite dogs. I did a quick estimate of the seating available: up to a thousand viewers could be on hand to marvel at the poodles, pointers, and pugs on display. Surrounding the ring area, several large sections were created by low walls, fitted with tables for the dog owners to use for grooming. The perimeters of these rooms were lined with crates, each fitted with bowls and a blanket for the dog, and, in front of the crate, a chair for the owner to use while awaiting her or his turn.

At the far end of the building, a spacious room was furnished with a davenport, several chairs with side tables, and in one corner, an ornate oak desk and chair on an Oriental carpet. An icebox stood nearby, and a cart containing glasses and pitchers, and a teapot with cups and saucers. This must be the judges' lounge, and it seemed no expense was being spared for their comfort.

Reynolds had told me an area would be set aside for me, and I scouted around until I saw a small campaign desk and fold-up chair taking up a portion of the outer ring. I nodded my approval. While nowhere near as fancy as the judges' area, it gave me a full view of the outer ring, and I could have a nice line of sight for anyone coming into or out of the show ring, grooming stalls, and judges' lounge.

"There you are! Glad to have you aboard, old man." Reynolds was approaching with his hand outstretched and a blazer over his other arm. "I've told people you were on loan from a club downstate, sent up to learn about the arrangements here. That should give you free rein to enter any area and ask questions, if you need to. I see you've found the little desk I scavenged up for your use. There's a clipboard in the left-hand drawer, and you can wear this blazer to look like an official member of the team."

I thanked him, and he offered to show me around, keeping up a running patter on the field of dogs vying for the honors.

"This area here will be important to keep an eye on. These are kennels for our most famous contestants. Champion Dolph Von Vurstenbruck is a police dog who's a champion here and in Germany. King Beauty, a little

Boston Terrier, has several blue ribbons, and key entrants in the wire-fox terrier and bulldog breeds have won multiple championships, including a ribbon from Westminster." He paused in front of the crates with their name plates on them. "The residents of these guest rooms will require a lot of attention."

He waved his hand, taking in the grooming areas. "All these areas will be packed with contestants, their owners and handlers, all getting ready for judging of the different groups, like the terriers, hounds, and sporting or hunting dogs. As soon as we have winners in each of those, we will have the Best-in-Show competition—the moment everybody's been waiting for."

In the judging ring, he stopped and pointed. "Over there will be a large table with all the silver trophies, and the dogs will parade around the ring for our Best-in-Show judge. At that moment, all eyes will be on the magnificent show dogs, and yours, Mr. Jerome, will be on the 'hardware.'"

I nodded my agreement. "You can count on me, Mr. Reynolds."

"Yes, Harry Jerome, 'the Hound.'" So, it had been the ad that appealed to the dog show organizer. This time, instead of a little sniff, I got half a smile, and counted it progress.

* * * *

The next day, I wandered the grooming area and surveyed the bleachers. People bought the cover story of a visiting dog-club member and seemed eager to show me around their grooming stations, where I could keep an eye on their belongings as I asked questions and stopped to pet the dogs. From time to time, I checked on the bleachers and show ring from a strategic vantage point near the entrance to the show site.

The day went along smoothly. Several groups were judged, and the winners' owners primped their charges for the Best-in-Show competition. Those with losing dogs packed up their grooming cases and headed for the bleachers to watch the rest of the competition.

Suddenly, I noticed a bit of commotion around the registration table. A late entry had arrived for the Airedale Terrier competition, and I could hear the volunteer at the desk arguing with the owner.

"This is highly irregular, sir." He said in an officious tone. "In fact, totally unheard of. We never allow late entries where we can't check their pedigree and verify their membership in a sister club."

The other man raised his voice. "Do you know who this is? It's Champion Always a Gentleman. He has several blue ribbons and even a Best-in-Show trophy. Surely, you've heard of the top Airedale in the Northeast? His call name is 'Raffles.'"

At the sound of his name, the dog cocked his majestic head, his mouth open in what could only be described as a grin. He wagged his tail and looked from his owner to the club official and back again.

I wandered over, taking it as part of my brief to quell any disturbance that would impede the flow of the show. I took a stance behind the officious volunteer and eyed the dog's owner. "Let's not have a fuss here, Mr.…."

"Justice," he said, with a haughty sneer in my direction. "Of the Newport, Rhode Island, Club."

The volunteer shrugged, indicating he'd never heard of the dog or owner.

That's when Mr. Reynolds appeared. "Gentlemen, please! What seems to be the problem here?"

The volunteer explained the situation, and Reynolds looked over the dog. "He's certainly a beauty," he said, as he ran his hands along the dog's back. "Let's let him in for now, Mr. Jerome, but you send a telegram to the Newport Club to verify his membership and the dog's pedigree. The Airedales go on last, so we're sure to have an answer by then."

The volunteer registered Justice and took Raffles over to one of the grooming areas, while I went to send the telegram as Reynolds ordered. On a hunch, I also sent another.

* * * *

It was about 8 p.m., and the Airedales were lining up for the breed judging, the organizers wisely having held the highly anticipated breed until the last to insure a good crowd. The audience was buzzing with anticipation of the Airedales' turn in the ring with their famous judge, when I heard a ruckus in the grooming area.

"My bracelet!" shrieked a matron in a blue silk dress. "It's missing!" I hurried over and asked her to describe the jewelry she'd lost. "It was a diamond bracelet, a gift from my husband," she said, sobbing into a lace handkerchief. "From Tiffany's, in New York City."

I tried to calm her down and asked where she had last seen the bracelet. "Well, it was right there just a few minutes ago. I remember taking it off to wash Gracie, my cocker."

She ran her hand absentmindedly through the spaniel's fur. "Then, Mr. Justice stopped by on his way to the ring, and I was petting that beautiful Airedale, Raffles," she said, pointing at the dog just entering the show ring. "When I turned to put my bracelet back on, it was gone."

Just then a messenger came up to me, waving two telegrams. A quick scan of the missives confirmed my suspicions.

Trying not to disrupt the dog show, I headed for the ring. Justice was just taking Raffles off the judging table when he saw me approach. Quickly, he pulled something out of his jacket pocket and clipped it to the Airedale's collar. As he did so, I noticed a flash of white sailing off toward the bleachers. "Raffles, GO!" Justice shouted, slapping the dog on its rump.

Raffles bolted to the edge of the ring and leaped over the low wall that separated it from the rest of the building. He dodged between the grooming tables and crates and made a beeline to where the canvas panels were rolled up to let in the evening breeze.

Yelling, "Stop that thief!" and pointing at Justice, I headed after Raffles. I'm no high jumper, so I took the long way around. As I came in sight of the door, I could glimpse the tip of a wiry-coated tail vanishing over the threshold. I followed.

I kept Raffles in sight but was no match for the Airedale's speed. My progress was further hampered when my way was blocked by a farmer trying to urge along a stubborn Holstein on the way to the dairy barn.

I could just see Raffles slipping around the Coliseum, housing the horse-show ring, when a band in white uniforms filled the roadway, playing a Sousa march on their way to the bandstand for an evening concert.

By the time I pushed through the tubas and trombones, Raffles had escaped the fairgrounds and was making his way across the maze of S&O train tracks.

On the other side of the tracks, the dog turned back in my direction. After looking both ways up and down the track, he stared right at me and barked, wagging his stubby tail. The diamonds clipped to his collar sparkled in the last rays of sunset.

I made for the tracks to give chase once again, but before I could reach the siding, a train came roaring through. Car after car of freight rattled by, while I stood helpless, cursing my luck.

As the caboose rolled past, I scanned the other side of the tracks, but my quarry was nowhere in sight. Raffles had escaped, along with the diamond bracelet.

I turned and trudged back toward the dog show site. There was still work to be done.

* * * *

Back in the tent, I stayed behind after the judging ended, watching the crowd disperse. When the last spectators walked out, I hurried over to the seating area, focused on completing my task before the cleaning crew arrived.

I combed the bleachers on my hands and knees, checking cavities and sticking my fingers in the spaces between boards. In the gap between two third-row seats, I spied a bit of white. Pocketing my prize with a satisfied nod, I headed over to the State Fair Diner.

* * * *

"Oh, Harry, say it isn't so!" Art kidded me as he brought over my customary free drink. "The Hound bested by an Airedale?"

"Afraid it's true, pal," I said, but not before I took a long sip of the rye.

Art shook his head. I could see he had a copy of the *Herald* on the bar, but he was a good enough friend to not read me the headlines I was sure trumpeted my failure to catch the canine crook.

"But what clued you in that Justice wasn't legit?" he asked.

"First of all, he was little too cocky with his choice of alias. He called the dog Champion Always a Gentleman, with a call name of Raffles. That put me in mind of those famous stories about the gentleman thief. Then, he gave his name as Mr. Justice, and something clicked. I remembered reading they were making a new movie called 'Mr. Justice Raffles,' based on those very books. When Reynolds told me to write to the Newport Dog Club, I sent a second telegram to the police station there. Both confirmed Justice was a fake. He'd targeted wealthy matrons at dog shows all over the Northeast, using the handsome Airedale as bait. While the ladies oohed and aahed over Raffles, Justice stole their jewels. By the time the victims noticed, he was usually long gone."

"So, the dog got away with the goods," Art said, casting a sympathetic look my way. "But did you at least catch the human thief?"

I shook my head. "When I shouted and Raffles jumped the fence, Justice tried to run out of the ring in the other direction. He got tangled up in the leashes of the dogs lining up for the Best-in-Show competition, going down in a pile of pooches. A quick-thinking handler grabbed him, and Reynolds called the police. Unfortunately, with the evidence gone with the dog, they had to let Justice go. He's probably in the next state by now."

Art brought me over a second glass of hooch. "I figured you could use another, buddy. It's not every day Harry Jerome sees his quarry get away."

"Not to worry, Art," I said. "Before I gave chase to Raffles, I saw something white fall from Justice's pocket as he clipped the bracelet to the Airedale's collar. The breeze picked it up and blew it toward the bleachers."

Art folded his arms and, leaning against the bar, shook his head. "Coulda been a clue, Harry. Bad luck for you, it got away, like that terrier."

"Art, my friend, you make the mistake many a crook has made. You underestimate just how dogged The Hound can be," I said, as I reached into my pocket. "After Raffles gave me the slip, I headed back into that tent, searched the empty bleachers and turned up this."

I smoothed out a crumpled piece of paper on the bar.

"Big deal," Art said, squinting at the sheet. "It's a receipt from the State Fair Diner. Somebody named A.J. had two hamburgers for lunch. I'm no detective, but even I can deduce that's not much of clue."

"In the books, A. J. are the Raffles character's initials." I explained. "The waitress at the diner confirmed it was Justice. She remembered him, because the second burger was for the Airedale. She said it was the funniest order she had all day."

I turned the receipt over with a flourish. On the back, Justice had scribbled a list of the dates and locations of fall dog shows up and down the East Coast, with notations by each one. The Philadelphia show had "Mrs. S., beagle, emerald necklace"; Baltimore was marked, "Mr. W., greyhound, gold watch."

I scooped up the paper and my glass in one quick motion. "So, even though Raffles may have escaped with the loot, and his master walked scot-free, I've got their itinerary for the next few weeks. I'll dog their steps and collar them soon enough!"

Michele Bazan Reed's Jazz Age private detective, Harry Jerome's debut case is "Lady in Black" in Flame Tree Publishing's *Detective Mysteries* anthology. His adventure of "The Ghost in Balcony B" appears in *Malice Domestic XV: Mystery Most Theatrical*. Michele's recent stories include "A Rum Turn," in the *Wrong Turn* anthology; "The Hitler Heist," in *Mid-Century Murder*; and "Udderly Mystified" in *Woman's World*. A member of the Guppy Chapter of Sisters in Crime and the Short Mystery Fiction Society, she is the 2017 Daphne winner for Unpublished Mainstream Mystery/Suspense. Michele and her husband split their time between Harry Jerome's Central New York stomping grounds and France.

TRUE COLORS

C. M. WEST

It was her eyes that got me. Just past the West Oakland station, I always watched the graffiti wall for anything new as the BART train ripped by. It was only a brief glimpse, but I saw 911 had thrown a new piece up, another stenciled portrait of a missing teen girl; with a halo of dark curls, this one had soulful light blue eyes set in a dark, mixed-race face. 911 spray-painted portraits of missing kids on walls throughout San Francisco, Oakland, San Jose, and Berkeley. It broke my heart whenever I saw them.

I didn't have kids, but I hoped someday I'd meet the right woman and would start a family. I imagined losing a child would be torture that would drive anyone mad. 911's portraits kept those kids' faces from being forgotten.

Back in my teens, I'd had my run as a skate park punk, and in Sacramento, I did my share of tagging. I even joined a crew for a while until my dad found out. My father worked military intelligence; nothing ever got past him, so I spent months scrubbing out graffiti and picking up trash around downtown on my weekends, after he found the spray cans in my backpack. Instead of a street artist or pro-skater, eventually, I became a sculptor. I thought 911 did important work, and I didn't care if images of missing kids showed up on someone's storefront or was pasted over some corporate ad on a billboard. I think most people agreed. Days later, I still couldn't get the image of that girl out of my head. So, I googled missing teens, but no one on the list matched those eyes.

* * * *

I have to admit that I pretty much forgot about it until, two weeks later, she showed up on the news. Butterfly was the only name anyone had for the fourteen-year-old homeless girl last seen in the encampments around where the Cypress freeway used to be, the area of overpass that collapsed in the Loma Prieta earthquake decades ago. Despite the pixelated snapshot of the girl, I recognized her eyes from the graffiti portrait. A girl like that would attract attention, and I worried about what kind.

Outside the cluster of tents and cardboard shanties, a reporter interviewed a man called Fresno. He said the girl would've come to his birthday party, because she arranged the whole thing. "She even managed to arrange a cake from Safeway. Don't know how she did that. Butterfly would've been here," he said, dabbing his eye with his sleeve, "but she wasn't. She was a great kid."

Was. Past tense. Fresno had that red, leathery complexion one gets from living rough, and it looked like someone had recently beat him up. He had a busted lip, and his right eye was swollen shut. The reporter continued her report, citing statistics of homeless children, runaway teens, and the abuses they faced, before she appealed to viewers to contact a hotline if anyone saw the child. However, I'd tuned out from the report as I did the math. 911's portrait of Butterfly was up at least a week before anyone reported her missing. So, why the delay? Immediately, I called my friend Steve, a county sheriff.

"Yeah, the MPR came through the station today, Tru." Steve crunched on something as he talked. "A runaway teen who skipped a birthday party at a homeless camp may not be considered missing in our eyes. But we're cross-checking national lists to find her real identity, of course. Hold on." He made some muffled reply to someone in the station. "Sorry. Honestly, a lot of teen runaways need somewhere else to go, because they run away from what you wouldn't call a home. She's a kid at-risk, even if she's not missing, so everybody is on the lookout." Steve probably saw a lot more shit than I could imagine, but he had a young daughter, so I figured this one would have his attention.

I wasn't sure why I cared so much, but something about it got to me. "She was pretty. That can be bad for a girl out there, right?"

"Is pretty. Yeah, that's bad." This time I could hear more concern in his voice. And I knew Steve was thinking about his daughter Mia.

"Steve, I may have a lead on this. I saw a graffiti portrait of that girl about two weeks ago. I'm pretty sure that was before anyone said she was missing. That street artist, 911—you must've heard of him. Well, if he jumped the gun on her disappearance, he must know something. You have to find him." As if that cracked the case. The absurdity of my call and the futility of solving the problems of teen runaways all began to sink in.

Steve was silent for too long, then he said, "Of course, I've heard of 911. Listen, Tru, my friend, graffiti artists don't exactly come forward to the cops. We have no idea who 911 is. But, if we did, he would've been hauled in for serious property crimes. Most taggers and graffiti gangs are looking at vandalism charges that have fines in triple digits."

"This painting was on a legal wall, so maybe 911 will come forward?" I knew it was hopeless.

"Well, where did you see this portrait?" Steve's voice had an edge to it that I couldn't decipher.

* * * *

Steve followed me into West Oakland in his own car. He had thirty minutes before he had to pick up his daughter from her mom's place in North Oakland. Other than spotting it from the train, I'd never set foot at the legal wall, so it took me some time to get my bearings on the streets. Steve was a sheriff in the Contra Costa County hills where we lived, so I supposed he was out of his jurisdiction. But he'd never let something like that keep him from following a lead.

He kept checking his watch and looking around uneasily. "You sure this is it?"

I knew we were in the right location but gaped at the wall in disbelief. The portrait of the girl was gone. More than just spot-jocking, huge colorful geometric patterns and an illustration of a giant robot rat entirely covered the wall just above the BART tracks. There was no trace of the other painting. I couldn't believe it. Usually people give 911's work a lot more runtime.

Steve shrugged. "You're sure it was by 911 and not just a picture of someone's girlfriend?"

"Well, no. But it had the characteristic drips…." I tried to remember if I'd seen a signature. Maybe I'd made an assumption that was dead wrong?

The Bart train roared above us as it passed on the elevated track. We stared at the wall. Steve's feet were planted wide in his cop stance. A teen rounded the corner of the wall, did an abrupt turn, and retreated again. With his dark skin and slouchy hoodie, Steve might've blended in around that part of Oakland, except his posture had a stillness that always reminded me of a bird of prey watching every movement around him. No point in hanging around, anyone would immediately peg him as a cop. No one would talk. Steve said I should leave this up to the cops, but he'd update me on progress with the case before he took off to get his daughter.

But Steve also said 911 would never talk to cops. I realized I wasn't far from the homeless encampment where Fresno did his interview. So, I cruised along Mandela Parkway until I saw the cluster of tents and cardboard huts near some sparse shrubs in the shadow of a big industrial warehouse. Several old RVs were parked at the curb. I drove my truck a few blocks farther before I parked, paused to stuff some bills in my jeans, then backtracked on foot to the tent city. Shopping carts loaded with belongings were wired together into a train that blocked the area between the sidewalk and the encampment. The few people leaning against the graffiti-covered wall visibly shrank and folded into themselves as I approached. I'm a big guy, and I'm used to that reaction when I walk down a tough street. It's either that or some punk decides he has something to prove. I usually avoid walking in areas where trouble will find me, but I marched right into it this time.

"I'm looking for Fresno. When was the last time anyone saw Butterfly?" I said to no one in particular.

"Fuck off," came a voice from the RV. The screen door squeaked open, and Fresno stood in the doorway. His face was in worse shape than the TV cameras showed. A bruise spread along his jaw, and his eye looked like it was becoming infected. He was also bigger than what he'd seemed on TV. "Like I told that last guy, I don't know where she is."

What last guy? "Did that guy beat the crap out of you?" I stepped forward.

That was when I noticed the knife in his hand. The interview was over before it began. A brick or something hit me in the back of the head, and I felt warm blood gush from my scalp. A few skinny guys stood behind the shopping cart blockade. One had a rock in his hands. They waited for my response with raised chins. I noticed the graffiti on the wall behind them dripped with fresh paint.

I pressed my hand to the head wound. "Look, I didn't come here to hurt anyone. That girl Butterfly was missing for longer than people know. If any of you know 911, I think he saw something. Tell 'im he should step up."

They stood their ground, and no one spoke. But I'd noticed the kid clutching a skateboard had reacted, startled a little, when I'd mentioned 911. He looked away when I stared at him. The skate deck was covered in stickers; one of them was arrow-shaped and read Lower Bobs. It was a skatepark and a street-art hangout close by. I wasn't willing to be killed over some teenage girl I didn't even know, so I left it at that and staggered back to my truck.

Fresno knew something and wasn't spilling it. The news report I'd watched went into detail about how sex trafficking and drugs were common traps for teenagers on the street. Someone had tried to beat information out of Fresno. Trafficking seemed possible. But I wondered whether Butterfly was taken by someone or had she run from someone? The cut on my head needed cleaning, and I didn't really want to go to the Lower Bobs skatepark on my own, so I headed over to my friend Nigel's artist live-work warehouse, which wasn't far.

* * * *

Nigel fixed me up with some antiseptic, ibuprofen, and a chunk of ice. We sat on folding chairs in his sculpture space. The cut turned out to be shallow, but head wounds bleed a lot. No big deal. The knot on my scalp was already reducing in size from the ice.

"You're always trying to save someone, my friend," Nigel shook his head.

I shrugged. "I guess. I need you to go with me to the Lower Bobs."

It was Nigel's turn to shrug. "Well, Detective Inspector Truitt James, what are your plans for that?"

Nigel is a British import, and his street art persona is Dr. Who; he regularly stencils steampunk gears, clocks, or a little blue Tardis image around town. He'd admitted he didn't know 911, but he knew a lot of people and could know who painted the rat. I showed him the photo.

"Can't say. Ask me, the work is shoddy, rough nozzles and scrappy detail. You really want to go to the Bobs? We'll be the creepy, old white dudes, but I'll bring a board and some cans. That might earn us some cred. Better take the fixies, unless you want your truck stripped while we're busy. Someone might talk to us there, mate."

* * * *

We rode Nigel's janky hipster bicycles about five minutes to reach The Lower Bobs, located in the aptly named Lower Bottoms area of West Oakland. Next to the 880 Freeway curve, it was the kind of place you imagined was, indeed, rock-bottom—a post-apocalyptic wasteland of asphalt, full of trash, old cars and, RVs, parked next to a mile of freeway wall covered in graffiti. However, some industrious kids had put effort into building the ratty skatepark. We entered the gate to the Bobs next to a trailer with a tag with Bob left spray-painted on the side. It was June; school was out for the summer. A group of teenagers idled at the far end of the bowl and scowled at us.

One of the black girls stepped away from the group and yelled, "Go home, pervs!"

Ignoring her, Nigel pulled a board from his backpack. He smoothly dipped off the rim and banked around the bowl, cruised the bumps, and then pulled an ollie and slid back next to me on the top of the deck. The boys in the group stopped talking and watched. Nigel picked up his backpack again and told me to follow him.

We walked to the long graffiti wall, and Nigel plucked some stencils from his pack. "Hold this right here," he said as he aimed a can of bronze paint at the stencil. I pushed on the stencil. Nigel worked the gear stencils carefully and built a complex Rube Goldberg machine on the freeway sound wall. I glanced back from time to time and saw the skaters edge closer to watch the action. He finished it off with a blue Tardis.

One of the kids stepped forward. "You're Dr. Who?"

Nigel stood back and kept his eyes on his work. "Maybe. Maybe not." Nigel nodded to me. I figured he meant this was the time for me to ask questions.

"I'm looking for Butterfly." I wiped my hands on my jeans and walked over to the kid. "You happen to know the rat who covered up 911's portrait of her?" I showed him the picture on my phone.

The kid scowled. "You some kind of narc?"

"Would a narc be painting here? 'Course not. We just wondered how 911 knew Butterfly was missing before anyone else did. Someone covered it up in a hurry with that robot rat."

"You knew Butterfly?" The kid pointed to something on the wall.

I looked at the stylized writing. Between tags, I made out a small painting of a Blue Morpho butterfly, then skirted his question. "You said knew, like in the past. Is she dead?"

The same girl who called us pervs crossed her arms. "What you want with Butterfly, perv?"

"Nothin'. A missing kid is serious. I just wondered if she's okay. Does anyone know?" The kids looked at each other. I tried again. "I wonder if she has any real friends, like people who look out for her. Maybe she was missing longer than what the cops think?" I made a mistake by mentioning the police, but I couldn't take it back.

"Path-et-ic." The outspoken girl put her hand on her hip. "Other pigs already came sniffing around here. We don't know nothin'."

The boy pulled on her elbow. "Come on, Mona, it's time to go. See you around, Dr. Who."

Nigel said, "My friend is all right. You should tell him what you know." He painted another gear.

The boy spoke to Nigel's back. "Butterfly only came around late at night. She's got a boyfriend she stays with, is what I hear. Maybe she just ran off with him." Nigel nodded. The boy walked back toward the skate area, and the others followed suit.

Except, one girl with lots of braids hung back as the others moved toward the skate park. "Butterfly joined the FV crew," she said quietly. Nigel made a kind of snort, and the girl stopped for a second. Then, she said, "She started hanging out with some new girl called Ria. I mean they were both new." The girl glanced at the retreating kids. "I liked Butterfly, but I didn't, like, know her. Besides, Mona was kinda jel—B. was totally gorg, you know, those blue eyes. Mona said they were, like, colored contacts, but I don't know if that's true. What you said about friends—well, I wanna know if B. is okay. Ria was, like, older and into some shit. I didn't trust her. I think she got B. into trouble."

"What's the FV crew?" I glanced at Nigel. He was busy packing up his cans but had a wicked smirk on his face.

The girl looked at the ground. "Fierce Vaginas," she said, and then, ran to catch up with the others.

Nigel laughed. "I know who to talk to next."

* * * *

Back on the orange fixies, Nigel led us several blocks back toward Seventh and to the Crucible, a metal-arts outfit in a huge warehouse. Nigel rode right in through the roll-up doors.

"Hey, Nigel." A Chinese American woman in her twenties with a razor-chopped haircut and too many piercings to count leaned against the tool room counter.

After he took off his helmet, Nigel smoothed his hair. "Hey, Jude, just the person I was looking for."

"It's Judy." Her mouth made a kind of skeptical curve. "What are you after, Nigel?"

Nigel raised both his hands in a gesture of surrender. "Nothing, love. I heard that the missing girl was on your vag crew is all. Tru, here, has made it his mission to find the little darling."

Judy swiveled her head and looked me up and down. "You've been here before, right?"

"Yeah, I come around to use the foundry sometimes. The Fierce Vaginas sound cool. Butterfly was on your crew?"

She laughed. "You did all right. Most guys can't say the name of my crew without cracking a joke. But you heard wrong. She wasn't on my crew. She just hung around when the FV made our piece on a woman's right to choose."

"I saw that. It was on the legal wall for a while, right? Someone said Butterfly had a boyfriend, but I also heard she hung out with this girl named Ria. Word is, Ria was into some stuff. I figured something serious happened to Butterfly, because I saw 911 made a portrait of her, but it was glossed over pretty quick. Something's not right."

Judy pulled her chin in. "No shit. Hit me with a brick."

"I kind of was just hit by a brick." I gently rubbed the back of my head.

Judy laughed, as if I'd made a joke. "Butterfly was young and totally gorg. She looked blasian, if you ask me, but damn knows how she got those blue eyes. I heard she was homeless, but then I also heard she stayed somewhere over in the Oakville housing project, which isn't bad. You're after the reward, huh?"

"Reward?" Was that the reason the homeless guys chased me off?

Nigel put his hands on his hips. "What reward, Tru?"

Judy looked from Nigel back to me again. "Oh, come on. Let me guess. You didn't want to share it with Nigel? What I could do with ten thousand dollars...." She caught my expression and paused. "What? Seriously, you didn't know?"

"No. Did her family come forward and put up a reward?" I hoped Butterfly had a loving family that wanted her back.

"Nuh-uh. Some anonymous donor put up cash through a missing-kid organization. I guess other people care, too. All I know is that Ria got tapped for some event, like a live, paint, street-artist thing. Although I never saw Ria paint. Supposedly, some marketing person wanted to add cachet to some fashion hip-hop party, or maybe it was, like, a high-tech start up? Anyway, Ria was trying to get some other girls to do it with her."

That could explain where the reward money came from. I looked at the spray paint lodged under her fingernails. "Do you know who 911 is? I'd like to talk to him, or her or, um, them."

Judy shook her head. "They'd be on the hook for literally hundreds of thousands of dollars in property damages if anyone knew. 911 would be up a creek if they got caught." She fiddled with a pen. "You're better off looking for Ria."

Something in her voice, her expression, I wasn't sure what exactly—call it instincts inherited from my dad—but I knew that Judy sure as hell knew who 911 was. "Well, do you know anything about Ria? What does she look like?" I wondered if the cops knew about that girl.

"Not much." Judy tapped the pen on the counter. "Young. They're all really young. I'd put her at eighteen or less. She's like, Latinx, long dark hair, and big boobs. She is new to the scene, kinda paranoid, probably illegal. Anyway, she always wears too much makeup and this jean jacket with an embroidered tiger on the back. She'd come around the wall sometimes, bragging about parties and trying to get the girls to go. I have no idea where you'd find her. I heard she turned tricks, but no judgment here. Her body, her business."

"Yeah, sure, unless she wasn't eighteen or didn't have a choice." I took the pen from Judy and wrote my number on the sign-in form. "Could Butterfly's boyfriend be a pimp?"

Judy shrugged. "Guess I'd go over to Oakville and ask around. But, good luck, white guy. Oh, I wouldn't turn down some of that reward if you get it."

Nigel coughed. "Darling, you've given us nothing. I'd love to chat, but I've got to get back to work." He put his helmet back on and turned his bike around.

The back of my head had a dull ache, and I didn't want to go poke around some housing project, looking like some jerk after a reward. Besides, it was nearly evening. I asked Judy to call me if she ever saw Ria. We pedaled back to Nigel's place. I thanked him, and then, packed it in and drove home.

* * * *

After grabbing a beer, I flipped on the evening news. Nearly dropped the bottle when the reporter, standing near the estuary in Jack London Square, with a grim expression said the body of a young woman was found dead in the water there. They estimated she'd been in the water for almost a week. They asked anyone with information to call the police. They had no identity for the girl, but he said police described her as in her late teens, Hispanic, and wearing a jean jacket with a tiger embroidered on the back. It wasn't Butterfly. It was Ria. I grabbed my keys and headed back to Oakland.

* * * *

The air smelled delicious, as various dinners cooked in the Oakville Projects. Some kids, probably middle-school-aged or so, sat outside on a stoop and clustered around a cell phone. The boy holding it concentrated intently and jammed his fingers rapidly on the buttons. I started to walk toward the group, but something else snagged my attention. To my right was a small community garden, and the wall of the little shed sported a mural of blue, stenciled butterflies. I took photos of the mural and stood staring for too long, because an elderly woman paused as she passed me.

"May I help you?" She said it in a way that indicated she did not want to provide any sort of help.

"Oh, I just...do you know who painted that mural? I saw something like it before."

"Logan painted that a few months ago. You don't live here. What are you doin' hanging around by those kids?" She frowned.

"I'm helping to look for that girl who disappeared. Have you heard about it? Someone told me a boy here, possibly Logan, might have been friends with her. I hope he can tell me anything that might help us find her. We're canvassing the neighborhood." I was sure this Logan had to know Butterfly.

"No, I haven't heard about a missing girl, but Logan is a good boy. You better go talk to his foster mom. She's in 616 B." The woman shuffled forward.

* * * *

Logan's foster mom answered the door but didn't invite me in after I told her what I wanted.

She hadn't watched the news that day. "He's not here." Her mouth had a grim set to it.

"When was the last time you saw him?" I had my hands in my pockets, trying to look non-threatening.

She let out an exasperated breath. "Look, it's summer, and school is out. It's not anything to worry about. He'll be back soon."

"Did he have a girlfriend?" I already explained what I wanted. "Someone said maybe he knew those girls."

"No. No girls ever come around for him," she said as she began to shut the door.

I wedged my boot in the way. "Listen, one girl is dead. Another is missing. I don't think he's involved. I just want to know any little thing that could help us find the other girl."

She looked down. "I never saw a girl, but he stole some stuff from me. Nothing fancy, just some hoop earrings and a dumb sparkly jacket. I don't even care about the stuff, but maybe he gave them to a girl? I've tried his phone, and he doesn't answer. He's only been with us for six months, but he's a good kid. He'll come back. I'm not calling social services yet. He's fifteen and independent. School just let out. He hasn't been gone long. The last thing a young black boy needs is to have the cops hassle him."

"Yeah, I get it. And, like you, I'm just trying to help a lost kid. I think he might have known these girls. Maybe he's trying to help one? How long has Logan been gone?" I started to worry Logan was in trouble too.

"Just a few days." She looked past me at something deep inside her mind. "It'd be just like Logan to try to help someone. Hold on." She left the door and was back in a minute. She handed me a sketchbook. "I never go through his stuff, but maybe there's something in here that will help. Just leave it on the doorstep when you're through. He will want it back. He goes to the School of the Arts. He draws all the time in that book. You said there's a hotline? I promise. I'll get him to call when he comes in. I mean, if he knew that dead girl. Oh, God rest her. Now, please remove your foot."

I did as she asked, and she shut the door. The kids were still on the stoop as I walked by.

"Hey, I hear Logan is missing. Any of you ever see a girl hanging out with him?" I looked directly at the oldest girl, maybe about twelve.

She tore her gaze away from the video game. "I ain't seen him for days. But yeah, I seen a girl go in or out his window sometimes, like late at night. His window is near mine. I heard it slide open kind of quiet. She was real sneaky."

I tried to gauge her response. She was about the right age to have a crush on a neighbor boy, especially a new one. "I heard Logan was a really nice guy, an artist. I suppose girls would be interested in him, makes sense if someone visited him. Did you ever get a good look at that girl? Was there more than one?"

"I don't know. It was dark." She tugged on a braid. "Logan is so cute. Never seen a black boy with eyes like that before."

* * * *

I sat in my truck, and the neighborhood settled into the dinner hour, as I flipped through the sketchbook. Many kinds of butterflies and Manga-style drawings of Geisha women with blue eyes filled the pages. He'd read Memoirs of a Geisha, according to his notes. He might've been obsessed with Butterfly. He designed an elaborate mural full of erotic, androgynous figures in Japanese kimonos, reminiscent of Egon Schiele portraits. The kid was a good illustrator, but there was no mention of any friends in his journal. It seemed like he lived in his drawings more than anywhere else.

I hadn't realized it was getting so dark outside, until my phone lit up the cab. A text from an unlisted number read, Look at Hustle & let B.—be. I made a mistake & I fixed it. 911.

I could only assume Judy passed along my message and my number to 911, the elusive street artist. A quick search on my phone told me Hustle was a tech startup that had some app-based business for entertainment industry booking for mostly rap artists and studio musicians. Their launch party was last week. Their Instagram posts showed people at the party posed in front of a large street artist mural. The text wouldn't take replies, but I knew what to do next. I called Steve, the sheriff in my corner.

He picked up right away.

"Hey, it's Tru. Don't ask me how I know, but I have a tip. Tell Oakland PD they need to look for a tech company called Hustle. They had a party sometime last week. I think it involved paid sex and probably underaged girls. I'd bet my shirt it was somewhere near Jack London where they found that dead girl, who I think is called Ria. And, I think Butterfly might be hiding, not missing." Well, I hoped that was the case.

* * * *

The bust made the news a week later. A sex trafficking ring blew open after an anonymous tip led the cops to some tech geeks, who bargained for clemency. They admitted hiring escorts for their launch party. They thought it would be ironic to have actual hustlers, but they swore they didn't know the girls were underage. They were scared when Ria turned up dead, but they seemed to convince authorities they hadn't done anything to her. The tech company had put up the reward money to find Butterfly. They confirmed she was at the party but said she had run away during the event. Apparently, Ria disappeared from the party with her handlers. I hoped Butterfly was hiding. In the message, 911 had said they'd made a mistake and fixed it. So, they must've erased their own mural. Maybe Butterfly was being sheltered by 911? I didn't know if Logan had returned home. Maybe he was hiding with her?

The report said the police busted the managers of a massage parlor along International Boulevard for recruiting homeless women and girls, and then, imprisoning them for sexual exploitation. From what Judy said, I figured Ria for a recruiter. It seemed she'd paid dearly when Butterfly escaped the net.

I watched the news report on my phone, as Nigel and I waited for the Richmond train at the 16th and Mission station in San Francisco. We'd attended a street-artist mural-and-music event at The Lab. Judy was there and had said "Hi." She was the one who told me to look at the news on the way home. I showed Nigel, relieved that Butterfly might be safe now.

The Fremont train pulled into the station, and I stepped back, so others could get on. Someone jostled me hard as they rushed onto the train, and I looked up from my screen. A pair of soulful blue eyes, on a boy with a shaved head and a dark complexion, stared at me through the glass as the doors snapped shut. And I finally understood. I knew that face. Now, I hoped, someday, Logan could stop hiding his true colors. The train took off before I noticed a small, blue, origami butterfly was pressed onto my sleeve.

In small print were the words, thank you.

C.M. West is the pseudonym for co-authors, Carol Elkovich and Mark Butler. Also visual artists, they draw from art subcultures of the San Francisco Bay Area to write dark-hearted stories about unconventional characters and the pursuit of justice. Other short stories, featuring artist sleuth character, Tru James, can be found in the Northern California Sisters in Crime Chapter anthology, *Fault Lines*, and in *Mystery Weekly Magazine*. Updates on their work can be found at partnersincrimefiction.com. They are currently working to publish their first novel.

ACKNOWLEDGEMENTS

The stories in *The Fish that Got Away* were much improved by the sharp eyes and good judgment of editor Linda Rodriguez. Linda Rodriguez's 11th book is *Fishy Business: The Fifth Guppy Anthology* (edited.)

Dark Sister: Poems is Rodriguez's 10th book. Plotting the Character-Driven Novel, based on her popular workshop, and The World Is One Place: Native American Poets Visit the Middle East, an anthology she co-edited, were published in 2017. Every Family Doubt, her fourth mystery featuring Cherokee detective, Skeet Bannion, and Revising the Character-Driven Novel will be published in 2021. Her three earlier Skeet novels—Every Hidden Fear, Every Broken Trust, Every Last Secret—and earlier books of poetry—Skin Hunger and Heart's Migration—have received critical recognition and awards, such as St. Martin's Press/Malice Domestic Best First Novel, International Latino Book Award, Latina Book Club Best Book of 2014, Midwest Voices & Visions, Elvira Cordero Cisneros Award, Thorpe Menn Award, and Ragdale and Macondo fellowships. Her short story, "The Good Neighbor," published in Kansas City Noir, has been optioned for film.

Rodriguez is past chair of the AWP Indigenous Writer's Caucus, past president of Border Crimes chapter of Sisters in Crime, founding board member of Latino Writers Collective and The Writers Place, and a member of International Thriller Writers, Native Writers Circle of the Americas, Wordcraft Circle of Native American Writers and Storytellers, and Kansas City Cherokee Community. Visit her at lindarodriguezwrites.blogspot.com.

Made in the USA
Monee, IL
06 August 2021

75092458R00121